How One Attempts To Chase Gravity

How One Attempts To Chase Gravity

Gem City Book 3

Nicole Campbell

Copyright (C) 2015 Nicole Campbell
Layout design and Copyright (C) 2018 Creativia
Published 2018 by Creativia
Cover art by Cover Mint
This book is a work of fiction. Names, characters, places, and incidents are the product of the author's imagination or are used fictitiously. Any resemblance to actual events, locales, or persons, living or dead, is purely coincidental.
All rights reserved. No part of this book may be reproduced or transmitted in any form or by any means, electronic or mechanical, including photocopying, recording, or by any information storage and retrieval system, without the author's permission.

*For my readers who fell in love with Ethan and Courtney. Your feedback, comments, and, sometimes, downright obsession have made this story into what it was supposed to be.
Thank You.*

♪ *"Magic's In The Makeup" – No Doubt*

Prologue

The feeling rolling around in Courtney's stomach as she read the letter for the third time could not decide if it was angry, nostalgic, or really, really sad.

Courtney,

I know how you feel about handwritten letters, so I hope this one is legible. Anyway, I wanted you to get something other than bills or junk in your mailbox when you first moved in. I wanted to cheer you up from the last time we talked. Thinking about you being as sad as I am makes me feel even sadder. Sorry I didn't try to use a synonym, sad was all I could think of.

I know we both said we would try not to make this harder on each other, so that's all I will say. I hope you have all of your pens organized and that you and Vanessa are having fun. Tell her I said hi.

Know you can call, Court.

Miss you,

Ben

Well... there's that. Not making things harder at all. A vision of Ben's easy smile floated into her mind, and the guilt sank like a rock from her chest to her stomach, when the actual scene set before her was a newly organized desk with Train tickets for that weekend sitting prominently on top. She slid the letter and the tickets into a drawer in order to make the solid adult decision to, well, ignore it, for the time being.

♪ *"Magic's In The Makeup"* – *No Doubt*

1

After the literal fourteenth outfit she put on, Courtney was near tears and giving up ever walking out the door. Vanessa stormed in moments later after pretend knocking.

"What *happened* in here?" V asked in disbelief at the state of the room.

"This is the product of the universe knowing it is a terrible idea for me to go to this concert." She took a deep breath, fully understanding that she was being ridiculous.

"To go to the concert or to go backstage and hook up with Fisher in some rock star's dressing room?"

"Does that even exist? Like, dressing rooms backstage? That seems fictional… But completely beside the point- I'm not hooking up with him, I've informed you of my stance on this."

"Yeah, you sound all sure of yourself in our kitchen. When he's not there."

"Whatever," she retorted, refusing to admit her friend's point. She went back to the closet for yet another try, and picked out a cream-colored lace sundress with a sweetheart neckline. While it was fancier than something she'd typically wear to a concert, it made her feel a little bit like a fairy, so it was deemed a winner. She and Vanessa were in the car fifteen minutes later.

"This dress is too much isn't it?"

"Oh. My. God. If you say one more thing about the dress, I am going to freaking lose it. You look fierce. Maybe if you'd just admit that you are having some sort of mental breakdown about seeing Fisher, all of your craziness would die down just a little. So try that."

Courtney exhaled. "Ok. I am having an absolutely freaking meltdown about seeing him." She didn't think it was helping. She felt even crazier than before, like she was introducing herself at an AA meeting.

"Because…"

"Because I don't know what will happen. I like knowing what's going to happen."

"That's boring. Can't you just embrace it? I love not knowing what's going to happen. Reason three on the list of why I broke up with Luke. Too predictable."

"You think *Luke* is predictable?"

"No, just our relationship was predictable. I want something exciting. And so should you. You're not attached anymore, Ben is in California, for Christ's sake. Ethan is… well, you know I hate to admit it, but he's beautiful. So just chill. Hook up, don't hook up, do whatever you gotta do, but for the love of all that is holy, will you just. Calm. Down?"

"I'll try," Courtney mumbled, knowing that was a near impossibility. The parking situation only increased her stress. Living and driving in a city she hadn't resided in for six years was nerve-wracking. They finally made it to their seats and the energy from the crowd helped to improve her mood. *You're going to freaking see Train,* she reminded herself, and she was going to be able to do it backstage if she wanted. They were there early, and her mind couldn't help but wander to Ethan and how he was faring, knowing he was about to perform.

♪ *"Lover of the Light"* – Mumford and Sons
"For Me, It's You" – Train
"We'll Pick Up Where We Left Off" – OAR
"Learning to Love Again" – Mat Kearney

2

His shoes squeaked on the sealed cement floor of Crawford's apartment while he paced. They were set to leave in less than thirty minutes, and his mind was racing. They were opening for Train. At the Riverbend Music Center. In front of a *lot* of freaking people. It would be great exposure for them, and he and Brian had been working tirelessly at designing a banner and getting t-shirts and other promos ready to go for weeks. The radio station was taking care of their merch sales as part of the contest win, and the thought of having his music out there for that many new people in one night was making him antsy. In a good way.

"Okay, man, I like you and all, but if you don't stop creating that sound, I am going to chuck your shoes out the window."

Ethan squeaked them loudly once more, but agreed to sit down afterward. "Sorry. Just ready." He knew that opening bands had the difficult task of warming up a crowd with songs they didn't really show up to hear; they were going to have to convince them to listen. The short set list had taken what seemed like ages to iron out, and they tried to showcase the range of what they could do. Southbound was on first, followed by The Fray- not his most favorite band, but he had respect for anyone touring and making money doing what they did. He had driven by the venue a few days before and taken a fairly embarrassing amount of photos of the band's name on the marquee. Everyone started loading equipment, and he was relieved with having something to do.

When they arrived at the RMC, he was surprised with how structured and organized everything was. The venue manager clearly had her shit together. They made it through sound check without issue, and Ethan was twirling one of his silver rings around his pointer finger while he listened to the rush of the pre-show around him. He checked his phone and lit up, seeing his messages.

> C: I tried not to text you, but I wanted to say I'm excited for you guys. You'll be great, and we will see you later with these fancy backstage passes :).
> E: I'm glad you didn't try too hard ;). Knowing you'll be here makes the crowd seem smaller. Thanks for the vote of confidence- you can message me any time.
> C: I'll keep that in mind.

He was feeling like he could conquer the world right about then. There was another text from his mom saying that she and Tay would be in their seats soon, and that made him feel better as well; he didn't really care if that was lame. He checked his appearance last minute- gray-washed jeans and a tight black t-shirt, and maybe more than his usual amount of jewelry. He liked his hair a bit longer, being that he could push it behind his ears when he inevitably had sweat dripping down his face.

"Fisher, we all know you're the fairest in the land, now can we go do what we came here to do?" Crawford teased him. His stomach dropped the way it did at the top of a roller coaster. He took a breath and nodded. Hearing their name announced made his heart pound in rhythm with some scattered applause throughout the arena. Most people were still milling around and securing their beers at this point in the show.

Here it goes then, he thought, and wished for a moment that the spots weren't so bright and he'd be able to see Courtney or his mom in the audience. His mind cleared when the drums sounded behind him and he played the opening riff. The difference in the sound system of the RMC and their usual haunts was like comparing a Sentra to a Maserati because they were both street legal. The applause got louder after each song, and his energy was through the roof for their closing. They ended with a song he'd written with Courtney in mind, and he hoped she got that it was for her.

"Thank you all so much, we appreciate it more than we can say. Have a great night!" Crawford finished for the crowd, and they made their way back from where they'd come. All of Ethan's nerves seemed to crash once they were off stage, and his hands were shaking.

"That was amazing- the best we've ever sounded, like ever," Brian relayed to the group.

Ethan breathed slowly, coming to terms with the fact that he'd just played the set of his life, several songs of his own creation, for a real audience. "Hell yeah it was," his cockiness returning as he grabbed a bottle of water.

The venue manager walked by on a mission, her headset pressed to her ear behind her short blond hair, but she stopped to tell them congratulations. "Great set guys, honestly. You're free to hang out here for the rest of the show, or the radio station has a suite, Number two twenty-seven, if you wanna head up there with your passes- totally up to you." She walked away, her heels clicking on the floor.

"Yeah, I'm going up to the suite- I'm pretty sure this is the life I was meant for," Brian joked. Chase and Jeremy went with him, but Ethan and Crawford stayed behind. Being backstage with a tour like this one wasn't likely something he'd be able to repeat in the near future. They listened to The Fray and scarfed down some sandwiches.

"I think I should probably thank you," Ethan said to his friend.

"Why?" Crawford questioned.

"I never would have gotten here if you hadn't called that day. Like I'm one-hundred percent sure of that. I mean, I would have kept playing, but nothing of this magnitude. It was a pipe dream, playing on a stage like this."

"If we're handing out some honest gratitude? We wouldn't have gotten here either."

"Nah, you guys were great before me."

"We were good. Now we're better, so at least appreciate that. Your songs killed out there, enjoy it." Crawford got up to talk to some of the label guys who were wandering around- the guy never quit. Ethan elected to relax instead.

"So, I'm pretty sure I've been missing out my whole life by not having all-access passes to everything. The treatment is amazing- like, I want VIP access to the grocery store now. This whole experience has corrupted me, I hope you know." A grin spread across Ethan's face before he turned around, knowing Vanessa was behind the semi-compliment. She stood there, looking entitled in four-inch heels and painted-on jeans, a royal blue top baring her midriff.

"Hi to you too, V. It's been a while." He stood up to greet her and held his arms out for a hug.

"Yeah, you're like *really* sweaty, so I'm going to just stay right here." He rolled his eyes, but started to lose his excitement when he looked around for Courtney. "Stop with the puppy-dog face, she's here. She went to find water. You're so obvious," She looked at him pointedly. "A word of advice though? Don't overstep tonight- she's in super-anxiety mode." He nodded his understanding as he saw her come around the corner, water in hand. Vanessa made herself scarce, and he sent her a silent wave of appreciation.

She looked... beautiful. She had ditched her usual jeans and a tank top for a cream-colored strapless number and heels. Before she saw him, her hands worked at repositioning the beaded headband across her forehead, her eyes unsure. "Hey, sprin... Courtney." He tried to recover awkwardly. He didn't know how she would feel about his former term of endearment. She covered a laugh at his expense.

"Hey there, rock star. Do you want me to tell you how amazing you were out there?" she asked, fluffing her short curls. His nerves were already overworked from being on stage, but they rose to the occasion when he thought about kissing her exposed neck.

"Of course I do, have you met me?"

She smiled. "Well, you were. Honestly- you guys were incredible. Very different than the last time I saw you play. This... well, it suits you better."

"Agreed. I'm a lot happier... I get to play a lot of my own stuff, and the guys are amazing. I'll introduce you to Crawford in a minute, he's around here somewhere. The rest of the guys are up in the radio station suite. You'll like them though, really."

"Well, look at you living the high life. I'm proud of you, you seem... steady." *If only you knew how long it took me to get here,* he thought, knowing she would not be as proud if she could have seen him six months earlier.

"Do you wanna hang out for a bit? Or we could go up to the suite..." He was trying so hard not to "overstep" as Vanessa had put it.

"Yeah, I'm down to hang out backstage at a Train concert, you know, no big deal." She grinned, showing her excitement. She practically skipped out of the lounge area so they could get an actual view of the stage. She seemed nervous, though she was playing it pretty cool. He caught glimpses of her glancing at him from under her lashes and biting her lip when she thought he wasn't looking. He wanted to fix it- the awkwardness of them not knowing how to act towards each other. They had never been just friends, not really, and he couldn't take the space between them. When Train took the stage and opened with one of her absolute favorite songs, he couldn't overthink his actions anymore.

Leaning over, he pressed his lips to her ear. "Dance with me," he told her, hoping she wasn't going to shut him down.

"Ethan..." she replied warily, looking up at him.

Ignoring her hesitation, he held out his hand. She took it slowly and he twirled her around before bringing her in closer. She laughed softly, and god, how he had missed that sound. Her hair smelled the same, and when her fingers traveled up the back of his neck, he could have been right back at the river, falling in love with her the first time. She ran her nails along his shoulder blades lightly, and he tried to keep his hands at a respectable position on her back.

"Have I told you I like your hair this way?"

"Not today." He pushed a stray curl behind her ear that had escaped from the headband, and tipped her face up towards him. Resting his forehead on hers, he tried to think of a good reason not to kiss her. Vanessa's words rang in his head, and he knew he had already left the territory of just pretending to be friendly. The song ended before he made a decision one way or the other, and she let go without making eye contact. Groaning silently, he looked toward the sky, kicking himself internally for not just going for it when he had the chance. She had walked a few paces ahead and he moved to follow her.

"Are you coming?" she asked plainly, holding out her hand.

"Of course," he answered, taking it without hesitation and intertwining their fingers. She led him through a few smaller clumps of people until they came to stop at a metal partition just off the side of the stage. He couldn't deny that it was a great view. She didn't drop the connection once they made it to their destination, and he squeezed slightly. She squeezed back. Two songs later when he moved over to let someone slide by them, she didn't try to stop him from wrapping his arms around her waist from behind. Instead, she ran her fingers across his forearm and pulled him around her tighter. He let his lips brush her neck, and was satisfied when she shivered. *Never underestimate the nostalgia-inducing power of a great song*, he thought, admitting to himself that one of her favorite bands playing live in front of them was probably contributing to her openness at the moment.

Courtney's phone vibrated in her purse and she pulled it out. She held it up for him to see that it was from Vanessa.

V: I'm tired of flirting, come find me.

He took it that she and Luke were in a separation period- it wasn't the first time- and followed Courtney back towards the main backstage area. She stopped abruptly before they walked through the gate and were still largely alone.

"Okay, so I didn't... I don't know what I thought, coming here tonight. You didn't lie... you're different, but it feels the same too. It's kind of messing with my head, and I don't know what you're thinking-"

Before he really thought it through, his hands were in her hair and his lips pressed against hers. Her fingers found their way hastily to his belt loops and she closed the gap still between them. He didn't pull back this time, like he had always done before; he kissed her with the magnitude of a year's worth of mistakes and wishing things were different until she stepped back for air, her hands on his chest.

"I'm sorry," he got out, catching his breath as well. Words began to rush out of his mouth, now that it was no longer occupied. "I don't want to mess with your head. You just said you didn't know what I was thinking, and that's what I was thinking... all night. I didn't mean to push." He couldn't stop the stream of jumbled-up thoughts finding their way into words. "Can I apologize? For everything? I will make you a list of every stupid thing I did last year if you want, just let me make it up to you. You're-"

"Shhhh."

"Okay?"

"Just, let's leave tonight alone. You opened for *Train*, we danced backstage, and that kiss was... well, I think it answered my question," she said. "Let's just go hang out with V. We will talk. I promise. Just not right now, okay?"

"Okay, yeah, of course. Whatever you want." He brushed her lips with his once more and grabbed her hand to walk through the gates. They found Vanessa chatting it up with Crawford on a sofa in the lounge. It did not escape his notice that Courtney dropped his hand when they crossed into their eye line.

"And where have you two been?" Vanessa asked knowingly as Courtney wiggled in next to her on the couch.

"Watching the band, obviously," Courtney replied evenly. Crawford walked up behind him and clapped him on the shoulder. "You didn't tell me you invited such enchanting ladies to the show tonight, Fisher. I had to come across this one all by myself when I overhead her talking about our band."

"Seriously, Ethan, your manners need work. You could have introduced us," Vanessa replied. Crawford handed Vanessa a beer and sat down across from her. Ethan tried to control the surprised look on his face; never in a million years would he have thought the two of them would hit it off.

"I am so sorry. I have been remiss. Courtney, this is Crawford, Crawford, Courtney... clearly, you already know Vanessa."

"Nice to meet you, you guys were seriously amazing tonight. Congratulations on the contest and this and everything," Courtney relayed sincerely, shaking his friend's hand.

"Nice to meet you too, and thank you- it wouldn't have happened without this guy," he replied, gesturing to Ethan. "So are you guys coming out with us then?"

"Out..." Vanessa raised an eyebrow.

"There's a party at this hotel, the radio station is running it. Not sure if those guys will be there," referencing the headliners, "but it should be a pretty good time."

"Um, yes," Vanessa replied without hesitation. Courtney cleared her throat.

"Hey there, V. Can I talk to you for just a sec?" Vanessa rolled her eyes slightly and let Courtney pull her around the corner. He couldn't help it. He had to try to overhear them. Shooting Crawford a look, he casually made his way closer to where they stood.

"...you know I've been missing Luke, I just wanna go out and blow off some steam. You don't have to come if you don't want, I'm sure I can ride with this hottie out here."

"Ugh. I am not doing a very good job of keeping my distance. You know he gets to me, I just don't think that going out and drinking, at a hotel no less, is the smartest thing I could do," Courtney admitted.

"So then don't be smart. You're always smart. I knew as soon as you were alone with him you'd turn into a pile of mush. Just have *fun*. You're in college and we're getting invited to a rad party and literally one of your favorite bands of all time could show up. Come on." Courtney took a breath, and he thought she was going to give in.

"Will you hate me if I just go home? Like, you can go, and I'll even come back and pick you up if you need a ride at four a.m., I just don't think I can do it." Vanessa gave an exasperated sigh.

"All right, girl, whatever makes you happy." Ethan quickly made his way back over to the couch and waited expectantly. The gears were already turning in his mind.

The girls walked back up, and before they could say anything, he said, "Hey, I think I'm gonna get a cab home or something, I don't know if I'm in the mood for a crowd tonight, but there'll be room in Crawford's car if you guys wanna go with him. You should, I'm sure it'll be a killer event." He tried to give off the most innocent vibe possible in that moment and counted on Vanessa to carry his plan to fruition.

"Works for me! I'm gonna take you up on the ride, if that's okay with you, Crawford. Courtney's not gonna come because she's allergic to fun, but she should be able to give you a ride home, then," Vanessa concluded with a devilish look. Courtney's eyes widened, and she shot daggers at her best friend. Vanessa promptly ignored her and slid into the seat next to Crawford, leaning into him flirtatiously.

"Yeah, absolutely. Are you sure, Fisher?" Crawford replied, putting his arm around Vanessa in response.

"Yeah, I'm sure. You guys have fun, though." He took a few steps toward a back room where their gear was stashed, and he felt Courtney's eyes on him. "Come with me, you can carry my guitar."

"There will be no carrying of anything in these shoes," she shot back at him, her face still holding a pissed-off look from the unspoken argument with Vanessa.

"Fine, I'll carry it, you keep me company." He knew he was pushing her, but he didn't care. She hesitated, but finally followed behind him.

"You don't have to drive me home. I'm fine taking a cab, honestly," he lied. He wanted more than anything to be alone with her. It was the only way he could picture ending this night.

"Stop, it's fine. I'd never pass up a chance to drive through Gem anyway. How come you didn't wanna go to the party?" *Because you didn't wanna go*, he thought.

"I don't know. This whole thing was kind of surreal, so I'm sort of in the mood to appreciate it where it's quiet. I'd also like to keep myself out of whatever's going on between V and Luke, so witnessing her make out with my band mate is not on my to-do list." He grabbed his guitar and made a mental note to apologize to his friends later for not helping load the rest of their stuff. They headed down the corridor towards the parking lot.

"Don't even get me started. You know they'll be back together by next weekend. I think she just wants to prove she can be on her own."

"It's happened before, and history would suggest that you're spot-on with that prediction." He held the door open and slid his hand into hers as she walked by. She shot him a sideways glance but did nothing. It took some time, not that he was complaining, but she finally found her little silver Mustang in the still-crowded parking lot. There were a couple of people who recognized him, thanks to the telltale sign that he was carrying his instrument, and complimented their performance. He even signed an autograph on one of the 7-11 Southbound t-shirts that had been for sale that night.

"So, how much are you loving all of the girly attention, then?" Courtney asked, amused.

He grinned at her, hoping it was a hint of jealousy he heard in her voice. "It's not terrible, but to tell you the truth? I'd really prefer the attention from just one girl," he said carefully, nudging her with his elbow not subtly at all. He placed his guitar in the trunk.

Her eyes rolled, but he had made her smile. "You think you're so smooth." When she turned on the car, his band's music came through the speakers. She quickly reached to turn it down.

"So you listened to the CD, then?" He smirked.

"Don't do that."

"Do what?"

"You know what. Don't look like that."

"I literally don't know what you're talking about, but I will try to stop looking however I was looking." He wasn't being entirely truthful. She had mentioned more than once when they were together what it did to her when he carried that expression. He wanted to pretend he didn't know why she was fighting so hard when the pull between them was overwhelming, but he knew exactly why. He felt a familiar sting in his chest when he thought about hurting her.

"Sure you don't." Soon, an old playlist was resounding through the car, and they were cruising up the highway with the windows down. They fell into the old habit of singing along with one another, and that performance felt just as important as winning the battle of the bands. *You cannot screw this up.*

She pulled up in front of his house, and he was ready to convince her why coming in was the best possible idea. "I can't tell you what it meant for you to be there tonight. I, well... I know you said we would talk another time, but really, when have I ever listened to your timelines? So will you come in? We can sit on the deck and drink decaf. I get your hesitation, I-"

"Yes, I'll come in. I was going to ask to anyway, but good job selling it." He breathed. Originally, he had hoped they'd be alone at her house, because he wanted her out of that dress in the worst way, but being at home with his mom and sister sleeping upstairs was much safer. Memories of the last time she'd stood in his kitchen were hard to ignore, but he washed them away with all of the words he'd practiced saying in his head a million times. A pot of coffee brewed while she sat on the porch, and he grabbed her a sweatshirt from his closet.

"Here, it's cold," he told her, handing it over.

"Oh, thanks, yeah, it's so crazy that this is summer. In Phoenix I'd still be sweating in one hundred degree heat at night."

"Yeah, but then there's the seventy degree Christmases to enjoy."

"True, I can't argue there." There was an expectant pause on both sides as he struggled with exactly what to say.

"Yeah, so...I don't really know how to start, but I'm so sorry for how things ended between us. I don't have any excuses for you, that's not why I wanted you to hear me out- I should have done a lot of things differently. I should have told you how I was feeling along the way instead of always acting like I was fine. It was stupid of me to think things were going to be easy, but I let it get to a point where I couldn't take it anymore, the distance."

"Ethan, I was heartbroken when we broke up, but I didn't begrudge you that decision. It *was* hard. Like, so hard. Just..."

"I know. The phone call. I can't. I don't have words. I was, I don't know, in a downward spiral of poor decisions, and I thought if you would just take me back everything would be fine, and that wasn't fair either. I am so sorry." His voice broke in delivering the last apology. Having her sitting in front of him and seeing the residual hurt in her eyes as she recalled that night was almost too much, but he knew it was what had to happen. "Can you at least believe that me calling you that night had everything to do with my own bullshit and nothing to do with wanting to cause you pain?"

She took a moment and he held his breath. "I can believe that, yeah. I didn't know how much I needed you to say it until right now. I sort of thought I had just put it behind me or risen above it or something, but being with you tonight? Put me right back into last year, and well, I needed it, I guess is the shortest explanation I can give."

He wanted to hold her, but knew she had to be the one to initiate it, and he got the feeling she wasn't quite finished yet. "Can we just be real for a minute?"

"As many minutes as you want, yeah, of course." He was afraid what she'd say next, and that she'd channel Vanessa and start yelling.

"Tonight felt good," she admitted, surprising him.

"Yeah, it did."

"And Vanessa was being a bitch because she's mad about Luke, but she said a couple of things that hit home for me, and I feel like we just need to get it all out on the table before I go home, or I won't be able to sleep tonight."

"Well? Lay it out there, then." She hesitated, but pressed on.

"I just got out of a relationship. It was a good relationship, and leaving Phoenix to come here was... difficult." His stomach tightened at listening to her talk about Ben. "But in the interest of full disclosure, I don't think it was as hard as leaving you after homecoming." He nodded in acknowledgement, not wanting to interrupt her. "Seeing you, and well, kissing you, felt... right, like it's how it was supposed to be all along, but in a lot of ways that seems like cheating." He sat back slightly, wondering what she meant. "Not like cheating on him, I mean, I'm single, don't take that the wrong way. It feels like cheating in a universal sense. Like it shouldn't be this easy to fall back into what we had. It can't be that easy, because if it is, then it seems like my relationship for the past seven months was a placeholder, and I need you to know that it wasn't. I'm not saying that to try to hurt you or to emphasize that I was with someone else. I just need to be clear, I guess, before we... I don't know what we're going to do. There have to be some rules or something."

He had forgotten how much she talked. "I knew that you were with someone else. Vanessa and I sort of had a, well, I wouldn't call it a confrontation, because she's the only one who did the confronting, but the point is that I knew. I don't expect-"

"She yelled at you?"

"Yeah, but I had it coming. Really, it's fine."

"No, I just sort of wish I could have seen it, that's all. Sorry, you were saying?"

He gave her a half-smile and laughed slightly at the memory. "I, uh, yeah. I was saying that I don't expect to like... pick up where we left off like nothing happened. I know that I missed the last seven months of your life, and I know that I'm very different now than I was then. Better, I hope, but different. Still, I can't lie and tell you I don't want to do this. I want you. You know that I do."

"And we can agree that there should be... rules? On how exactly to do this?"

"Yes, anything," he said, though he sincerely wondered what possible "ground rules" she had in mind. In the grand scheme of things, it just didn't matter. She stood up and stepped towards the chair where he sat.

"Then I guess we can discuss those tomorrow." She smiled and climbed onto his lap. Her eyes searched his and her expression betrayed her seemingly cool exterior. This moment, with the stars barely visible overhead in the cloudy night sky, it was important. With that, her lips pressed into his tentatively, and he reacquainted himself with the way his hands felt on her skin. Heat spread across his chest when her fingertips found their way there. He had never been more thankful for the invention of sundresses in all his life; her legs were so much better in person than in memory. He didn't ask for anything more, and let her show him what she needed. They continued their reunion tour for almost an hour. He finally stopped distracting her when she said she had to leave for the ^^ forty-seventh time and his lips were near swollen from their intensity. Dizzily, he walked her out to her car.

"When can I see you again?" He was not ashamed of his eagerness.

"When do you wanna see me again?"

"Right now." He kissed her playfully. She laughed against his lips and stepped back.

"I don't have anything going on tomorrow, unless I have to go pick up Vanessa somewhere."

"Nah, Crawford will make sure she gets home. He's a good guy. Can I take you somewhere? Like somewhere good. I canceled all of my lessons and got someone to cover my shift at the pool because I wasn't sure how late I'd be out tonight. Let's go to King's Island and ride roller coasters and eat funnel cake."

Her eyes lit up, and she seemed to have agreed even before he'd said "funnel cake." He kissed her again, his hands unable to stay out of her hair, and let her drive away. *You are the luckiest idiot ever,* he thought, not believing the good fortune that had finally shown up that night.

He ran this thumb over his bottom lip and appreciated the fact that he thought he'd never get to feel that way again.

♪ *"Sparks Fly" – Taylor Swift*
Performed by Landon Austin or Alex G

3

Have you fallen down the freaking rabbit hole? What the hell just happened? She had a good ten minutes of uninterrupted bliss after the tryst with Ethan, but now her brain was working overtime questioning what she'd done. It wasn't even like he had *done* anything. They had been sitting there, discussing things. Serious, important things, and all her mind could focus in on was the way his hair brushed his jaw line and the woodsy smell of him on the sweatshirt he'd lent her, and the reminder of what his lips had felt like earlier that night. Before the concert, she'd promised herself there would be *no* kissing. That they could be friends, or at least friendly. *Pretty sure what happened out on the deck could be classified as friendly,* she thought, groaning inwardly. When he looked at her with that stupid, irresistible, 'I-know-what-you-look-like-naked,' tempting-as-hell *smile,* she lost all sense of logic.

She looked at her phone, ready to call him, though she couldn't be sure if it was to tell him it had all been a mistake and they were better off as friends, or to tell him to get in his car and drive to her house so she could reacquaint herself with the veins that ran down his forearms. *Annnnd your effing lock screen is still a picture of you and Ben from graduation. How are you this terrible a person?* Not even T-Swift could calm her brain at that moment. She was kidding herself if she thought she could walk away from him, though. It was impossible to be entirely sure which feeling was stronger- the nostalgia or the near-hiccups her heartbeat experienced when he touched her, but mixed together, they were completely intoxicating; it was a force of nature. *Just go home and go to sleep. Maybe you will magically know what to do in the morning.* She almost laughed out loud, knowing that telling herself to sleep was ridiculous. There would be no sleep with her mind racing as it was. The whole night had already been a roller coaster, and she knew the next day would be even more so- both figuratively and literally. *You don't have to go tomorrow,* she thought rationally. Cancelling was not out of the question. Except that it was. She couldn't ever envision herself wanting to go sky-diving, but imagined the feeling in her stomach when his kiss had finally found her again was probably the same level of adrenaline and fear-inducing excitement.

Despite putting forth a significant effort to reprimand herself for what could only be considered reckless behavior, she found her lips turning up into a smile without realizing it. The whole night really had been incredible. *God, he is a good kisser.*

* * *

She had been tossing and turning for three hours when she finally heard Vanessa's keys in the front door. She jumped out of bed like there was a sale at Anthropologie and practically pounced on her best friend at the top of the stairs.

"Jesus Christ, Court! Don't DO that!" Vanessa yelled, gripping the banister.

"I'm sorry, I'm sorry, just. Ugh! I have to talk to you!"

"Apparently! Talk while I take off my make-up. And speak slowly. I'm not one-hundred percent sober." Courtney followed her eagerly into the bathroom.

"How did things go, anyway, with Crawford?" Courtney questioned, feeling bad that she didn't think to ask first.

"I'll tell you tomorrow. Just get out whatever crazy thing you're gonna say before I pass out." Courtney grinned sheepishly.

"I sort of...well, I, I don't know what to do, I guess. I need perspective."

"Did you sleep with him?"

"No." She wanted to be offended, but knew it hadn't been out of the question. "I may have reacquainted myself with some of his other... talents." She bit her lip, feeling guilty again.

"Okay...did you at least talk to him about last year?" Vanessa asked with an air of disapproval while she brushed out her hair.

"Yeah, actually, we talked for a while. I think we ended up in a good place. I don't know. It's all so surreal, being around him again. I feel... I don't know how I feel. Yes, I do. I feel horrible because Ben and I just... broke up? Left? It's such a messed up situation." Vanessa looked at her pointedly, and she knew a lecture was coming.

"Okay, so normally I'd let you go on with your crazy theories and analyses about right and wrong and black and white until you ultimately end up at the sensible conclusion. But well? I'm tired, and my buzz is wearing off quickly. So here it is." Courtney sat on the edge of the claw-footed tub, waiting for her friend to impart her wisdom. "Stop feeling guilty about Ben. Like, just stop it. Is he here?"

"No, but-"

"But what? Are you planning on transferring to Irvine at some point in the next four years, or even crazier, stay single for that long and hope he does too?"

"Well, no. I just don't want to bounce from one relationship to another. Isn't that... I don't know, frowned upon?"

"By whom? Yeah, I said whom, so you know I'm freaking serious. For once in your life, just do something because it feels *good*. I saw him looking at you at the concert, and it even made me blush, so I know whatever went down afterwards was probably *very good*. So can we skip the analysis? For real, like, just ignore it."

Courtney started to interrupt, to defend her particular brand of crazy and its overall effectiveness, but she got distracted thinking about the *very good* from the deck earlier that night. *It can't be that easy, though. Nothing ever is.*

"I can see that you're not sold, but here's what's going to happen if you don't take my advice. You're going to keep feeling guilty for no reason about Ben, which is going to make things awkward with Ethan. Then you will convince yourself the awkwardness is a sign that you shouldn't be with him, or that your star charts aren't aligned, or there is a moonbeam interfering with your love numerology- I honestly don't know where you get some of the stuff you worry about, but maybe, instead of all of that, you could just give yourself a real shot with him. Like just go for it. Be crazy in love, don't worry if it will end in a messy, fiery explosion, and let the guilt go." There could have been a mic drop at the end of that monologue, but instead, Vanessa smoothed her hair and sat down next to Courtney on the ledge.

"You're kind of persuasive. Maybe you should be pre-law instead of me."

"Nah. I'll stay in the land of everything that's pretty. You know I love you. Just choose to be happy. And stop driving me insane." Vanessa yawned loudly and shuffled to her room. *I guess that settles that,* Courtney thought, unable to come up with a decent argument against V's advice. She gave in to the emotional side of her brain and texted him before she went to bed, convincing herself she didn't need to feel bad about it later. *Give yourself a real shot with him.* She repeated Vanessa's words in her head, and for the moment, they were enough to allow her to fall asleep.

♪ *"How Far We've Come" – Matchbox Twenty*
"You Are The Best Thing" – Ray LaMontagne
"Hurricane" – Something Corporate
"Love Song For No One" – John Mayer

4

He awoke to his alarm and a mile long queue of text messages the following morning. He hadn't slept that hard in a long time. Before looking at any of them, he did a brief reality check about what had occurred the previous evening. *It actually all happened.* He wasn't even sure which had been more unlikely- opening for a band as well known as Train, or ending the night with Courtney's mouth pressed against his. After allowing sufficient time to relish in that memory, he gave his attention to his phone.

> Crawford: How have you been holding out on me that you have a single friend this hot? What's her story?
>
> E: Too long to text, man. Will catch you up when I see you.

* * *

> Brian: Dude, I can't believe you skipped the party last night- completely insane. Hope you scored with whatever chick took you home.

Nicole Campbell

* * *

V: So, I kind of like your friend. Maybe. I don't know. If you say anything to Luke, I swear to god you will think the last time I yelled at you was a tea party.

Ethan laughed at that one. He had no desire to tell Luke anything, regardless.

* * *

L: Bro, Vanessa and I sort of broke up…again. I know. Anyway, we need to go out, and you are relegated to wingman duty, not that any girl in her right mind would choose you over me, but I wanted to make that clear.

E: Sure man, we can go out. But for real are you okay? Of all people, I'll get it if you're not. You pick the place, I'll buy- tomorrow night.

L: No, I'm not. But I'm not going to have a breakdown like someone I know. I'll hook up with a hot chick and go on a weeklong bender like a normal person, and be good to go in time for classes to start next month.

E: Whatever you say, I'll pick you up tomorrow night.

* * *

C: I just wanted to say that tonight was amazing. The concert, you, everything. I'll see you tomorrow.

E: Just woke up- had to make sure last night was real. Thanks for confirming :). I will pick you up in like an hour. Do you want me to bring coffee?

C: Good morning :). And what a silly question.

E: Haha, okay. Coffee it is.

How One Attempts To Chase Gravity

He got dressed quickly in swim trunks and a t-shirt, throwing a change of clothes into a bag just in case. A hat and a pair of sunglasses later, he was on his way out. His mom was in the laundry room and talking to him before he could slip out the back door.

"I didn't even hear you come in last night, I would have told you that you guys were awesome. I know I'm not, like, hip to your musical tastes or whatever, but it was... well, it made me proud, seeing you perform in that place. Sorry we couldn't stick around for the rest of the concert, Tay had swim team at six this morning... and where are you going?" *Why does she always have to ask questions?*

"Aw, Mom, you're plenty hip, don't sell yourself short. And thanks, it was a rush, I'm not gonna lie. I'm going to King's Island since I had already taken the day off from work."

"With..."

"Mom, I'm not fourteen, you don't have to know everything about everything."

"Yeah, yeah, I'll take it things went well with Courtney last night. You're horrible at misdirection." He couldn't help but smile in response. "Have fun. Bring her home for dinner if you want."

"I will eventually, no promises today. I'll text you when I'm on my way back, though, promise." He rushed to his car, intent on grabbing a mocha and doughnuts on his way to her house. Coffee and pastries in hand, he rang the bell. He felt a jolt of electricity when she opened the door in a very small, white ruffled bikini top and cut offs- the swimsuit bottoms peeking above the waistband of her shorts.

"Hi, I'm sorry, I'm almost ready, I swear," she promised, sticking bobby pins into her hair frantically.

He stepped across the threshold and leaned down to kiss her anyway, despite her hurry. He felt her relax as she kissed back. "Don't apologize, there is no rush. Take a breath... and feel free to run around here as long as you want dressed in this," he flirted.

"You like it?" she asked playfully, doing a twirl.

"I like you, but yes, this doesn't hurt." He looked around as she disappeared into a room off the entryway. He heard the dryer door open and she reappeared wearing a black tank top and applying lip-gloss. "So, am I to wander your house freely, or are you going to give me a tour?"

"Oh my gosh, yes, I'm sorry. Come here." She flitted across the house, barefoot, and he followed. The floor plan was small, but laid out well. Dark stained wood floors and original details stood out as he looked around, coming into the kitchen. There was a table large enough for four made of what looked like reclaimed wood. He pulled out a rounded silver chair and sat down. "I need coffee, and then I'll show you the rest, but this is our kitchen- all décor choices are credited to Vanessa, she's a genius, but I like it... it feels homey." The cabinets were painted a pale yellow and all accents were white and metallic. It was girly, but it looked good. There was definitely a comfort vibe about it. She scooted out the chair next to his, but he pulled her into his lap instead.

"I just wanted to say good morning," he teased her, his lips making contact with her cheek. She tensed up slightly, and he let her go, shooting her a confused look. "What's wrong?"

"Nothing, just ah, adjusting. This is new. And not so new, I guess." She smiled, seeming somewhat more relaxed. She looked pensive, and he wondered if he should have let her set the tone when he arrived. Thankfully, she surprised him by leaning back into his chest and turning his hat around so it could not interfere with her plans. Her lips parted and pressed against his with a purpose. Suddenly, King's Island seemed like an afterthought, and all he wanted to do was see her bedroom. She eventually pulled back and slid into the other chair.

All mornings should start that way. "I missed you." She stated it like it was a confession, sipping her coffee.

"No complaints here, I'm good with that becoming our traditional greeting." They chatted over doughnuts, and she determined she was awake enough to finish getting ready and head to the theme park.

"Come with me, I'll show you the upstairs and grab my bag, then we're good to go!" He followed her as she trotted up the stairs on her toes, enjoying the view. "Vanessa's room is there, but she'll kill me if

I show it to you right now. She's in hangover rescue mode." She kept walking. "This is our bathroom, and here is my room." She paused briefly and opened the white painted door to reveal a small but airy space. The breeze was flowing through the window, playing with the white cotton curtains next to her desk. Her bed set up against a gray tufted headboard, and the white comforter had more ruffles than he'd ever seen in one place. It was adorned with several sparkly pillows, and he grinned.

"This is the Courtney-est room I could have imagined." She smiled shyly.

"Well, V decorated, but she knows me better than anyone, so that makes sense, I guess. You really like it?"

"I do. I'll have to ask her to do my room next." He sat casually on the end of her bed while she threw things into an oversized purse, willing her to walk over to him.

"Okay, I think I'm ready." She finished, topping her head with a pair of large sunglasses.

"I think you'll have to help me up," he stated, holding out his hand. She shook her head, not buying it for a moment, and marched over to him. She placed her hand in his and he pulled her in close. He dropped kisses on her forehead, her nose, her eyelids, and finally reached her mouth. She pushed his hat all the way off this time and let her nails run through his hair. The feeling of being with her and knowing there was no one there to check on them was strange. Even though he was nineteen and about to enter college, living at home took away some of the "adulthood" of the transition. He looked up at her and continued down her neck in the way she liked. His hands moved up the back of her shirt and he started to pull on the strings that tied her bikini together.

"Ground rules." She breathed, stepping back and placing her hands on his elbows.

"Ground rules?" he asked, not wanting to stop.

"Yes. We need to agree on some things. We talked about this."

"Yes, you're right. Let's do that," he agreed, coming down from the high he got when he made physical contact with her.

"We can talk and drive. You're not getting out of taking me on roller coasters, no matter how distracting you can be. I haven't been to King's Island since I was eleven, so you better follow through."

"Does this mean you're going to ride them fearlessly with me? I don't really appreciate whining on roller coasters."

"Oh, you don't even know with whom you're dealing," she answered playfully.

"Really, Shakespeare? With whom I am dealing?"

"Well, it's the proper way to say it."

"Ah, sprinkles. I missed you."

She grabbed his hand and pulled him off the bed and down the stairs. He was excited about spending the day with her no matter what, but began to worry about these guidelines she had in mind. *Whatever they are, they don't matter. She's giving you another shot. That's enough.*

They drove and she sang and he worried, which made him wonder when their roles had reversed.

"What's wrong?" she asked him finally, turning down the music.

"Nothing." He grinned purposefully at her.

"Well then, let's talk. I want us to have fun today, so no dark clouds ahead. Deal?"

"Deal. Lay it on me." She took a long inhale after that, and his concern deepened.

"Okay, so, like, I know that we can't start fresh, and I wouldn't want to even if we could. We have a history, and it's not one I want to forget. Being with you… it brings back good things."

"But…" He waited.

"But, we haven't really spoken, or hung out, in seven months."

"True."

"So, I don't think I'm in a place where us being… *together* for the first time… well, the first time again… I don't want it be a quickie before we go to King's Island. I'm sorry, I don't know how else to say it." She blurted it out so quickly, it took him a moment to catch up. Things started to make sense in his head.

"You're right. I'm sorry. I didn't mean to make you feel like... I don't know, like I just expected..."

"Don't apologize, I just think we should, I don't know, slow it down a bit. Yeah? I want it to be..."

"I get it, I absolutely get it. Okay? I want it to be that too."

"Okay, good. That's item number one."

"How many items do you have on that list in your head? Just so we're on the same page. They do all fit on one page, yes?"

"Only one more, I think, so no need to be snarky."

"All right, all right, shoot."

"I just wanted to put it out there, before either of us says something and it gets, like, awkward..." She sat there for a long moment, not saying anything, and he started to get nervous again.

"Court, you're starting to freak me out, just tell me."

"I'm sorry, it's just a weird thing to say. I don't know if we say 'I love you,' anymore, or if we wait, or even how you feel, and this is the most uncomfortable conversation I think I've ever had." Her cheeks were red, and that made his heart swell even more. He grabbed her hand and kissed the back of it as he drove down the highway.

"That one's easy for me."

"It is?" she asked, still struggling to look him in the eyes.

"I've loved you since I met you. When we danced at the river? I knew that was it for me, so there's no going back on my end. If you don't want me to say it because it's too soon, or too much pressure, then I won't. But I don't want you to be unsure of my feelings for you." He pressed his lips to her hand again, hoping he hadn't gone too far, but words always seemed to just find their way off his tongue when he was with her.

"You never told me that before," she spoke softly.

"That I loved you?" he asked, confused.

"No. About the river. That's when I knew too."

"Oh, no, I guess I didn't. We never really talked about it." She paused for a beat.

"I love you, too. Still. I worked really hard not to, but when I saw you at orientation…"

"You knew you had failed miserably and wanted to make me your love slave until the end of time?"

"That was my exact thought, yes." She grinned. "I went out and bought handcuffs immediately after my advisor meeting." Her eyes sparkled at him and he knew the serious part of their talk was done. He did want to know more about these handcuffs though. He flirted shamelessly with her until they arrived in the parking lot. She hadn't lied about going on every roller coaster, and had apparently searched the Internet for the best schedule to hit every ride with the shortest wait times and the least amount of walking in between.

"Only you would schedule your fun this intensely. You know that, right?"

"Yes. I'm one of a kind- this is why you love me."

"All right, all right, where to first, then?"

"Seriously? Like it's not obvious?"

"I'm on pins and needles." She shoved him playfully.

"We start on The Beast. You've read the Goosebumps book, right? When you were a kid?"

"Um, no. There was a book about the ride?"

"Yes! Oh my god, I'm going to buy it for you, but anyways, it's King's Island's claim to fame, so that is our starting point. An oldie but a goodie."

They spent the day riding every coaster in the park, some twice, and making out on the "Boo Blaster" ride.

She convinced him to take photo booth pictures, even though he warned her he couldn't be trusted in a small-enclosed space. She pulled him in anyway, and the photos came out a little R-rated.

"Well, these are not scrapbook-acceptable, are they?" She smiled contentedly when they finally exited the booth.

"That would depend entirely on the theme of the scrapbook. If it is 'hot faces Courtney makes when Ethan is-' "

"Yeah, okay, thanks for that," she said, clamping her hand over his mouth. "Are you ready to call it a day or you wanna wind down at the water park?"

"If we go to the water park, will you be wearing that bikini?"

"That is the plan."

"Then that is where we are going. You wanna ride?" He turned around to offer her his back, and she hopped on willingly. She took his hat off and put it on her own head while he carried her towards Soak City.

"I look super edgy now in this hat. I just need an eyebrow piercing and a tattoo and I might actually fit in with your people."

"Well, we can take care of that today, babe. There's a tattoo studio not far from campus. We'll stop and get them both done at the same time. Plus, Ethan is really easy to spell, so they should be able to finish it pretty quickly for you."

"It's a good thing you're so pretty, because your jokes suck," she told him, shoving the hat back on his head. They conquered water slides and lounged by the pool until they were both too worn out to carry on. As they shuffled to his car, he walked behind her and rested his chin on her head. Once on the road, the music was mellow and they held hands quietly, both tired from their adventure.

"I need a nap." She yawned as they pulled up in front of her house.

"A nap sounds good," he realized, his whole body moving slowly from the heat.

"Well, do you have to be home for any specific reason?" she asked.

"No, I don't suppose I do."

"Then come, let's sleep and rally. Vanessa and I can make dinner tonight. And when I say make dinner, I mean we'll order in food."

"That very seriously sounds like the best idea you've ever had."

Courtney let Vanessa in on their plan, and she agreed, but informed them she'd be inviting Luke over too.

"Are you for real? How long did that last, like, thirty-six hours?" he asked incredulously. "You literally texted me this morning that you liked Crawford."

"I did like Crawford, but that made me realize I love Luke. Keep your comments to yourself, Judgy McJudgerton."

"Whatever you say- just let me sleep." He went upstairs while Courtney got all of the soap-opera-esque details from her friend about how she and Luke got back together. He slid under the covers and was very nearly asleep when she entered the room.

"Hey, I'm gonna jump in the shower, I'll be right back," she informed him, grabbing a towel from the back of her desk chair.

"Hoooold up. You did not just come in here and tell me you'd be in the shower and think you were gonna walk out, did you?"

"Well, yeah, that was my plan."

"I'm coming too, I am very in need of a shower. With you."

"Ethan, we just talked about the ground rules-"

"I am acutely aware of the rules. I will remain in my swim trunks the entire time, and you can wear that thing you claim is a bathing suit. No rule breaking, Scouts' Honor."

"No way you were ever a boy scout."

"Do you want me to swear a musician's oath or something?"

She was quiet for a moment. "No rule breaking?"

"I promise." She smiled and made her way out of the room. He took the lack of argument as a yes and grabbed a towel to follow her. It was, without a doubt, the hottest shower he'd ever taken, and it had nothing to do with the temperature. He didn't break the rules, but he didn't even try to keep his hands to himself. She eventually kicked him out, claiming his wandering fingertips and their habit of tickling her were not conducive to her washing her hair. He couldn't help it. She slid in next to him minutes later after putting something-or-the-other on her skin that made her smell like a cupcake, and found the spot where she fit on his shoulder. Her tank top and shorts were soft and he briefly thought about why only girls got really comfy loungewear. Coming back to earth, he was beginning to wonder if he'd wake up and realize all of this had happened in his head- it was too perfect for words. They fell asleep quickly and awoke to the doorbell, the moon high in the sky outside her window.

Courtney stretched next to him, and he took the opportunity to tickle her sides again.

"Not fair!" She giggled. "I hate that you're not ticklish."

"Well, at least not anywhere you've tried so far. I totally encourage you to keep searching." She rolled her eyes and hit him with a pillow.

"You are relentless. Now go downstairs and keep Luke company, I need to do my makeup and put on real clothes."

"That is ridiculous. You look amazing, even when you just wake up. Which is something I like, by the way… seeing you next to me when I open my eyes." He kissed her shoulder, then her collarbone, and her neck up to her ear and she shivered involuntarily.

"Relentless," she sighed, kissing him back.

"Hey, friends, long time no see!" Luke bellowed as he burst through the door. He looked like a surfer, his hair lighter than last Ethan saw him. He was going to give him so much shit for getting highlights.

"Luke! Get out of my-" but he continued like Courtney didn't exist.

"Nice room… I dig it. Hey, V! Good job in here, I like the essence of girliness," he finished, yelling down to his once-again-girlfriend. "See how I'm taking an interest in her future career? That's what good boyfriends do. You should make a note of that, bro."

"Dude, can you vacate the premises? We will be down in a minute." Ethan scolded his friend, but it was difficult because he looked so stupidly happy. Ignored… again.

"So, Courtney Ross, I see that you wasted no time in luring my man Fisher back into bed? You've lived here for what, two weeks? Tsk tsk, I expected more from you." He would not stop grinning.

"Oh my god, get out of my room!" Courtney tried to sound stern as well, but she couldn't wipe the smile off her face. She chucked a pillow at Luke's head, but he dodged it easily.

"Well, I can see where I'm not wanted, but now you've hurt my feelings, so I may not share the insane amount of Mexican food I brought over from that place down the street. Just think about that before you throw anything else at me." He gave Courtney an "I'm watching you" gesture and finally lumbered out of her room and back down the stairs.

"Are you sure it's a good thing that they're back together?" Courtney asked Ethan.

"Not at all. But he kind of grows on you, you know?"

"Yeah. Don't tell him that. Anyway, I'm really going to do something to my face. And then eat a lot of Mexican food."

"Fine fine. I'll go. I'm starving." He was slow to get moving, but shuffled down the stairs and into the kitchen to find Luke and Vanessa in a compromising position.

"Ah-hem." He cleared his throat.

"Hi Ethan," Vanessa said slowly as she untangled her legs from around Luke's waist and hopped down from the counter. "You want some food? A margarita? We bought a new blender," she explained proudly.

"Food, yes, gonna pass on the beverage. I'll have to head home in a bit here." He wanted to stay with Courtney, but he knew she had to be the one to suggest it, and he also knew he would wait as long as she needed. The entire day had been better than any pseudo-reality he'd ever created in his head, because it was real and she challenged him every step of the way. Now dressed in black and white polka dotted shorts and a white tank top that just barely showed her stomach, Courtney joined them and complained passionately about the quality of the food, or lack thereof, and insisted that any restaurant in Phoenix would be better. It didn't stop her from eating more than her fair share, however, as they sat around the large whitewashed coffee table in their living room.

"Hey, boyfriend, we need to go to the rec center or something… otherwise the Freshman Fifteen is going to turn into the Freshman Fifty." He looked at her without answering. "What? Do I have cilantro in my teeth or something?"

"No, your teeth are perfect. Can you just repeat what you said to me, though?" he asked, baiting her.

"That we should hit the gym? Is that, like, insulting to you or something? I mean I know you've got those abs, but doing some cardio wouldn't- OH!" He watched as realization sank in that she had called him "boyfriend." Whether out of habit or not, he loved the look of embarrassment she was giving him. Luke and Vanessa just exchanged a look and kept right on eating. "Yeah, I'm just gonna grab some water, or something... that is not in this room" She hopped up and headed for the kitchen. He followed her, a smirk on his face.

"Babe, it's okay. I was just giving you a hard time," he assured her once they were alone.

"I know, I know. Is that what we are, though?"

"I recited a monologue today about the depth of my feelings for you, so I think the word 'boyfriend' is appropriate, if you want. I'm not here to rush things. I'm not going anywhere, I promise. So we'll do what you want to do."

"You always make everything sound so simple."

"It is simple."

"For you... you think with your heart and then seem surprised when your head catches up." Ethan was taken aback by the harshness of her words.

"Um, okay?"

"No, no, I don't mean it negatively... just an observation. It's what makes you a great musician, and great at a lot of other things that I'm *very* appreciative of. You do what feels good and it seems to make decisions very easy for you. But you know me. I'm an over-analyzer, and all I keep thinking is that we start college in a couple of weeks, and I know it's not the same as before, because we're both here, but what if it doesn't work? And we have to see each other all of the time. I... well, it hurt. A lot. Trying to get over you before, and I don't know if I can do it again... the last couple of days have been-"

"Baby, breathe. Please." He put his hands on her shoulders and rubbed her arms, trying to be a calming force. "You're worrying about something that hasn't happened."

"That's sort of what worrying is all about. I know. It's insane."

He laughed slightly, feeling some of the tension release from her body. "I know you think I don't worry, and I guess compared to what's going on in your head, I really don't, but I've spent a lot of time worrying about us. That you'd refuse to speak to me, or that what was between us wouldn't be the same. But it is. It's still you and me, and I don't need to analyze it."

"What it must be like to live in your head." She sighed. "Do you realize we've never even had a fight? Not really, anyway. Like what kind of couple doesn't argue? How do we even know if we can do it properly?" Now she was just being ridiculous. He decided the best approach was to demonstrate.

"Well, let's do it, then. Ummm, glitter is stupid. It's to be used for children's art projects and not as an accessory."

She let out a mock gasp. "Take it back, Ethan Fisher."

"Nope, sorry. When I get into an argument, I stand my ground until my girlfriend distracts me. Also? I lied to you the night we met. I don't really like John Mayer. I mean, he's super dreamy and all, but at that point in our very short relationship? I was trying to get in your pants, so I said I did."

"What kind of monster are you?" she shot back playfully.

He grinned. "Can we stop this nonsense now? Like, if we argue, then we'll argue. And then we'll make up. And it will be okay. I am getting an overwhelming sense of déjà vu trying to convince you to be my girlfriend, so I'm not going to push anymore, you just let me know what you want and when you want it, and I'll do that. Okay?"

"I want to go and eat another horribly prepared empanada."

"Done." He grabbed her hand and pulled her back in the direction of the living room, glad that conversation was over for the time being.

"Thank you... *boyfriend.*" He left the kitchen with the same smirk he wore when he entered. They walked in to an empty sofa and music floating down the stairwell from Vanessa's room. "I'll take it they are done hanging out with us."

"It would appear that way." He sank down into their woven charcoal sofa and waited while she opened the front windows.

"I will never get tired of summer nights here," she expressed wistfully.

"Me either," he responded, though he suspected their definitions of the word "here" might be different. He watched her stare into the night sky and wondered what she was thinking. "Come here. Tell me what classes you're taking," he said, seeing her textbooks stacked up neatly next to the couch. That brought her back to him, and she plopped down to his right, already spouting off class descriptions and everything she'd learned from skimming through the texts. He had never seen anyone that excited about school. She was registered as Political Science/Pre-Law, and that was kind of a turn on for him. Thinking about her in a courtroom in a suit or something, it was working. As a freshman, she was disappointed she couldn't take too many classes in her major, but seemed jazzed about English and math just the same.

"Tell me about yours," she said when she had run out of things to tell him about Poli Sci 110.

"Well, I don't think I'm quite as well versed in my course syllabi just yet, but I talked to my advisor about majoring in Marketing and minoring in Music Technology. I don't know exactly what I'd do with it, but it sounds cool?"

"That's perfect for you!"

"Yeah?"

"Of course, people love you. You'd be great doing publicity or marketing for a label or indie bands or something. Seriously, it's genius."

"Well thank you, I do try." He shrugged his shoulders in mock arrogance.

She kissed him unexpectedly. "This has been one of the best days ever. I know I'm a nerd, but thank you for listening to my spiel about classes and school. I've been holding it in, but I just can't believe we're going to be on the same campus every day."

Her excitement was contagious. Even he was looking forward to beginning the semester and moving towards something real, something he might actually want to do with his life. "You're kind of amazing, sprinkles. I love you." He kissed her forehead sweetly. "And today has been the best day I've had in a long time. But unfortunately, I need to head home." *Just tell me to stay,* he thought, but he knew that she wouldn't. Things were going well, and he accepted that her head needed time to catch up to his heart. "Walk me out?"

She slid to the door and tiptoed out to his car, barefoot. "What does your week look like?"

"I've gotta be at the pool pretty much every morning, and I have lessons tomorrow and Wednesday…band practice on Tuesdays and Thursdays, but I can rearrange almost anything if you have something specific in mind," he promised, leaning against his car.

"I've got, like, six job interviews lined up this week, but maybe we could have dinner or something? One night that you don't have practice?"

"Of course. Do you wanna go out or come to my house for family dinner?" He was joking about the latter, but he wanted to get a reaction.

"Come to your house," she blurted out unexpectedly.

"Really? I was sort of kidding, I can take you to dinner."

"Yeah, well, Vanessa and I really don't know how to cook, so going out to dinner doesn't even compare to how a home cooked meal sounds right now. Plus, I kind of like your family. I'm totally wearing my Time Turner necklace to impress your sister."

"Well then, family dinner it is. I'll double check with my mom, but Wednesday is probably good."

"Yay!" She clapped. "I love you, too, by the way. I think I only said it in my head before. Drive safe. Text me later, or tomorrow, or-"

"You know I will. Don't stress." He bent down and brushed her lips with his before getting in the car. "I'll talk to you later." She blew him a kiss as he backed out of the driveway, and he couldn't remember ever feeling as steady as he was in that moment. He even found a playlist she had made for him last fall and let the barrage of John Mayer songs wash over him for good measure on the way home.

♪ *"Caught Up In You" – Kate Voegele (feat. Inland Sky)*

5

She hurried back into the house, no longer a single girl. *Were you ever really single after you saw him, anyway?* Her heart and her brain had been at odds since orientation- maybe before. She had crafted such careful reasons for why it was better for her to start college being on her own. *How is it that he always knows what to say when you have a seemingly logical argument?* The things she fretted over for hours in the middle of the night were casually erased by a single phrase. Everything was just so clear-cut for him. He did what he wanted- it seemed so simple, but she always had seven layers of crap piled on top of what she wanted: *Why do you want it? What will happen if you don't get it? Even crazier, what will happen if you do get it? How long will it last? Is it the best thing to even want? What if, what if, what if?* It was exhausting being in her own mind. *No wonder Vanessa thinks you're insane.* She couldn't have been more grateful that she had sought her friend's advice the night before, though- that conversation was absolutely to thank for the near-perfect day she had just experienced.

Despite all the chatter, her body was lit up from the heat between them. It was all-consuming, but she'd missed it. When he was touching her, she couldn't worry about anything else. He was a really beautiful version of an anti-anxiety drug. She realized she had been pacing between the kitchen and living room, and knew she had to just let it go- there were job interviews to stress over instead.

She spent what was left of her productive hours online, reviewing common questions for the thousandth time, looking up information about the two companies she had lined up for tomorrow, and trying to come up with non-cheesy ways to make herself sound awesome.

* * *

Courtney pranced nervously around her room in a gray pencil skirt and a yellow silk blouse, feeling like she was impersonating a grown up. Finally making her way downstairs, she felt more like throwing up than eating. She came upon Luke with his head in their refrigerator. "Ah-hem," she said, waiting to pass through to the coffee.

"Well, aren't you looking fancy this morning? Are you auditioning to be a librarian?" he asked quite seriously.

"Ugh, no. I have a job interview at a law firm. Do I really look like a librarian?"

"Yeah. Just a little though. Are the lawyers men or women?"

"Men. Why?"

"Then you need to unbutton about three of those," he gestured to her top.

"Shut up. No, I don't. They're, like, old."

"Uh-huh. You should unbutton them. I'm not talking like wardrobe-malfunction, but not so stuffy. Just one guy's opinion, but well, it's the right one, so take it or leave it," he stated, as though it were written in stone, before finally moving out of her way. She sighed, annoyed that this was her first conversation of the morning.

Vanessa wandered in looking like she was in need of caffeine as well, and Luke asked her opinion on the matter. "Well. It's what I would do, but you're a lot more... proper than I am, so you do what you want. They'll probably hire you either way." Courtney stuck out her tongue in a very mature fashion at Luke and grabbed a mug. She just wanted the interviews to be over and to have a job already. Her mom had sent her no less than four good luck texts in the past twelve hours, and it wasn't helping her stress level. *Get. It. Together.* She knew she would be fine once she was sitting in their office, answering questions because the adrenaline would take over. She always performed well under pressure; it was the lead-up that killed her. Quickly, she looked at her phone to gauge how much time she had left before needing to head out, and saw a familiar name in her message log.

> B: Hey Court, just wanted to say good luck on your interviews today- don't stress, all right? You'll knock 'em dead.

Her heart ached at Ben's sweetness. She'd forgotten even mentioning the interview to him last week over an iChat. He didn't know she had even seen Ethan, and it was probably kinder to keep it that way, but it crossed her mind that Ethan might not be as impressed with Ben's words of encouragement. *That is a worry for another time,* she told herself. Her brain was at capacity.

> C: Thank you! Heading out soon, thanks for the vote of confidence.
>
> B: I miss you, you know? I know we said we wouldn't make this harder on each other than it needed to be…I just had to tell you that. I've got an early practice so I'm headed out of here soon. Lemme know how they go.
>
> C: I miss you too. Have a good practice.

It wasn't a lie. She did miss him. She also felt like the scum of the earth for not telling him she was seeing someone. *Another thing to worry about later.* The "later" list was becoming a little scary. She practiced deep breathing and got ready to leave. Her heart skipped a little when Ethan messaged her on her way out. *Sigh.*

♪ *"The Page" – The Appleseed Cast*
"First Day of My Life" – Bright Eyes
"Fast Car" – Tracy Chapman
(Performed by: Boyce Avenue Feat. Kina Grannis)

6

E: So I take it we are not going out for you to pick up on drunk women tonight?

L: Yeah probably not in my best interest.

E: You guys are so predictable.

L: Ah yes, compared to you and Courtney, the wild card couple? Please. I knew she'd take you back. You're too pretty.

E: Yeah yeah, don't hate. Nice highlights by the way, speaking of being pretty. If you wanna go out anyway, sans wingman duty for me, lemme know.

L: Shut up. I'm down, text me later

Ethan got ready for his shift at the pool, a new band he'd just come across blaring in his ears. He made a mental note to see if he had any talent whatsoever for playing harmonica when he went into Vinyl that afternoon. He had a few sets of lyrics that had been pissing him off, and now knew it was because they needed that specific sound behind them. Playing with Southbound had expanded his musical horizons more in the first month than playing with Tin Roof had in a year. His friends' tastes ranged from The Ramones to The Appleseed Cast to Mr. Bungle, and he was finding new music every day. He had forgotten what it was like to discover an album for the first time and find himself in it.

> E: My mom said Wednesday is good. Do I really have to wait until then to see you? I'm going out with Luke tonight, but I can't stand you being this close and not looking at your face.
>
> C: I'll have to see what I can do :).
>
> E: And good luck on your interviews today. Anywhere promising?
>
> C: One law firm with a PT receptionist opening. That would be awesome, but we'll see. I'm so nervous! I've only ever interviewed to be a babysitter or for Krispy Kreme.
>
> E: You're like the most proper and professional person I've ever met. They would be crazy not to hire you.
>
> C: <3 I'll let you know how it goes, and see if I can come visit you for a minute today or tomorrow.
>
> E: Perfect. Talk to you then.

He ate his breakfast in the car and headed to the pool. It was semi-overcast out, so he hoped it would be a slow day. He got his wish, and spent most of the morning shooting his co-workers with a water gun from his post by the diving board. Nearing the end of his half-day shift, he blew the whistle for an adult swim break, and may have sprayed some of the younger kids climbing out of the pool with the Super Soaker.

"Is that really considered appropriate life-guard behavior? I mean, you are literally supposed to be guarding *lives*."

He was smiling before he even looked at her. He motioned to one of the other guys that he was taking five and climbed down. "Just enjoying my work, sprinkles. And speaking of... this is very sexy secretary of you." He was not used to seeing her in professional attire. He twirled her around and admired her butt in a tight belted skirt. He liked when she wore heels and he didn't have to bend down so far to kiss her. She smiled against his lips.

"Well, I gotta say I like your work clothes better. I may become a permanent fixture here at the pool just to stake out my territory."

"Anytime, babe. Is this lunch you're offering?" he asked, pointing to the bag she was holding. "And how was your interview?"

"Yes, and good. Really good, actually. You are looking at the newest receptionist for Kramer and Green, Attorneys at Law. At least on Tuesdays and Thursdays." She beamed.

"Seriously? On the spot? That's great, Court. I told you they'd hire you!" He pulled her in for a slightly sweaty hug, but she didn't complain. "I'm off in, like, fifteen minutes, you want me to meet you in the park and we can toast our sodas to your success?"

"Perfect, I'll scope out a good spot." He blew the whistle to let the anxious swimmers back into the pool, and waited for shift change. Thankfully, his replacement got there right on time, and he was showered and on his way to the park. It still took a second for him to register that she was his when he saw her. Part of his brain still lived in the recent past when he didn't know if she'd speak to him again. Life was good.

He sat down beside her, kissing her like they weren't in the middle of the city park, and checked out the spread. "Nice. I was kind of expecting burgers and fries."

"Nope. Soup and salad- I wasn't kidding about needing to work out. Vanessa is a horrible influence on my food choices."

"Sure. Vanessa's at fault for your crazy eating habits. Whatever you wanna tell yourself."

"Shush."

He made her tell him all about her new job, which she apparently would begin training for the following week. He was excited for her, and selfishly happy she'd be working somewhere that had regular business hours. That meant her nights would be mostly free.

"If memory serves me correctly... and I can assure you that this particular one is pretty accurate, you have a birthday very soon. What are we doing?"

"Meh, whatever."

"Hold on, I have to decipher the girl code. Bear with me, it's been a while. So, you want me to serenade you outside of your window and then whisk you off to a romantic dinner and dancing?"

"Serenade? Maybe, but, like, on my back patio, not under my window. Dinner sure, dancing... what kind? I'm not hitting up the club with you or something."

"Did you just say 'hitting up the club'? Like, that right there proves that you're not allowed to go to any club. Anywhere. Maybe a country club. They'd like you there... all those guys named Biff in their starched polos."

"Biff sounds nice, I bet he'd teach me to golf."

"So, for your birthday, you want golfing lessons from a guy named Biff at the country club. You are an odd girl, but I'm glad that's settled."

"You are in a super special mood today, boyfriend," she said, smiling.

"Yeah, you kind of do that to me."

"In all seriousness... can we just have a repeat of last year's birthday? That was the best one I've ever had." She held his gaze for a meaningful beat, and he stopped messing with her.

"Consider it done."

They finished their picnic and solidified plans for Wednesday. He said goodbye to her for so long standing outside her car that he was two minutes late for his first lesson, but he felt confident that it was worth it.

* * *

He left Vinyl with a harmonica in hand, intending to text Luke. He had three missed calls from Crawford, which was more than a little out of character, so he returned those before even pulling out of the parking lot.

"Hey, I saw you called, what's up?"

"Yeah, man, I sort of have some bad news, well, difficult news to deliver, anyway." Ethan's nervous energy kicked in and he started tapping his foot on the floorboard.

"Well, spit it out."

"We heard from Benny today, and he's done subbing on tour with Revelation... but the tour manager offered Southbound a spot to open for the ten shows they added on to the end of the run if we want it. The label approved it, and it's sort of... well a huge opportunity. But."

"But Benny will be taking his spot back," Ethan finished for him, trying to keep his voice even.

"Dude, I'm so sorry, like, Southbound isn't even the same band without you. I just don't know how to pass up this break."

"No, I get it. And you were upfront from the beginning that he could come back and it would be up in the air. I mean, it blows. Like, playing with you guys has been...I don't know, I felt like everything finally clicked, you know? But I'm not gonna be pissed at you or anything."

"It might make me feel like less of a sell-out if you were."

"It's not selling out to try to get out there. You guys will be great. We'll need to figure out which songs you need to pull from the set list, but we can sit down or talk about it whenever."

"Yeah man, for sure, all of your stuff is yours, but we can make sure we're on the same page. If anything opens up or we actually get anywhere with this label, know that you're at the top of my list- I will sing your praises to anyone who will listen and maybe you can get a leg up, yeah?"

"I appreciate it, call me when you know when you're leaving and we'll chill before then. I'm happy for you, honestly, don't feel bad."

"Well, you're a better man than I, but thanks for everything. I'll call you."

Ethan clicked and dropped his phone, leaning his head back and staring at the ceiling in his car. Exhaling loudly, he felt like he was deflating. He tried to convince himself that this was for the best before the reality of it came crashing down. School was starting in a matter of weeks, and going on tour would have screwed all of that up. He wished it wasn't so damned close to the dream he'd had pre-college. Touring, especially with guys like that, who got him, had been his vision for so many years, and it was hard to see it happening for someone else. This wasn't the first band he'd walked away from, but it was never like this. Crawford had saved him when he was floundering for a new direction, and kept him from burning out trying to find it on his own. He sat for a while in the parking lot, arguing with himself. There was the part of him that knew he'd need to man up and let it go. He had known this was a possible outcome since the beginning. The other part of him wanted to cancel plans with Luke and be alone. And probably high. *Maybe you need to develop a new coping mechanism.* Despite the knowledge that it wasn't his fault, the weight of failure was crushing. He thought about calling Courtney, but hated the idea of sounding this pathetic to her, not when she was out treating herself to a pedicure or something with Vanessa.

He finally acted on one of those thoughts and texted Luke that he was on his way.

"So, where to?" Luke asked cheerfully.

"Wherever," he replied, unable to match his friend's tone.

"Are you PMSing again?"

"Nope."

"You are a moody son of a bitch sometimes, you know that?"

"I know." He felt gutted. He was trying so hard to snap out of it, but the weight of losing the place where he fit was hard to shake.

"All right, I know where we're going. A place off the 75, just drive and I'll tell you where to go."

"Okay? I'm not going to a strip club."

"It's not a strip club, Fisher, have you ever even *met* V? I would literally be dead if she found out I took you to... Jesus, just trust me."

They arrived at a sort of hole-in-the-wall pub off the highway and went in after Luke finally dragged out of him the reason behind his sudden turn in mood. A large-chested waitress came to take their order. She eyed them both appreciatively before speaking.

"How are you guys doing tonight? My name's Sandra, I'll be taking care of you." Ethan knew it was probably her typical script, but the way she said it had other implications.

"Hi, Sandra. I am doing just fine, but my buddy here has gotten some bad news, I'm afraid, and is in need of cheering up. I told him we had to eat at this place tonight because they have the hottest servers, so I'm glad to see I didn't end up a liar," Luke flirted with her. She rolled her eyes but shot him a seductive smile. "Is there any way you could get the bar tender to mix us up something to get this guy out of his funk? I, for one, can only take so much more of his whining, so it's sort of an emergency." Luke was laying it on so thick Ethan didn't think there was any way she was going to do it without carding them, but five minutes later there were two "Mind Benders" sitting in front of them. After letting the first drink burn its way down his throat, it was apparent that the drink was approximately ten parts alcohol to one part pineapple juice. Luke's napkin had a phone number added to it, which pleased him endlessly.

"You have no shame."

"Whatever, at least now we have drinks. You're welcome, by the way. Secondly, they have an open mic in about twenty minutes, if you had bothered to even look at the sign, and you're gonna play something ridiculously lame, get drunk with me, and then our girlfriends will come pick us up and you'll get over this sad sack routine about your band." It wasn't posed as a question. Luke tossed back what was left of his Mind Bender and ordered them both another. He regaled Ethan with the details of his initial meet and greet with his new team, the coaches, the practice schedule, really everything he never wanted to know about BG basketball.

"Oh, and check this out, I got to meet my roommate."

"And…?"

"He's cool, I like him. I mean, he's on the team too, they have us all room together... something about keeping each other on track or whatnot. He's from like Omaha or some shit, I don't know. His name's Derek, I'll bring him out one night."

"Cool, man, I'm excited for you." The alcohol had started to course through his system, and he was feeling a bit lighter. He knew he'd eventually recover from this blow, just getting over the thought of starting all over again seemed insurmountable. A woman's voice came through the speakers set up in a corner of the bar and announced that open mic night was officially open for sign-ups. A few people, whom he assumed were their regulars, made their way to the table.

"Not sure what you're waiting for- go get your guitar, because I know it's in your trunk, and do whatever it is that you do."

"Nah, I don't need to play, I'm all right, honestly."

"Well, when you were taking a piss, I sort of told the waitress you were going to play something for her, and these last two drinks were free. So maybe you do one song."

Ethan couldn't help but laugh through his sigh. "You are a lot of things, Miller."

"Yeah, I know. All of them awesome." Ethan shook his head and ambled over to the table, deciding to play something by Bright Eyes. "The First Day of My Life" seemed appropriate, and listening to that band had gotten him through worse. Two glorified karaoke performances and one decent poetry reading later, he was on stage with his guitar. He didn't really know how much he needed it until the lyrics were off of his chest, but by the time he strummed the last chord, he felt more certain that he would be ok. A cheer scattered throughout the sparsely populated restaurant, and he stepped down to make room for the next singer. He found Luke grinning when he returned, two new drinks at their table. Ethan passed on his; he was already past the point of just being buzzed, and he was pretty certain his friend mentioned their women would be taking them home, so sobering up sounded like a grand plan.

He ordered a coffee, but didn't need it when he heard the voice of the next performer weaving through the restaurant. Even with the crappy speakers and even worse acoustics, her voice was clear and strong, singing "Fast Car," by Tracy Chapman. He laughed when he saw she was playing his instrument, and Luke's insistence on taking it back to the car for him suddenly made a lot more sense. He let out a whoop when she finished, and she curtseyed for the crowd adorably, her blond streaked curls falling in her face. She looked hotter than he'd ever seen her, and it wasn't just because she was holding his guitar. There was an off-the-shoulder black dress involved that hugged her in all the right places. She beamed at him, and after motioning to Vanessa; they came and joined them at their table, much to Sandra's chagrin.

"You are... well, you are sneaky, but other than that, you are the keeper of my heart. Do you get that?" he told her seriously, not caring who heard him.

"Aw, baby, you're a little bit drunk, but thank you. I'm gonna write that down for later when you insist you never said it." She laughed, but wrapped her arms around him.

"No need, I'll remember. You're kind of a Romeo when you're blitzed, Fisher," Vanessa chided him.

"Luke texted and said you needed cheering up, so I figured either the song or the dress would do the trick, but what's up? Are you okay?"

"Yeah. I'm okay. We can talk about it later, I'm just happy you're here." He breathed her in and ordered her cake and a soda before paying the tab as he'd promised.

♪ *"Neon" – John Mayer*

7

Courtney and Vanessa made a production of showing off their toes before they agreed to drive the boys home.

"I'll bring you back tomorrow, no worries. I canceled the rest of my interviews, obviously, and I don't start training until next week."

"You're not gonna make me walk? You're so good to me," Ethan joked. He seemed to be feeling better from whatever it was he was dealing with. They had all piled into her Mustang for the ride home.

"Don't be sassy."

"I wouldn't dream of it."

"Could the two of you just, like, get a room? You're making me nauseous," Luke spat.

"Dude, that's the four 'Mind Benders' you charmed out of the waitress." Courtney looked at Vanessa in her rear-view, wondering if she was about to unleash a torrent of expletives.

"I can't help it that I'm naturally charming, Jesus." Luke defended himself, slurring the words slightly.

"Naturally charming? Please. I've seen you lay it on when you want something. Did he throw out a little bit of a southern accent and flex his biceps casually? I feel sorry for the girl." *At least V knows whom she's dating,* Courtney thought, thankful there was no backlash from Ethan's admission.

"I do no such things. I'm just a likable guy. Apparently that's a crime now."

"Whatever, no one believes you," Vanessa said confidently. The breeze felt good across Courtney's face, and though Ethan was quiet, he squeezed her hand periodically, as if to let her know he was still there. Upon their arrival at the little Victorian, she slipped her hand into his, and he followed her into the house. *You can always drive him home later,* she kidded herself.

"Maybe another pot of coffee would be a decent idea?" Courtney suggested when she led him into the kitchen.

"Mmmm, yes." She didn't really know where their friends had disappeared to, but neither of them seemed to care. She was still buzzing from her performance, and just his general presence. The closer he got, the antsier she felt, not knowing if she wanted him to slow things down or speed them the hell up. When he started rubbing her shoulders slowly, the strength in his fingers willing the tension she carried there to melt away, she knew exactly which direction she wanted things to go.

♪ *"For Me This Is Heaven" – Jimmy Eat World*

8

He did everything in his power to distract his girlfriend, looking sexy-as-hell while she prepped the coffee maker. "Thank you. For coming tonight. Not just picking me up, but for singing, it was..."

"Of course, I like singing for you. I never feel that nervous when I know you're there." She smiled at him and fluffed her hair. "Do you wanna tell me what happened to prompt your little departure from reality this evening though? You could have called. You can always call me, you know that."

"I know. I was just trying to figure shit out in my own head. I, um, I lost my spot in the band, I guess you could say."

"*What?*" she said, clearly offended for him.

"No, I mean, I didn't, like, get kicked out... I just had to give it back." He wasn't explaining it well, but he eventually got out the whole story so she understood.

"I am so sorry. I can't say that I know how you feel, but I wish you didn't have to feel it." She sat next to him on the couch, running her fingernails through his hair and down his neck, giving him goose bumps every time. "I know it won't be the same, but if you want to work on lyrics or have someone come with you when you record to give feedback..."

"Really? That would be good, I think. I just need to find my footing again. I'll be okay though, really. Especially if you come in and record a song *with* me."

"With? Like you want me to sing on a track?"

"Hell yeah, like Sonny and Cher. During their good years."

"Well, I don't know about that, but we can talk about it when you're more apt to remember the conversation."

"Nah, I'm fine, babe. Honestly, Luke had way more to drink than me, and I've had almost as much coffee, I'm good." He assumed this was the part where she'd offer to drive him home, but she kissed him instead. And kissed him again. And again, longer and harder. Her legs were taunting him in a dress that short, and he thought back to the first time he ever contemplated having them wrapped around him, following her up the stairs at Vanessa's. He guided her onto his lap and she pressed against him. When she slipped off her heels and they clattered onto the hardwood, he started to get the relieving feeling that she had no intention of taking him home.

She gazed at him intently, pulling back. "Do you wanna stay here tonight?" The question was heavy with memories of their past and the rules governing their present. He nodded wordlessly and let his hands follow the seam of the painted on dress until he could feel her shiver when he reached her thighs. Her uneven breath urged him on, and he stood up, taking her with him, and climbed the stairs. His hands never left her body as they felt their way down the hall to her room and fell into a mound of ruffles. He proceeded with caution, knowing that while they'd been together before, they were kind of back at the starting line. He kissed a pathway down her body, really liking the sound she let out between her teeth. His hesitation proved to be unfounded, as the woman before him was more confident and sexy than he had ever imagined. A thought tugged at him, reminding him that she'd gained that confidence while with someone else, but he shut it down. She was there with him now.

Some of the things she murmured in his ear made his head spin, and he lost himself in her.

How One Attempts To Chase Gravity

* * *

When the sun hit his eyes the next morning, the fact that her body was curled into his overpowered any lingering resentment he suffered while remembering that he wouldn't have band practice that evening. Or maybe ever. She was wearing his t-shirt from the night before, and though it made him feel like they were part of a country song, he liked it. She was his. He let her sleep, the clock on the wall letting him know he had a good hour before he needed to get his car to make it to work on time. He started to extricate himself from her, intending to make them breakfast, but she sleepily grabbed his forearm and pulled it tightly around her.

"No leaving," she murmured without opening her eyes.

"I was going to make you breakfast. Something with protein even, not just sugar."

"Not interested." She smiled, looking up at him. "You don't get to look like this when you first wake up. It's not fair," she complained, messing with his hair.

"I, for one, like your fluffy morning hair." He kissed her forehead.

"Ugh. Let me do something with it. You can go ahead and make me breakfast if you insist, but there has to be *some* sugar. I think there are cinnamon rolls in the fridge."

He brushed his teeth with one of an alarming number of extra toothbrushes she kept in her bathroom, and started on eggs and cinnamon rolls. She and Vanessa actually had pretty decent cookware, though he suspected the set was purchased more because the pieces were turquoise and pretty than because they were high quality.

She made her way into the kitchen and slung his t-shirt over his shoulder. "For the record, you should cook all meals without a shirt. Actually, you should do almost everything without a shirt." She demonstrated her opinion by wrapping her arms around his waist and lightly scratching his stomach. He chuckled softly.

"Anything you want, sprinkles."

"Hmmm, I want to eat these cinnamon rolls and then find a way to burn off the calories." She was flirting hard, her fingers tracing the waistband of his boxers.

"Well now you're just making me want to call in sick to work. I never thought I'd say this, but you're a bad influence on me."

"Stupid pool. Can't the kids save themselves?"

"Courtney Ross, don't you care about the safety of the *children*?"

"Yes, yes, I care about the children. I vow to take you to your car as soon as you're done serving me breakfast," she finished with a grin. Her mood was playful, and he was glad. He had needed to pull her out of a cloud of anxiety on more than a few occasions lately; it was nice to see her like this. "I'm excited for dinner tonight. What should I wear?"

"Whatever makes you happy. There's really not a dress code at the Fisher house."

"Yeah, but I want your mom to like me. Oh my god, she doesn't, like, hate me now or something, does she? Maybe you turned her against me when we broke up."

"You have far too much time on your hands if you're worried about stuff like that. No, she doesn't hate you. She probably likes you more than me, okay?"

"If you say so, okay." He brought eggs, cinnamon rolls, and pre-cooked bacon to the table, making a note to show her how to grocery shop properly at a later date.

"Bon appetite," he said with a flourish.

"Yummy! Thank you." She dove in for the center cinnamon roll first. "So, would it be weird or stalkerish if Vanessa and I went to the pool today? It's either that or more shopping, and well, the pool is cheaper... and it has you there. But if you want a break from me, that's okay."

"Never," he reassured her, leaning over and kissing her sugary lips. She took a whole three bites of egg before deciding she was finished.

"Lemme go get dressed appropriately and we can go."

When she returned, he had to laugh. He remembered the bright yellow bathing suit well underneath a barely-there cover-up, and he knew work was going to be a difficult task. "That's your definition of getting dressed appropriately?"

"Well, not if I were going to a lecture on the origins of the universe, no, but to spend a day at the pool? Yes."

"Whatever you say, babe. Let's rock and roll." She grabbed an overstuffed beach bag and yelled up the stairs to Vanessa.

"V! I'm leaving- meet me at the pool when you actually get out of bed, yes?"

"Yeah, yeah," Vanessa called back down.

"She loves me so much." Courtney smiled and hopped her way to the car.

♪ *"Forget It"* – *Breaking Benjamin*
"Beautiful Soul" – *Jesse McCartney*

9

She dropped Ethan at his car and promised to see him later. *Maybe we should adopt a dating schedule.* She really didn't want him to get sick of her. She also imagined his reaction if she were to voice this suggestion out loud. *School will start soon; we'll both be busy. Relax.* The list of "things to worry about later" was floating on the edge of her focus, making her stomach turn slightly because she knew what had to be done.

Pulling into the lot by the pool, she ensured that Ethan was already there and inside the gates before taking out her phone. She took three quick breaths and pressed Ben's number.

"Hey there, I was just thinking about you," he answered.

"Hey yourself, how's it going? I hope I didn't catch you at a bad time."

"No such thing for you. What are you up to?" She could have sworn her skin was literally breaking out in hives from the stress of how much she did NOT want to have this conversation.

"Just getting ready to go to the pool for a bit. I got that job the other day, so I don't have too much summer vacation left, I guess."

"That's awesome, congratulations! I knew you'd get it though."

"Well, it's probably all because you sent me a good luck text, obviously."

"Clearly. You owe me dinner or something over Thanksgiving for my part in all of it." *Just tell him, Courtney... this is painful.*

"You got it, we'll get Mexican food. The selection here sucks. But, I um, well, I called for a reason."

"Sure, go for it," he responded, some of the cheerfulness leaving his voice.

"I don't really know what the protocol is, but I figured honesty was the way to go, no matter what, so, just, I wanted to tell you that I sort of started seeing someone here. I..." She really didn't have much else to say, other than wanting to ask his forgiveness. He was quiet for a moment.

"Wow, um, okay? I guess I didn't really see that coming this soon. Obviously, I mean, I didn't expect you to stay single, we talked about this, I know, and... just, wow." He let out a breath.

"I'm so sorry if I'm hurting you. I don't want that. Ever. I just didn't know if it was worse to keep it from you. Please don't hate me, you are so important to me, and I can't..." she begged, tears now escaping down her cheeks. Their relationship was playing like a highlight reel behind her eyes, full of tender moments and memorable nights. He was so good to her.

"Court, I will never hate you. I was surprised, that's all. And yes, it hurts; I'm not going to pretend it doesn't. I love you. This is hard, but we knew that going in. I kind of feel like flying there and kicking this guy's ass right now, but I think it'll pass. Maybe," he finished, lightening the mood.

"I love you too. I do. I know that seems ridiculous to say, but I don't want us to, like, not be friends. We were friends before..."

"We'll get there. I don't want us to not be friends either. Maybe just give it some time, okay?"

"Yeah. Okay, I can do that. And I wasn't just saying it before, about dinner at Thanksgiving. It's an open invite." She hiccupped out the last of her tears.

"If you ever need me, it's never off-limits for you to call, all right?" He avoided giving her an answer about seeing each other, but she knew she should quit while she was ahead.

"Okay. I'll talk to you soon?"

"Of course," he assured her, but she knew he was probably lying.

"Bye, Ben," she whispered.

When she'd first left Phoenix to go to UD, she had kind of held the idea that they would both stay single. She couldn't really imagine being with anyone but him. Except Ethan. Ethan was the only person she would have made that call for. Feeling beyond drained, she tried to regain the magic of waking up that morning with Ethan's warmth wrapped around her and headed into the pool, sunglasses securely affixed to her face.

She found a shady spot after waving to her boyfriend and made herself comfortable. Even in her current state, there were butterflies when she looked at him. There was a small happiness found in her new glitter sunscreen, and she took out the paperback she'd picked up the week before. The anxiety of speaking to Ben was gone, but there was a hollow feeling left in her stomach in its absence. The book managed to hold her attention for fifteen minutes or so, but in the back of her mind, she continued replaying their conversation in her head. *Did he sound okay?* It was difficult to understand how she could be so happy with Ethan but feel so incredibly guilty. She glanced up, feeling her boyfriend's eyes on her, and blew him a quick kiss. The book eventually lost its effectiveness as a means of distraction, and she hopped up to buy a soda, wishing Vanessa would show up already. A hand grazed her back, and she jumped, almost spilling her drink.

"Just me, I'm sorry, didn't mean to sneak up on you. You were kind of in your own world there- everything okay?" Ethan asked, concern coming through in his voice. She realized that on the outside, she had just appeared to show up at the pool an introvert, when they had been in bed together not two hours before. She tried to fix her expression.

"Yeah, everything's fine, sorry, I was just daydreaming, I guess."

"Really? You seemed... I don't know, sad, from where I was sitting. You can tell me if something's up, honestly." With his warm brown eyes searching hers, she felt the calm she'd so carefully achieved start to wilt. She took a deep breath. *You cannot cry to him about Ben. You will not cry, you will not cry.*

"Really, it's nothing. I'm fine. I didn't come here to keep you from work, I'm sorry." Her face started to heat up, and she knew she had to stop talking about it.

"I can take five minutes, don't apologize. Talk to me." She could tell he was starting to worry, and she just piled that guilt on top of all the rest.

"I just, uh, well, I called Ben, after I dropped you off this morning. I needed to tell him that we are together. It was just, I don't know, the right thing to do, but it was... hard. I'm sorry if it's weird that I'm telling you this... I thought I would be able to let it go once I got through the hard part, but hurting him was... I'm sorry."

"Court, seriously, please stop apologizing. Sit." He motioned to one of the picnic tables nearby. He breathed and she worried. "I don't think I've been fair in really understanding that you just got out of a relationship, so I'm sorry if you felt like you couldn't talk to me... I get that you wanted to be the one to tell him that we are together. You're just a good person." He held her hand and she wiped her eyes, breathing deeply. *Everything is fine, just calm down.*

"I'm okay, honestly. It just hit me harder than I thought, that's all. He and I were friends for a long time before anything else. I wanted to be respectful, I guess. That's it."

"Of course. You're sure you're okay, though? Do you still want to do dinner tonight?"

"Yes, silly. You're not going to take away my lasagna." She grinned sincerely, and he squeezed her hand.

"Okay, good. I know it's weird, but I'm kind of looking forward to you coming over to hang with my family. And thank you, for telling me what was up. Don't be afraid to talk to me, all right?" He kissed her still-damp cheek and made his way back to his post. Some of the stress she'd built up that morning started to subside slowly as she sipped what was left of her lemon-lime fizz. Vanessa strolled in not long after, looking beautiful but mildly annoyed as usual.

"Hey girl," she stated breathlessly as she dragged another chair into the shade.

"Hey, cute suit," she commented, feeling somewhat envious of her friend's twig-ish figure. Her top was a deep purple and the bottoms emerald green, made to look like scales a la *The Little Mermaid*.

"Thanks! You know how I feel about mermaids." Vanessa had been obsessed with Ariel since they were young. Courtney vividly remembered her mermaid sleeping bag at their first overnight in second grade.

"Yes, I seem to recall something about that." She smiled. Vanessa proceeded to talk her ear off about how things were going now that she and Luke were back together. Apparently the few days apart had made a lasting impact. Courtney wasn't sure she bought it, but they both seemed happy. The conversation eventually came back to her, and she filled in her friend about the emotional status of her morning.

"Eeee, that sounds intense. But kudos to Ethan for handling it well, it sounds like."

"What do you mean?"

"Like, responding without the jealousy factor."

"What would he be jealous about? The whole reason I made the call was to tell Ben I was with Ethan."

"Well? You still cared enough and are in contact enough to call, I guess. I'm not saying I blame you- I don't, it's a difficult situation, I'm just saying it seems like everything worked out as well as it could have."

"Yeah. I guess it could have been worse." Courtney really hadn't contemplated Ethan feeling jealous. Ever, actually. He was so sure of himself, but she supposed it wouldn't hurt to make her feelings clear to him later on. They spent the remainder of the morning swimming and lounging, feeling like they had all the time in the world. Because maybe they did. That was the beauty of summer vacation.

♪ *"Girlfriend" – Streets of Laredo*
"You and I" - Johnnyswim

10

The sun felt good on his back that morning, despite the heaviness of the humid air. He felt better after Vanessa showed up, as Courtney seemed to return to herself a while later. Their conversation from earlier gnawed at him. He hated the feeling that there was someone else involved in their relationship, and there was nothing he could do about it. *They have a history,* he realized, when she commented that they had been friends for a long time. In his mind, this Ben person had always just been a side-note. Someone to hate because he was taking care of Courtney- but that wasn't actually the case. The relationship hadn't been a side-note to her.

Just let it go. You got the girl. He wavered between wanting to know more and wishing he knew less. He landed on longing for less and moved forward with that. After his shift, he elected to stay and hang out with the girls for a bit before heading to the music store. He dove in off the low board, maybe showing off a little with a jack-knife, and he popped up from under the water just shy from where she was watching him. He closed the gap between them and kissed her head sweetly. It was a far cry from how he wanted to greet her, but he didn't imagine that carrying out the things running through his mind about that damned yellow bikini would please the management too much. He just needed to know that she was his.

"I think I can beat that diving board performance," she challenged, leaving her arms around his waist.

"Oh you do, huh? Are you willing to put your money where your mouth is?"

"I think so. Name your terms."

"All right. Three dives each, and... Crystal and Jeff can judge." He motioned towards two of the other lifeguards.

"Well, they are your friends, so I'm not sure that's entirely fair. Vanessa needs to judge too."

"Not that confident huh? It's okay, I get that my awesomeness is intimidating."

"Oh shut it. I agree to your terms, plus Vanessa. Now what do I get when I win?"

"You really want me to go into that... *here*?" he teased, speaking slowly into her ear.

"*Please*, you'll give me that either way. If I win, you have to learn, sing, and record for me an eighties hairband song."

"You seem pretty sure of yourself. I'm going to have to start making you work for my affections," he kidded. "But I guess I better not lose then. What do I get if I win?"

"I'll record a song with you." He raised his eyebrows. "Among other things."

"That's better," he replied and kissed her squarely on the mouth. "Let's do it then." Climbing the rough steps to the diving board, he felt more secure in her feelings for him. *She just needed a moment, everything's good.* He started off simple with an inverted dive, and she countered with some form of cheerleader jump with a half twist at the end. The "judges" noted their scores. He went next with a front flip into the pool, and she came back with a back tuck off the edge of the board. He got the feeling he might be rocking to the 80s relatively soon. In the end, he gave up and went with the best cannon ball he had into the water. She laughed and shook her head before pulling off a full twist.

"There are just so many great bands to choose from. Do I go with Mr. Big or Def Leopard or Extreme… I'm going to have to give it some thought," she teased him as they dried off.

"Maybe I just have a secret desire to play overly dramatic guitar solos. You don't know."

"Sure, that's what it is," she said. "You know I'll still record a song with you, though, right?" She pulled on his towel and he stepped into her space, liking the way her hair was already curling at the ends.

"Yeah?"

"Of course. You knew I would before you asked. It's hard to say no to this face," she admitted, playfully running her thumb along his chin. He smirked, causing her to shoot him a look.

"I had a feeling you might consider my request." His lips found hers and more of his worry from earlier fell away.

"Do you guys ever stop making out? Like, you would think your lips would need some type of physical therapy after a while. Are you about ready to go. Court? I wanna hit the mall for a minute, Sephora is having a sale," Vanessa said, stomping over to them. Courtney sighed.

"Yes, V." Courtney kissed him again and promised to see him that night. His afternoon lessons went well, but he was just looking forward to dinner. Something about having her in his house with his family made it all feel real, that they were together again. *What has happened to you?* he thought, almost amused at what his former self would think of his transformation into collegiate-boyfriend Ethan. He felt a pang in his chest when he realized the new him no longer included "guitarist in a band."

* * *

The smell of lasagna hit him when he opened the door, and his stomach growled.

"Hey Mom," he called, setting his guitar on the staircase.

"Hey kid, come in here and make yourself useful." She appeared a little frazzled, and if he wasn't mistaken, she was making brownies. From scratch.

"Are you *baking?* Like, not from Betty Crocker?"

"*Yes.* I bake. You said her birthday was next week. I thought it would be nice to have a dessert. Don't act so surprised, it annoys me." Ethan laughed.

"I honestly think you're more nervous than she is about her coming over. Chill. Everything smells awesome in here. What do you want me to do?"

"Well, we have to impress her, Ethan, otherwise you might bring back that Sara girl, or someone even worse. Chop up that lettuce for the salad," she directed, gesturing with her head toward the counter.

"Don't hold back, tell me how you really feel about my taste in women." She just shrugged back at him.

"I can't be sorry when it's the truth." He just shook his head. The mention of Courtney's birthday sparked the realization that he needed to get her a present. He wasn't going to punk out this year and give her something homemade; it was going to be a real present.

"So Mom."

"Oh god, what?"

"What do you mean, 'oh god'? I haven't even said anything yet!"

"Sorry, I just envisioned you having something awful to tell me after beginning that way."

"Ye of little faith, Mother. I was going to ask your advice, but forget it if you're going to be crazy."

"No no, I won't be crazy. Ask away, I'm sorry."

"As I was saying. *So Mom,* what do I get Courtney for her birthday? Like, it's gotta be something good."

"Well? What does she like?"

"Well, she already has me." He grinned. His mom swatted him with her oven mitt.

"What *else* does she like, son?"

"Glitter? Harry Potter, anything with sugar in it, school, nineties music."

"Well if she likes things that sparkle, as all women do, I hate to tell you, get her a piece of jewelry. Don't go crazy, she's nineteen, but get her something fun."

"I can do that. Like, at the mall?"

"Ummmm, try that 'Reclaimed Charm' store in the square. They have some cool stuff. Way better than you'll find at the mall."

"Got it. Okay, sweet." He chopped lettuce happily and ran up to take a quick shower before Courtney arrived. When he came back down, he found her already in the kitchen, chatting animatedly with his mom. He slowed his pace, wanting to hear what they were talking about.

"Well, I'm sure it's hard being away from home. How's your mom doing?" his mom asked Courtney.

"Oh, she's okay. She has graduated to calling me only three times a day instead of once an hour," Courtney joked, "but I miss her. I'm sure once school starts, and I get a routine going, it will get easier, but the transition is hard."

"Well if you are ever in need of a stand-in, feel free to call. I know it's not the same, but, well, you make Ethan so happy, and you're welcome here anytime." His mom started to launch into her own recounting of going away to college, and Ethan realized what an idiot he was. *She just left her entire life, and you've asked her how she was doing maybe once? And now you're jealous because she had the decency to call her ex to break the news that you're back together? Jesus Christ.* As he walked into the kitchen, he resolved to take better care of her.

"Hey, sprinkles," he greeted, leaning down to kiss her briefly. He never got over how she constantly smelled like a confectionary treat. She had a tiny yellow bow in her hair that matched a yellow sundress. "You look pretty," he complimented, running his thumb across the bow affectionately.

"Thank you, you're looking awfully pretty yourself." She tugged gently on his gray button down.

"You do look nice, but your hair is too long. You're starting to resemble a pirate," his mom reprimanded, finishing up icing the brownies.

"Thanks, Mom," he replied, pushing his hair out of his face. "Maybe I'll get it cut before school starts, new year and all that." He sat down across from Courtney at the table.

"Ohhhh, I wanna come! Getting your hair cut has to have the fear factor for you that, like, camping does for me. I'll hold your hand," Courtney promised, grinning.

"Sounds good to me."

"So, where's your sister? I brought her a present."

"Let's see- TAY!" he yelled. He heard her door open and feet stomping down the stairs.

"I'm coming, I'm coming." Courtney pulled a small black velvet bag out of her purse. "Hi, Courtney!" she added cheerfully upon entering, looking like herself in a "Keep Calm and Read More Books" T-shirt. His sister had grown out of some of her awkwardness after turning fifteen. Her hair had grown out, and he was pretty certain she'd started wearing make-up, judging by the amount of crap all over their bathroom. She was still a nerd, but he thought she owned it a bit more now.

"Hey, it's good to see you again! I, um, I brought you a present."

"Me? Isn't it, like, your birthday or something?"

"Well, soon, yes, but I saw this and thought you would like it," Courtney explained, handing her the bag. Taylor took out a silver lightning bolt pendant with a rhinestone at the end, dangling on a shimmery ribbon. Her fingers ran over the charm and her eyes widened.

"Oh my GOD, this is awesome! I've never even seen one like it before. Thank you so much!" Surprisingly, she threw her arms around Courtney and ran to the mirror in the hallway to put it on. His girlfriend looked happy, and he thought his face might freeze in a grin from watching her interact with his family. She just fit there. He stood up to lean across the table and kiss her on the cheek. She blushed, but shot him a smile, clearly happy with Taylor's reaction. His mom finally joined them with the salad and lasagna, and they chatted about books and school and movies. All three of them tried to give him advice about what to do with his hair, and even worse, his music crisis, but he wouldn't have changed any of it. They finished eating, but the conversation continued on.

"Um, so will you guys think I'm a huge nerd if I suggest a board game?" Courtney asked, blinking nervously.

"Well, I already know you're a huge nerd, so suggest away, but I'm not even sure what we have." She threw her napkin at him from across the table.

"I may have stuck the *Harry Potter* version of *Clue* in my car before coming over tonight," she admitted, biting her lip.

"Sold. Game Night it is, brother," Taylor told him, already out of her seat and clearing the table.

"Well, I guess that's that. Don't be sad when I beat both of you, though. I won't tell anyone."

"Yeah, there's that arrogance resurfacing again, but I'm pretty sure I'm one-and-oh today when it comes to competing with you."

"Oh, I like this girl," his mom said, amused. He walked out with Courtney to grab the game; it just may have taken longer than necessary due to his urge to explain to her what she meant to him. With his tongue. She leaned against the Mustang, and her giggles escaped into the night air while he kissed her collarbone.

"Not that I'm complaining," she said breathlessly, "but you know your sister is going to come out here and pry this game out of my hands, right?"

"Then put it down and use your hands for something else," he flirted between kisses.

"Ethan!" she half-scolded him.

"Just tell me I can stay at your place tonight, and I swear we can go back in."

"No way your mom is just going to be okay with you driving to my house for no reason."

"Oh, it's not for no reason," he assured her, feeling her shiver when he kissed her neck.

"Relentless."

"Is that a yes?"

"If you figure out how to make it sound reasonable, then you tell your mom whatever you want. It's my house, so I'm going there either way." He and his mom hadn't really had a heart-to-heart about his sleeping over with Courtney, but he was nineteen and not that worried about it. He *was* worried about making it through the next hour of *Clue* without touching her.

They played an intense round of the game, and Taylor ended up winning, which pleased her to no end. She insisted the lightning charm brought her good luck. Courtney started packing up to leave and thanked his mother for dinner.

"Anytime, sweetheart, drive safely," his mom said. He walked her back to her car.

"Tonight was actually really fun," he confessed, pushing his hair out of his eyes again.

"It was. I told you it would be."

"My family might like you more than they like me."

"You might be right, but try not to feel too bad about it," she teased, making him laugh slightly.

"I am so in love with you." He kissed her intently.

"I love you, too. Thank you for tonight. I needed some family time, even if it wasn't my own."

"I want you to know that I'm going to be a better boyfriend," he let out, though he hadn't really intended on sharing his revelation from earlier with her.

"Better than what?"

"Better than I've been. I've been so happy being with you that I haven't even bothered to respect that fact that you just moved two thousand miles to a new place and are on your own for the first time. Like, I want to make things easier for you, not more stressful." He looked at her seriously, searching her eyes for a reaction.

"You do make my life easier. When I'm with you, I feel like I'm home, not away from home."

He kissed her again, wrapping his arms around her waist. "Well, I'm still going to teach you how to cook. And grocery shop. You and V will never survive going on like you are."

"Okay, fair enough."

"All right, I'll text you when I'm on my way over."

"Ah, so you're sticking with the idea that you're just going to waltz in there and tell your mom you're leaving to come to my house... to sleep."

"You just let me worry about it. Drive safely and I'll see you in a bit." She got in her car and was gone.

The screen door slammed behind him upon his reentry to the house, and he came in to find his mom doing the dishes. "Hey, I got these. You can go and relax."

"What do you want?"

"I just might head out for a bit. I thought I'd help clean up first."

"Head out where?"

"Well, Courtney and I were talking about wandering over to campus in the morning to map out our schedules, find the best coffee, whatever, so I thought I'd just-"

"Okay, kid. I get that you're nineteen, and there's not a whole hell of a lot I can do to stop you from sleeping at your girlfriend's house, but let's not pretend you're going over there to get a jumpstart on your college mapping adventure, okay?" Ethan pressed his lips together, but didn't try to argue. "Can I offer a word of advice?"

"Advise away."

"Don't suffocate each other. I know having your first taste of freedom as an adult is kind of intoxicating, but everyone needs time alone too. Including her and including you. So give yourself that, or you'll end up driving each other crazy."

"Understood."

"And yes, you can finish these dishes before you leave. I'm going to have a cup of tea."

"Sounds good, you deserve it."

"Don't overdo it."

"Sorry." He grinned. The dishes were done in record time, and he grabbed a bag and some clothes for the next day.

> E: I'm on my way, I'll see you soon. Please tell me you're still wearing the dress you had on tonight.
>
> C: Lol, I haven't changed yet, just chatting with V. I take it you liked it?
>
> E: You could say that. I'll be there soon. <3

♪ *"Crazy Beautiful"* – Hanson

11

Vanessa had her head between her knees and was brushing out her long blonde locks upside-down. "So, should we have a party? Like for our birthdays or a housewarming or something?"

"Well. I literally know three people here, and you're one of them, so I'd say if you want a party for your birthday, sure. But I think I'm all set doing a quiet dinner with Ethan."

"You guys are like an old married couple already. You don't have to know anyone; you walk around campus and say the word 'party.' People will come."

"And having a bunch of strangers drunk in my house sounds so much like something I'd enjoy?"

"Touché. Well, you do what you want. I think we should go out dancing for my birthday, then. There's gotta be an eighteen and over club around here somewhere," she said, flipping her head back over.

"Oh god, you want to go to a club? Really? The eighteen and over nights are so lame."

"Well, then I guess we'll need some IDs to go to a 'not so lame' one, won't we?"

"Whatever you say, girl." As she heard a car pull into their driveway, there was an automatic pick-up in her heart rate. He had been so attentive all night; she liked seeing him around his family. Clearly he was good to his mom, and she felt like it said something about him as a man. Prancing to the door, still wearing the capped-sleeve sundress, she swung it open. He had a bag slung over the shoulder of his gray collared shirt and was leaning casually against the side of her house. "I suppose I shouldn't have doubted your ability to talk anyone into anything," she admitted, happy he was there.

"Oh, you don't even know." He smirked, and then he was kissing her before she had time to react to the smile.

"You do actually have a room. It's right up the stairs, so feel free to use it," Vanessa interjected, now painting her nails.

"Such a great suggestion, V, thank you for your wisdom." He picked Courtney up unexpectedly, balancing her on his other shoulder and heading towards the staircase.

"I actually can walk up those stairs, I swear," she teased him once he flipped her onto her bed and she stopped giggling.

"Mhm." He ignored her, kissing her shoulder. She let him shower her in adoration for as long as he wanted. She had missed the charge between them. Her skin sang where his fingers traced winding trails to various destinations. She sank into the sensation of it all. For the first time since they'd met, it finally felt like timing was on their side. They had the next four years together if they wanted them. But having him whisper confessions of his feelings for her in her ear made her wonder if any amount of time would be enough.

They finally fell asleep some time before sunrise, and she awoke the next morning with his arms still possessively wrapped around her frame. She untangled herself and slipped into the bathroom to brush her teeth and torture her short hair into submission. When she came back, he was looking at his phone.

"Hey, love," he said, looking up.

"Whatcha doin'?"

"Just making sure I have coverage for work this weekend so we can celebrate your birthday properly, with no alarms before ten a.m."

"That sounds good. We're just doing something low-key, right? On Saturday night? I don't want a hullaballoo."

"There will be no hullaballoo. Who uses that word by the way?"

"I do."

"So you do," he accepted. "I will be taking you grocery shopping, though, and introducing you to something called a recipe. You'll love it."

"Ha. Ha. Ha." He grinned and grabbed her wrist to pull her back into the bed. He laced their fingers and pressed his forehead to hers. "I would stay here with you forever," he said softly. "That freaks me out a little bit, but I thought I'd share."

"I think I would let you," she said back, matching his tone, "and that freaks me out a little bit too." She kissed him sweetly, and they let it go at that. He proceeded to get ready for work, and she checked her "Pre-Back-To-School" to-do list for the millionth time, determined to knock some things off it that day.

"Do you want me to make you breakfast before I go?" he asked.

"Nah, I'm okay. I can pick something up." He looked at her pointedly. "I'll get something with protein! I swear it won't be a doughnut."

"I don't actually care. Do what makes you happy." He kissed her forehead while she sat on the edge of her ruffled bed.

"Will I see you tonight?"

"Up to you. I'll always be here if you want me, but I don't wanna take all of your alone time." When he said those words, visions of a hot bath and candles and one of the fifty books she'd downloaded but hadn't gotten to yet filled her mind.

"Hmm. Alone time, you say? I may explore this concept."

"Sounds good. I need to start figuring out which songs I can still use and what I'm actually planning on doing with them. I'll call you, though?"

"Of course. Have fun lifeguarding. Keep the community safe."

"All in a day's work, babe." He kissed her again and headed out. She flopped back onto her bed and exhaled. *How did things get this freaking good?* This thought was immediately followed by, *how long can things possibly stay this good?* She chastised her inner voice for being a pessimist and took her time getting ready and straightening up the room. The first thing on her list for the day? School supplies. It was going to be like a kid in a candy store. *Maybe I'll hit up the candy store too.* She sighed contentedly.

* * *

The remainder of that afternoon was dedicated to organizing her colored pens just so, and utilizing every single pocket of her new yellow messenger bag for various supplies. It didn't even bother her that her Type-A syndrome was in full effect. She and Vanessa took advantage of the down time that evening and picked up Greek food for their back-to-school movie marathon. All of the token high school favorites were accounted for- *She's All That, 10 Things I Hate About You, Can't Hardly Wait,* and *Cruel Intentions.* Admittedly, they only watched their favorite parts of each before moving on, but the night seemed to give Courtney the breather she needed. It felt like time had sped up since she arrived, especially after her mom flew home.

"This snack experiment is like one of your top ten greatest ideas," Vanessa declared, stuffing her face with a handful of peanut butter popcorn.

"Truer words have never been spoken, my friend. This is freaking amazing." Around them sat six bowls of popped kernels, all with different toppings ranging from mint chocolate chip to taco. She wasn't sure how she was going to feel in about two hours, but it was worth it.

"And who says we can't cook? This totally counts as cooking."

"Did it involve heat? Yes. Ergo, it is cooking."

"Ergo, you are a dork," Vanessa replied, calling her out on her Latin word usage.

"Whatever, just hand that one over here."

"So tell me," Vanessa commanded pointedly.

"Tell you what?"

"You know exactly what. How are things? Actually, just how is the one thing?" Courtney laughed and shook her head.

"Things are good. And the sex is...well, he's quite attentive."

"He'd better be. He should kiss the ground you walk on," Vanessa said, satisfied with her information.

"And things with Luke?"

"Good. Better. I don't know. I think I just wanted to know he was serious... when I broke up with him. I'm glad it didn't stick."

Courtney raised an eyebrow at her friend's admission- she usually didn't own up to her overly-dramatic nature. "For the record, I'm glad it didn't stick too. I kind of like Luke," Courtney confessed.

"For the record? I'm kind of glad you folded like a house of cards when you saw Fisher. I gotta say you're just more... yourself, with him. I mean, I would have held the grudge against him forever, obviously, but I'm glad I didn't have to," Vanessa explained, smiling knowingly and turning her attention back to their movie.

♪ *"Best I Ever Had"* – Gavin DeGraw

12

Almost all of his downtime was now devoted to teaching himself to play harmonica. He was also attempting to weave together any inspired moments found in his notebook. His feelings of defeat after the band had moved on without him were slowly transforming into feelings of resistance, which he hoped would lead to motivation. Now on his own, he realized the only limitations placed on his music as far as influence or genre or feel were self-imposed, and that was sort of freeing.

Since the split from Southbound, he'd begun to dive into any music he'd never heard of. He didn't care if it was a band listed on a flyer in the hole-in-the-wall Chinese food place by campus; he listened to them. Some of these adventures were a bust, obviously, but he came across some cool tracks along the way.

His mission for that particular day, however, was to find Courtney's birthday present. He had already decided to take her to out to eat that night, and then added on the excursion of a karaoke bar when Vanessa showed up that weekend with new IDs for all of them. He also promised her that before dinner, he'd let her take him to a salon to get his hair cut. That made him more nervous than finding a gift.

The door chimed when he walked into "Reclaimed Charm," and after appreciating the complex vanilla-cinnamon-sandalwood scent combination of the place, he sincerely hoped the salesperson would point him in the right direction. It was one of those shops with endless amounts of just *stuff*, and he didn't know if he had the energy to sift through all of it.

"Hello!" He heard a cheerful voice. "I'm over here behind the antique dolls," it called again. Not something he heard during a typical shopping experience, but he went with it and navigated back towards the creepy doll eyes. There was a short, frail-looking woman with cropped gray hair trying to navigate a rather large crate across the floor.

"Do you want some help?" he asked, doubtful she could have moved it at all. She sighed.

"Well, I think I'm supposed to ask you that, but under the circumstances, yes. Can you help me get this over there?" she pointed to under a bench in the corner of the room.

"Sure thing," he offered, and together they moved it into place. He wasn't even sure what it was full of- it looked like old metal gears and handles, but he didn't suppose it mattered.

"Thank you, young man, now what can I help you with, as it were?"

"Well? I'm looking for a birthday present for my girlfriend, jewelry probably, and my mom suggested I try here first."

"Perfect! I can help with that!" She hustled around to a large antique china hutch and opened it up. Inside hung hundreds of necklaces, bracelets, and rings. *Well that's good, because there's no way in hell I'm navigating through that.*

"Who's your mom by the way?"

"Mary Fisher." He was finally used to people asking these types of questions- it was a small town thing.

"Oh yes! Nice lady. You must be Ethan then." Again, weird, but no longer surprising.

"That's me."

"Excellent! Now tell me about this girl. Is she something special, or is this what you kids call a fling?"

It felt like he was talking to his grandma- he was mildly uncomfortable but more amused than anything. "No no, she's the real deal, not a fling. Um, she loves glitter, and books, and sugar." He almost laughed because it sounded like he was describing an eight year old. He was going to have to tell Courtney to develop more grown-up hobbies. The lady looked at him over her glasses, eyebrows up.

"Interesting list," she commented.

"I know. I swear she's nineteen, she's just, well, different." He meant it in the best way possible.

"Different is good," she assured him, searching the recesses of the forest of jewelry. "And here is the one I was thinking of." She handed him a necklace with a simple spherical glass pendant on the end of a silver chain, but this particular piece was filled with square-cut pieces of silver glitter. They caught the light and made sparkles dance on the wall.

"This is kind of...perfect," he stated, in awe.

"Yes. I have a gift."

"You do, seriously. I'll take it. I never would have found this in there." He paid for it happily and she even wrapped it for him. *So much better than the mall.*

He went home in a great mood and did some preliminary recordings of a few chunks of music on his laptop to test out on Courtney later. He couldn't decide if he was getting better or worse with the harmonica. In realizing the time, he rushed to get ready. He dressed a bit more casually, wearing a soft green t-shirt she always commented on and a pair of worn-in jeans. He found the necklace she'd bought for him when they first got back together and grabbed her presents off of his desk.

> E: Hey birthday girl, I'm on my way.
>
> C: :) I'm getting ready. Enjoy the wind in your hair in the car.

He smiled and shook his head. He did find himself looking in the rearview several times, wondering if the style change was a bad idea. His hair was sort of his thing, but Courtney swore she had scoured the Internet and found "super sexy" looks for him to peruse. *She's sort of the one who has to look at you, anyway,* he admitted, running his fingers along his hairline. He pulled up to the house, and she was already on the porch waiting for him. She flitted down the front steps and skipped to his car. He wasn't sure he'd ever seen her like this.

"I would have come up to get you. Now I don't feel like a gentleman."

"Nope, too excited! And for the record, I don't remember you acting very gentlemanly last time you were here." She arched her eyebrows at him, making him laugh. She made her way around to the passenger side, straightening her floral top. He admired the view offered by her tight jeans. As soon as she sat down, she ran her fingers through his hair and kissed him on the cheek. "Just want to do that while I can," she admitted, buckling her seatbelt.

"Well hopefully I still have some left when you're done with me, but you do realize I've had my hair cut before right? Like, you seem to be laboring under the impression that this is a first for me," he teased. She was still bouncy even sitting in her seat, and he waited a moment, just watching her.

"You're not the least bit excited?" she asked, seeming genuinely concerned she might not get her anticipated makeover-reveal opportunity.

"Sure I am, babe. I'm just waiting for you to calm down enough so I can kiss you and tell you happy birthday."

"Oh! Yes, you can do that."

"Then happy birthday," he said, pressing his lips to hers. She relaxed into him and he felt satisfied. "Okay. Now we can go."

♪ *"You Get Me" – Michelle Branch*

13

Courtney directed him to a salon called Razors. The name was bit much, but Vanessa had insisted they go there. Her nerves kicked in, and she fretted that it would be one of those places with sterile white surroundings and awful electronica music, and that Ethan would be less than pleased. But the worry was unfounded. The vibe was welcoming, and she appreciated the mid-century décor. It was clean, but not stark. She dealt with the receptionist and found Ethan in his own world, standing in the waiting area.

"Come back to Earth."

"Sorry, I'm here," he replied, squeezing her hand. The stylist's name was Jenn, and her appearance wasn't too hipster-y, which Courtney appreciated. No over-sized glasses in sight. She also didn't look at Ethan like she hoped Courtney was his sister. Hopping into the empty chair at the next station, Courtney felt positively giddy about the whole experience. It was like having a real-life Ken doll.

"So, Ethan. What are we doing here?" Jenn asked casually, raking her fingers through his hair. Courtney knew it was the girl's job, but there was a pull in her stomach watching someone else do that.

"Mullet," he replied intently.

"Stop it," Courtney interjected.

"No? I think I could sort of rock it… you did say something about eighties hair bands the other day- I just wanna look the part."

"No more talking." He resigned himself to her control.

"Whatever the girlfriend says. Within reason," he clarified.

"Brave man. All right. You are the girlfriend I take it?" Jenn asked, turning to Courtney.

"That I am! Tell me what you think of some of these." She flipped through several photos on her screen.

"This one's good, a little more edgy. He's kind of pretty, so you don't wanna go too soft."

"I'm pretty? And only *kind of* at that?" Ethan questioned. "Would you be happier with very pretty?" Jenn shot back.

"Yeah, I think I would."

"Fine, you're extra pretty, so you can carry an edgier haircut. Do you wanna see the picture or be surprised?"

"I might as well go all out and be surprised, right? Although I'm not sure how surprising hair can be. I hope you're not going to make me look like a zebra."

"No zoo animals today. Let's go wash your hair, Rapunzel." Courtney kind of liked this Jenn character. Looking up from her magazine when they returned, she quite literally perched on the edge of the seat for the entire process.

"You are making me more nervous than anything. You're going to fall out of the chair."

"No I'm not. I have exceptional balance. And don't be nervous." She watched him cringe when Jenn took out the clippers, but tried to pretend she didn't notice. To distract him, she talked about school and her new job, though neither had started yet, because, well, that was just who she was. Even thinking about her first day of work was enough to make her stomach tie itself in knots. She hated not knowing what she was doing. He just grinned in the way that made her head rush.

"You'll do great, baby. And I know you will anyway, but try not to stress. Everything will go swimmingly." He looked at her so sincerely, she almost believed it too.

"All right, kid, you ready?" Jenn asked, raising her eyebrows. It was shaved close on one side and left longer on the top and the other side.

Impossibly, he looked even more delicious than before. Jenn had been correct in her assessment; it did make him look a little less pretty. The stylist turned him around, but his expression was difficult to read. She found herself holding her breath, wanting to know what he thought. He put his hands through it and didn't look angry. Courtney felt like she was about to explode next to him.

"Well?!"

"It's cool, I like it," he responded.

"Oh my god, you are such a guy," she let out, all of her anticipation coming to an anti-climactic end.

"Do you want me to cry or something?" He laughed. "It looks good! I'm sorry, I'm not aware of proper makeover protocol, I guess."

"Clearly! Well, I like it, anyway. You look older. Like sexy older, not yuck older."

"Thank god. I don't know what 'yuck older' is, but I don't want to be it." He swung his arm around her shoulder and they went up to pay. She noticed he kept touching the shaved side of his head and smiled. He *did* like it. She stood back and contemplated briefly if the popcorn feeling she got in her stomach when she caught his eye would ever stop. *People don't just have this feeling forever, do they? They're married fifty years and get all fluttery when one just looks at the other?* She checked her own appearance in one of the available mirrors and wondered if he felt the same. *Who marries their first… everything? Isn't the bad boy musician supposed to be a phase?* she mused.

"You look perfect," he said, coming up behind her. More butterflies. She hoped this phase lasted forever. "Come on, birthday girl, let's get the actual celebration underway, shall we?" She floated out the doorway with him.

♪ *"To Be With You"* – Mr. Big

14

He took her to dinner at an Italian restaurant that the owner of Vinyl had raved about. As was their custom, they started working on song lyrics while waiting for food.

"So, when do I get to actually *hear* one of these bad boys, huh?"

"I recorded some stuff today just at my house, you can hear it whenever. I am afraid I'm really not good at playing harmonica."

"Well you've been playing for, like, a week, I can't imagine why you're not an expert already." She nudged him with her foot.

"Okay, okay, I know. But I know you get what I'm saying, Miss 'I quit guitar after six months because I wasn't a prodigy,' " he said, calling her out.

"Let's just keep the focus on you," she deflected. They continued on through appetizers and their meal, but when they brought out the cake, he closed the notebook and took the small purple package he'd been carrying in his pocket. The other gift was left in the car for later.

"Is now a good time for your present?"

"Ethan! I told you not to get me anything. I already made you get your hair cut and you-"

"Just say, 'Yes, now is an awesome time for gift-giving.' " She paused a moment.

"Yes, now is an awesome time for presents. You are amazing." He handed her the box and waited, hoping he'd hit the mark. She opened it carefully and pulled the lid off of the box. She dangled the chain between her fingers and examined the glass charm. "Is this... is this filled with *glitter?*" she asked, her voice rising a good octave on the word glitter.

"It is."

"Oh my god, it's, like, the best thing ever created! I'm going to wear it every day!" She stood and held it out to him to fasten around her neck, and he obliged. Rather than sitting down, she surprised him by falling into his lap and wrapping her arms around his neck. "I love you," she said in a low voice, kissing him on the mouth.

"I love you too, I'm glad you like it."

"Like is simply not a strong enough word. I literally get to wear glitter all the time now. It's perfect. You are the best boyfriend in the world," she declared, kissing him once more before returning to her seat. Hearing her say that, he felt a source of tension leave his shoulders.

"Well, I may have one surprise left for you, but after that reaction, I'm not sure which one will win the night."

"I can't even wait. Seriously, a quiet night with you anywhere would have been enough, but today... tonight... the last couple of weeks have been... They've been everything I imagined when I was planning it all out in my head last year. Better than, even." With that, she cut the cake in half and offered him the smaller side. He just laughed and sank his fork into the layers of chocolate.

* * *

He was sure they both looked ridiculous trying to use their fake IDs for the first time, but they were able to enter the bar just the same. Keeping the karaoke part a secret was impossible once they drove up, but at least his performance would be a surprise. He ordered her something girly-sounding.

"What are you going to sing?" she asked, actively scouring the song list.

"I guess you'll find out." He headed towards the small stage to turn in his sign-up slip to the DJ. Vanessa and Luke strolled in a while later, which earned him some affection from his girl.

"I like it," Vanessa stated without a greeting, staring at his new haircut.

"Thanks for the seal of approval."

"I don't, you look ridiculous," Luke threw out just as bluntly.

"Geez, man, don't be afraid to hurt my feelings or anything." "What is the world coming to? Don't talk to me about your feelings, Fisher. Someone has to be honest in this pansy-ass universe we live in." Ethan laughed, not even sure what to make of this version of Luke, and wondered what the hell had gotten into him. His friend got up to find their server, apparently unable to wait for a drink. He gave Vanessa a questioning look. She turned to make sure Luke was out of earshot before continuing.

"He got hit on by the bouncer when he was waiting for me to fix my makeup in the bathroom." Vanessa grinned. "He was cool about it to the guy, I am just thinking he now wants to assert his masculinity."

"That is the best thing I've heard all night." Courtney beamed. "But really, he should have been flattered- that bouncer is hot."

"Is he now?" Ethan asked.

"You know he is, no sense in denying it. Not as hot as you though, lover." She planted a dramatic kiss on his cheek, and he assumed her drink had kicked in. *She is such a lightweight.* Luke returned, still in a mood, but happier with a hand on his beer and an arm possessively around Vanessa. Ethan decided to wait until a buzz had set in before giving him any shit about it.

The DJ came on the mic and announced that karaoke would begin shortly. Ethan was thinking he must have lost his mind in gearing up to do what he was about to do, but Courtney had always kind of had that effect on him.

"To open up the night here at Northside Rebellion, we have a Mr. Ethan Fisher!" the DJ announced. He hopped up to grab the microphone amidst an encouraging round of applause and resisted the urge to roll his eyes about the song he knew was about to be displayed behind him on screens all over the bar.

"I feel like I should mention that this particular performance is dedicated to my amazing girlfriend, whose birthday happens to be today, and is also the result of losing a hard-fought bet, so please forgive me." He smirked, and several whistles went up from various bar patrons. Courtney's eyes went wide when he mentioned the bet, and she sat up a little straighter. The opening beat of "To Be With You," by Mr. Big sounded in the bar and he took one last breath before putting everything he had into that stupid song. He ended up playing air guitar through most of the instrumental, because one can't just sing an eighties ballad without going all out. The look in her eyes was one of amusement and love when she kissed him in front of the entire bar at the end. The DJ came for the mic and continued on down the list.

"Are you *kidding me?*" she asked in disbelief, her blue eyes shining at him.

"Well, a bet is a bet," he answered. "I recorded a version of it for you at work earlier this week, as I believe those were the terms."

"You are but a shell of your former self," Luke admonished.

"Don't be bitter, Luke, I'm sure we could get your new friend to dedicate a song to you when his shift is over."

Luke's fists clenched, and Ethan worried for a minute he'd chosen his moment incorrectly, but his friend downed the rest of his drink and replied, "Whatever, noticing he didn't ask for *your* number with your stupid new haircut. I'm just going to have to carry being the pretty one from now on."

"I'll make sure to send over my tiara." The DJ called up Courtney to sing next, and she got a warm reception after being the center of attention earlier. She rocked out to a country song he'd never heard before, but he liked it anytime she sang. After several more performers, some more entertaining than others, Vanessa announced that she and Luke were headed across town.

"We are going dancing," she asserted with a smile that looked like victory. Luke nodded, but appeared he'd rather do almost anything else. "You guys can come if you want." Ethan prayed the answer would be no; he just wanted to take her home.

"Nah, I think we're good. Thank you so much for surprising me and coming out though. You guys have fun." *Thank you, Jesus.* She scooted closer to him once they were alone and played with his hair. "So, are you about ready to get out of here, then?" He laced his fingers through hers, and noticed for the first time that she was wearing his ring from last summer. He twirled it around her thumb and pulled her even closer.

"I thought maybe you'd thrown it off of a bridge." Knowing she kept it even when they weren't together triggered a wave of nostalgia for almost exactly a year ago when he'd given it to her. They were both very different people than they'd been that night, but the energy between them felt the same. His fingertips found their way under her shimmery floral top, and he let them travel up her sides, making her squirm slightly. "I can't say the thought didn't cross my mind," she murmured. He smiled against her lips, and motioned to their server to bring the check.

♪ *"Free Fallin'" - Tom Petty*
Performed by: John Mayer

15

Nineteen was her favorite year, hands down. "This was the best birthday ever," she told him on their way out of the karaoke bar. His performance was something out of an eighties movie, and it was perfection.

"Ever?" he asked pointedly, bringing up images of their first actual date the year before. Despite the importance held in that night for her, this was better. There was no black cloud up ahead, there was no nervousness about what being with him would be like; she could just relax. She'd waited a long time to have this with him.

"Well, you still have some time to really solidify that assessment when we get back to my house," she flirted, leaning against the passenger side of his car.

"Challenge accepted." He whispered in her ear what he had in mind and tugged on her belt. She shivered and leaned into him, now very interested in getting home. "And stop biting your lip or we won't make it there," he teased her, pulling it out from between her teeth with his thumb. Her pulse quickened as she slid into the car. She stopped him before he turned the key in the ignition and kissed him with a renewed sense of urgency, wishing they were already in her room. Her fingers danced down the soft fabric of his shirt and lingered longer than necessary on his stomach. She undid his belt while maintaining their intensity, and with an act of contortionism gave him a quality 'thank you' for her birthday gifts. His eyes widened. "Jesus Christ, Courtney," he exhaled sharply, and she liked that she had the ability to shock him. Purposefully, she left him wanting as motivation to get them home faster. It worked. He was unbuttoning her jeans while she was still fumbling with the lock on the front door. She pulled off his shirt on the way up the stairs, and he walked her backwards down the hall and into her room.

"I love you." His fingers were traveling the arch of her spine.

"I love you too," she managed, her breath catching in her throat. There was an edge in his mood tonight, but it matched hers. It was a far cry from the slow and the sweet of their encounter the year before, but that made the contented exhaustion at the end even better. "I stand by my earlier claim," she told him, still marveling at his new appearance. He had gone from looking like an Abercrombie ad to a Calvin Klein Underwear model.

"I will agree. Wholeheartedly," he responded, his arms still secured around her. She traced the veins at the surface of his skin around his biceps, not sure why she found their existence so appealing.

"I'm gonna go grab some water," she said softly. "Do you want anything?"

"Nah, I'm good." He yawned. She put on his soft green shirt, fully intending to steal it from him at some point, and a pair of sweats. She found Vanessa in the kitchen in a similar get-up, eating a bowl of Cap'n Crunch.

"Hey, how was dancing?"

"It was fun for the whole forty minutes we were there." V shook her head.

"Why only forty minutes?" Courtney questioned, getting out a glass.

"Because when Luke went to grab me a drink, some guy got all up in my business, and I politely declined, but he wasn't really fond of that answer."

"Oh my god, what is wrong with people?"

"I have no idea, but I was in the midst of declining a bit more forcefully when Luke got back, and well? You can imagine how smoothly that went when he saw the moron's hands on me. I was able to drag him out of there before it became a felony situation, but that was the end of dancing."

"Where is Luke now?"

"Asleep. Ethan?"

"Probably the same. You tired?"

"Nah, why?"

"Feel like going for a drive?"

"Sure. Lemme go grab my phone."

"K, I'm gonna get a sweatshirt." Courtney slid back into her room and found Ethan passed out in her bed. She wrote him a quick note in case he woke up and thought she disappeared and met Vanessa back downstairs.

"Why does it feel like we're sneaking out of our own house?" she wondered aloud, climbing in the Camaro.

"I know, right? It seems like some things lose their appeal when you're on your own."

"Agreed. Although we really should go night canoeing someday." Vanessa grinned.

"I think I'm good with that being a once-in-a-lifetime experience," Courtney assured her, opening the moon roof. Her friend filled the car with a slower playlist, but it seemed to match her mood. "You okay?"

"Yeah, just annoyed."

"At Luke?"

"No, no, not at all. He is who he is. I'm lucky he didn't assault the guy. Just the whole situation. I don't like my boyfriend having to come to my rescue or something. I swear I'm going to start taking Krav Maga."

"That's a mildly terrifying thought," Courtney relayed, taking in the unfamiliar surroundings of their route. She vaguely wondered if Vanessa knew where she was going.

"I know I never really told you about the shit that went down when I was with Zack, but this just made me feel like I was right back there, some scared little sophomore who couldn't stand up for herself," Vanessa confessed, not meeting Courtney's eyes. Courtney turned the music down instinctively.

"What do you mean?" Concern filled her voice. The thought of some guy hurting V sparked fire inside of her. She would kill him.

"I don't wanna get into all of it right now, and it's nothing catastrophic, so don't let your mind go there, it just wasn't a good situation. Luke sort of saved me then, too." Even without the whole story, things about their relationship were starting to click for Courtney. She felt a deep seeded sense of guilt that she hadn't been around to help Vanessa then.

"I'm sorry, V. If you do wanna get into it ever, you can tell me, you know that. You don't always have to be the one listening to my crap, you know?"

"Oh trust me, I know. One day I'm cashing in, and you're going to have to listen to me analyze the minutia of Luke's every comment and give me advice for hours," she teased, the atmosphere around them evening out.

"Yeah yeah, so funny. But I will take Krav-whatever with you if you want. Or self-defense or something. Just let me know when and where. I kind of like the idea of being a ninja."

Vanessa drove around a bit more, but it didn't hold the same magic as their back-road adventures the summer before. Stop lights and late-night stragglers making their way home kind of ruined the idea of being free from the world. They made a pact to go again one night after dinner at V's parents' house.

The Camaro idled in the driveway a little after one am, and Courtney was looking forward to curling up next to Ethan and falling asleep.

♪ *"Sugar We're Goin' Down"- Fall Out Boy*

16

He sat on the edge of her bed tapping his foot nervously. He didn't know which emotion was the strongest at the moment: jealousy or guilt. After hearing the front door open, he knew he was going to have to choose one quickly before she walked into the room.

They had woken him up while leaving, and he had found her note. It was sort of cute that they'd snuck out to have an adventure, even if he wished it were with him. He had grabbed her phone on the nightstand to check the time, but found a text message on the screen instead. It was from Ben.

> B: Hey Court. I debated whether or not to text you. I know things are kind of awkward between us right now, but I wanted to tell you happy birthday. I hope you did something worthy of your awesomeness :). You don't have to write me back, just wanted you to know I was thinking about you. <3.

It took every ounce of strength and forethought that he possessed not to write back to tell him she had been well taken care of that evening. *What the hell can be done about this guy?* He knew there was nothing particularly telling in that message, but it struck the match to a much greater fire. He had sat and stared at her phone for a long time, knowing it was a bad idea to go there. The knowledge that she and Ben had been together just over a month ago began to take over the more rational parts of his brain. *It doesn't matter, she's with you, just let it go.* But he couldn't. He needed to know what she'd felt for him; he couldn't stand the idea of her *loving* someone else. He unlocked the phone and was determined just to find one piece of evidence that proved… he didn't exactly know what, but something that would make the hostility die down in his chest. He scrolled back to June, glad to see there weren't many recent conversations.

> June 16th
>
> B: What movie do you wanna see tonight? We can grab dinner first if you want.
>
> C: None of the above.
>
> B: Okay? What'd you have in mind?
>
> C: I don't know. Can we just drive up South Mountain or something?
>
> B: We can do that. You okay?
>
> C: No. I don't want to go to Ohio. Like I just wanna go to Irvine with you.
>
> B: Court. I'll be right over- don't be sad. You know you're psyched about school. Give me five minutes, we'll do whatever you want tonight.
>
> C: Even watch girly movies?
>
> B: Even watch girly movies. Again. I love you.
>
> C: I love you too

This was not better. This was much, much worse. He knew he had to stop, but then it became a compulsion. He scrolled through photos of them together and a couple other conversations until his palms were sweating and his mind was racing. He put the phone on the other side of the room to distance himself from the newfound discovery.

The thought struck him of wanting his old hair back when he ran his fingers through it nervously. *What the hell is taking them so long?* Although the other half of him was glad because he had no idea what he was going to say. He didn't think he could just pretend to be asleep; his whole body was reacting to the thought of her still having feelings for Ben. *You'll just ask her, straight out. Simply explain you accidentally saw the text. No need to go into anything else.*

That's what he had decided to do when she tiptoed into the room.

"I'm up, don't worry."

"Oh! Sorry, you scared me. Did you get my note?"

"Yeah, no worries. I, um. I need to talk to you," he got out, his foot tapping again.

"Ok? What's up?" she asked, turning on the overhead light. She was wearing his t-shirt, and it gave him a needed reminder that she'd just spent the last several hours tangled up with him and no one else. He took a breath.

"I woke up when you guys left- I saw your note, and I clicked the home button on your phone just to see what time it was, but..."

"But what?"

"There was a text on the screen? So I read it."

"Okay. Who was it from?" Her tone was confused.

"Ben."

"Oh. Okay, well that explains the drama of you sitting here in the dark then, I guess. What did it say? I haven't spoken to him since I told him we were together, just so you know... I'm not keeping anything from you."

She wasn't keeping anything from him, not really. He knew she had been honest that she'd just gotten out of a relationship when he pushed her for something more. It just hit him like a ton of bricks that she had a whole other life in Arizona.

"No, I trust you. I just need..." He breathed out. *This is so not a good idea.* "I need to know if you still have feelings for him. I'm sorry if that's unfair, it's just... reading that? It's killing me, thinking about you with him."

"Ethan, you knew I was with someone in Phoenix. This isn't like breaking news. What did the text say?" she asked again, looking around for her phone.

"It's over there. It just said happy birthday and that he was thinking of you. I'm not going to lie and say I didn't sit here for a while and come up with various things to text back." She shot him a hard look that reminded him of how he'd looked at Sara in an uncomfortably similar situation. "I didn't. Just… Please get how hard it is that there's some other guy out there thinking about you tonight and that you loved him not so very long ago. So please answer my question."

"You didn't ask one." A cold edge crept into her tone.

"Semantics, Court. Do you still have feelings for him?"

"I'm having some new feelings towards you right now." Her voice was now iced over. She started pacing and he knew that wasn't favorable. He waited. "I'm not going to tell you that I feel nothing for Ben. He has been my friend since I was twelve, so it would be a lie for me to say I am completely indifferent towards him now. He's a good guy, a good person. But I'm *in love* with you." She didn't look particularly pleased with that fact at the moment, but he felt his pulse slowing. He knew he was being completely unreasonable. She hadn't begrudged him his past when they were together. His guilt was now overtaking his jealousy, and he couldn't even look at her. He had crossed a serious line into her privacy, and all it had done was make him look insane.

"I'm sorry. I *hate* that he felt comfortable texting you in the middle of the night, but I hate it more that I let it get in my head." *If she only knew,* he thought, his actions seeming more and more unacceptable by the moment. "I may have also gone through some of your photos," he confessed for absolutely no good reason. She whipped around mid-pace and stared at him.

"So you went through my phone?"

"No, not exactly. I don't know what I was hoping to see… maybe that you didn't look as happy with him as you do with me? I know it was stupid. I don't have anything to say in my defense, I just couldn't stand it."

"Ethan! You can't just go through my stuff because you get jealous! You have to *talk* to me. And I have no control over what time someone messages me! Jesus Christ. Do I even want to know what I'd find if I went through your phone?" *Nothing,* he replied in his head. But that was only because he'd deleted anything incriminating. "Ugh, this was like the best night ever, and that seriously wasn't enough for you to *know* how I feel about us?" He wished she would stand still. "This is not what I want to remember about my birthday."

"Technically it's not your birthday anymore," he let out, realizing after that wasn't her point.

"*Semantics*, Ethan," she shot back, pivoting towards him. He decided to stop saying words. "I knew it couldn't be this easy. And for the record, between the two of us? I'm the one who should be jealous- not you. Take note that I haven't asked you about your activities while we were apart. Because I. Don't. Wanna. Know," she declared, more to the ceiling than to him, and he started to get nervous.

"Court, I'm sorry. I should have just waited for you to get back and talked to you. Please don't start questioning our entire relationship right now."

"Is that not what you were doing? Sitting here thinking I was still in love with Ben?" He sincerely hoped those weren't tears in her eyes, because he didn't think he could handle any more. Abruptly, he stood up and interrupted her pacing.

"Baby, I'm sorry. I screwed up when I unlocked your phone. I swear I trust you, and I don't need more proof of your feelings for me." She glared at him, but at least it was eye contact. He felt bold enough to put his hands on her shoulders, and when she didn't shrug him off, he felt better. They stood like that for several breaths. He carefully unfolded her arms and put them around his waist, dropping a kiss on her head. "I just love you. And there was no one of importance. When we were apart. Just so you know," he finished quietly.

She sighed, but he felt a considerable amount of tension leave her body. "I just love you too," she responded, and he breathed a sigh of relief. She let him hold her for a minute and he felt her nails along his back. "You sang Mr. Big to me tonight." She was much calmer now. Her big eyes looked up at him, apparently giving in to forgiveness.

"I did. I kind of rocked it if I say so myself."

"Can we go to bed now? With no more crazy?"

"Yeah." He found her lips and kissed her lightly. She held him there and bit his lip, and soon all of the heat from their argument slowly shifted into something else entirely. He picked her up, and they found their way back to solid ground.

♪ *"Dreams" – The Cranberries*

17

Despite the outrage she'd experienced walking into Ethan's jealous meltdown the night before, his feeling guilty had its advantages. His worry wasn't necessary, but at least he knew how it felt for her to watch girls tripping over themselves to be next to him.

He was incredibly attentive the few weeks before classes began, and she had to admit that it was helping with her homesickness. She missed her mom, and her house, and it was even to a point where she missed the heat. Starting a new job helped keep her mind busy, though, and she realized all of her stress about it had been silly. Her responsibilities were simple, as long as she could get past the awkwardness of accepting collect calls from their clients in jail. And the matter of then speaking to them politely as if she didn't know they were wearing an orange jumpsuit on the other end of the line.

Both of her bosses were pretty casual, and didn't care if she was on her phone or searching the internet for clothes as long as they got their messages. They even talked about having their paralegal show her how to draft simple motions in order to lighten up the paperwork. Really, she couldn't have landed a better gig, and could only hope her classes would be as good of a fit.

Ethan had planned a relaxing day together the Sunday before the beginning of the fall term. Well, relaxing for him. For her it was a bit nerve-wracking.

"You good, babe?" he asked her, getting situated in the small space.

"Yeah. Just, what do I look at while I'm singing?" His eyebrows gave her a confused expression. "I don't want to look dumb if I'm supposed to be watching for like a cue or something that I suck and should stop."

"There is no such cue, sprinkles. You can look wherever you want. Here," he resolved, shifting the position of the microphone, "you can look at me."

"Okay," she nodded nervously, chewing the inside of her cheek. They had been working on a song to sing together off and on since he mentioned it, and he had gotten her to agree to record it that day, before the craziness of homework started. She knew it was a terrible idea- her brain was already suffering from the-day-before-school anxiety and the fear she would get lost on campus or show up in the wrong class and everyone would stare at her.

"The look on your face is painful. This is going to be fun, *relax*. Please." He placed his hands on the back of her neck and put some pressure there. *He smells good,* she thought, breathing in his white cotton t-shirt as she closed her eyes. "Better?"

"Better." The song they'd written, and well, a lot of the new stuff he'd been messing around with, had kind of an Americana feel to it. Ethan walked out to talk to his friend from the record store that was running the soundboard. She took a breath and made up her mind to appear calm and collected no matter how she felt. His excitement for this project was palpable, and she had to admit that working with him on it gave her a sense of satisfaction- to create something from nothing.

"You ready to rock, baby?" he asked lightly when he walked back in. She took the three strides across the small space and stood on her toes to kiss him. He returned the sentiment and she flitted back to her spot.

"Now I am." She smiled, her nerves calmer. She thought her first run-through was awful, but by the third time, she was warm and happier with it. He was incredible as usual. In regular life he was so laid back, but in there he was a machine.

"I love you," he told her after listening to the playback for the sixth time. "If you don't wanna stick around for the rest of it, you don't have to. I had one other song I wanted to get done, so I won't be offended if you go home and organize your pens in color order." He grinned at her, the happiest she'd seen him in a while.

"Okay, one? You know my pens are already in color order. And two? I may go and buy a candy bar next door, but other than that, no way I'm leaving before I get to hear the final product." She messed up his hair slightly, and he didn't even try to stop her.

"Well, add two more candy bars to that, and you have a deal." She kissed his cheek and he went right back his conversation with his friend.

* * *

Stepping over bolts of fabric and a teetering stack of magazines, she navigated a path into her entryway upon arriving at home. Vanessa had started school the week before, and was already eyeballs deep in projects.

"Hey V? Do you want some help with this stuff?" she called, hoping the answer was yes.

"Yes! I'm in the den." Courtney picked up what she could and made her way there. After seeing the sheer amount of *crap* Vanessa would be working on all year, they had decided she should take over the home office as her workspace. It was coming along- she had shelves and all manner of tool and craft supplies imaginable organized on the walls.

"Where would you like these?"

"Fabric shelf," she responded as though it were obvious.

"Of course." She helped her move the rest of the mountain into the designated spaces, and she didn't hear from Vanessa again that night. It was kind of refreshing to see both V and Ethan so focused, though in Vanessa's case she wondered how much of her motivation was stemming from the fact that Luke was now two hours away at Bowling Green, settling into his dorm.

Courtney made herself a salad, courtesy of Ethan's insistence on taking her grocery shopping for acceptably nutritious food, and checked her schedule and map again. Just to be sure.

> E: Stop whatever nerdy thing you're doing and come outside.
>
> C: Are you stalking me?
>
> E: Absolutely.
>
> C: I'm good with that :).
>
> E: Wear shoes you can walk in, please.

She slipped on a pair of Chucks and adjusted her appearance on the way out the door. Her glitter necklace bounced against the black tank top when bounding down the stairs. Ethan was sitting on her porch railing, making a white t-shirt and jeans somehow look like a revelation.

"How is it possible that I missed you when I just saw you three hours ago?" he asked, hopping down and eliminating the space between them.

"Wrong person to ask. I keep waiting for you to become less appealing, but it hasn't happened yet."

"Don't be mean, not when I'm here to rid you of your inevitable insomnia later tonight."

"Say what?"

"Just come on." She shook her head and got in the car. The sun was setting, and it hit her that it was the last day of their summer. She could only hope that the next season brought with it as much gorgeous anticipation. Ethan pulled into one of the lots on campus and got out.

"You know school doesn't start until tomorrow, right?"

"I do, yes. But you've been prepping for tomorrow like it's the apocalypse, so we're here to walk to all of your classes. Again. I have also taken the liberty of cross-referencing your schedule with mine and creating a color coded map so you know where to find me if you want to make out under a tree or something between English and Greek Mythology."

"Did you just use the words 'cross-referencing,' 'color-coded,' and 'make-out' in the same sentence?"

"Yup. I'm just a nerd, living in this super hot body. It's a curse, honestly."

"I don't know that I have ever wanted you as much as I do right now." She grinned, snatching the map out of his hand. They walked the campus, and having him with her just brought back all of the happy feelings of possibility she'd experienced when she'd first visited, and she knew she belonged there. The cobblestones, the brick, the chime of the clock in the center of campus… and him.

♪ *"You and Me" – Sara Watkins*

18

A laugh escaped his throat when he dropped Courtney off at home and she said she had a back-to-school present for him. He had initially hoped it involved less clothing for both of them, but his girlfriend didn't really joke about school, he'd learned. She ran up to her room and came back down with a very sleek looking gray canvas backpack. Originally, he'd intended on just carrying his notebooks, but she insisted he needed something to help him stay organized, and be able to hold her hand and a coffee at the same time if required.

"I like it, seriously, this is cool." It was modern looking.

"You do? Good. I was nervous. But you haven't opened it yet," she prodded.

"Of course you've stocked my backpack for me." He laughed and pulled open the front zipper. It was filled with pens in all manner of color, highlighters, a mini-stapler even. The larger portion had even more stuff in it, and he didn't think he had been that prepared for academic success since age six. "You're the coolest, nerdiest girlfriend in the whole world, and I love you, thank you," he told her, wrapping her in a hug. Her cheek rested where his heart was, and it felt like home.

* * *

"Are you nervous?" his mom asked at dinner.

"To eat this thing you're calling a burger? Yes." He grimaced at his plate.

"Shut up, it's a quinoa burger. It's good for you. And you know what I mean."

"Whatever you say. And no, not really. I mean, the first day is easy, right? I'll be nervous come mid-terms."

"Yeah, that's sort of the attitude that worries me."

"Mom, please not a lecture."

"Just a short one. I know you're smart and capable when you wanna be, but the thing is that now you need to be that all the time. I went to school there, and it was a great experience, but it's not like you can just skate by and not do homework- it's not high school."

"I know, I swear. I'll do it, all of the homework, the papers, whatever. I know what it's costing in tuition. I won't screw it up, okay? Here, look-" He got up from the table and grabbed his new backpack from the car. Upon setting it in front of her, his mom looked confused. "Open it up."

"You're inviting me to go through your backpack? Do I need gloves?"

"Just do it." She did, and confusion turned to surprise.

"You did this?" she responded skeptically.

"Of course not. Courtney did it. But the point is that I'm ready for school, okay?"

"Okay, okay, don't be so defensive."

* * *

The first weeks actually went by quickly. He was a big fan of not being at school all day, every day. For the most part, he was able to keep up with the reading, except when it put him to sleep, and still have time to do a few open mic nights a month, teach his guitar students, and be with Courtney. He almost wasn't jealous that Southbound was on tour. Almost.

He did keep in touch with Crawford occasionally- things appeared to be going well for them. He sent his friend an email anytime he had any new music to share, and Crawford swore he'd keep passing it along to anyone who would listen.

Towards the beginning of October, he got a call to perform a couple of songs at the Fall Follies- a fairly popular event in Gem.

"That's awesome, baby, Fall Follies is my favorite festival- pardon the alliteration, I sound like a nursery rhyme," she rambled when he told her.

"Then you should be even more excited to be performing at it."

"Me?"

"Well, just the one song, yeah. Please?" He saw the hesitation swimming in her eyes and knew he had to act quickly. "It's so good, and you're so good, and I will make you feel so good if you'll say yes," he pleaded, kissing her neck in the spot she liked. He was not above bribing her.

"Unfair," she sighed, agreeing without any further hesitation. He was wearing her down.

"Thank you, baby." He smiled.

She changed her mind several times over the weeks leading up to the performance, but he was able to convince her of the benefits of singing with him. Namely that it would make him really happy. She tried to claim that she was too busy studying for mid-terms to practice, but in all reality, he had never seen someone so efficient at time management. He knew she was stressed, but it worked for her. He was at least done with one paper and halfway through the other two, though he wasn't sure if he really knew what the professors were looking for. *One way to find out,*.

Courtney met him in the library one afternoon and took out the scariest collection of flashcards he'd ever seen. He tried to pretend it was normal, but his face gave away his trepidation.

"What? How do you study vocab?" she asked him.

"Um, I don't? I mean, I read through the notes and stuff, but that is *a lot* of flashcards."

"I like to be prepared," she said in her defense. He was finishing up his last paper and did need to study for the multiple-choice tests coming up in the next week, but he couldn't imagine the effort. They even looked color-coded.

"Lemme read your paper," she commanded, taking a break. "What class is it for?"

"Yeah, no." He closed the screen of his laptop slightly.

"What? Why not?" she asked, genuinely offended.

"Because you're like Miss Verbal SAT and I don't want you to."

"That's precisely why you *should* want me to. I can proof a paper in, like, twenty minutes. You'll thank me later."

"What are the chances you'll let this go?"

"Slim to none. And then I will blame you when I fail my own exams because all of the effort that should have gone towards studying will have gone towards convincing you to share your paper." He wordlessly pushed the laptop over to her.

"Thank you." She grinned victoriously.

"It's for English. It's a narrative essay on my understanding of life, it's a stupid assignment. Don't judge me."

"Oh I will absolutely judge you, but I'll still love you." He resigned himself to his fate, trying to recall what he had written and how bad it was. She was quiet other than the occasional clicking sound of the "delete" button and replacement text going in.

"Done," she said fifteen minutes later.

"And?" he asked, trying to prepare himself for feeling like crap.

"It was kind of beautiful."

"Beautiful?"

"I mean, it's narrative, and you write lyrics all the time, so it sort of reads poetically. I cleaned up your grammar and formatting a bit, and I highlighted two sections that I thought were confusing, but otherwise, I liked it. Don't be such a weenie."

"Okay, then. Well, thanks," he told her, still skeptical.

* * *

He ended up getting an eighty-eight on that paper, but Cs on the two he didn't have her proof. He could tell she was biting her tongue when he shared that piece of news. They were in his car on the way back to The Fall Follies after watching the parade that morning, and she either wasn't as nervous as he'd anticipated, or she was getting better at hiding it from him. The weather had turned chilly, but the benefit to that was seeing his girlfriend in tight pants and leather boots.

"You look pretty," he told her, somewhat randomly.

"Really? This isn't too much with the lace and the belt?" she asked, referring to her ruffled black shirt. He didn't know what she meant by "too much," but he liked it, so he assumed it wasn't.

"Ummm, no? I just see pretty."

"Such a boy."

"That is one of the things you like about me, right?" he asked, rubbing her knee.

"I suppose you could say that." She smiled, shaking her head. They arrived at the festival and spoke with the coordinator.

"So if I'm completely off-key and ruin your whole performance, will you still love me?" she asked in true Courtney fashion. *There's my girl.* He had begun to think she'd disappeared beneath a calm and cool exterior.

"Nope. This is it." She shoved him. He kissed her cheeks, her eyelids, her nose, and her mouth. "You know I love you. I'm just excited." The director motioned to him and he sauntered out on stage alone to perform two of his solo songs. He hadn't tried the harmonica in front of a real crowd before, and he sincerely hoped it sounded how he wanted. Being on stage in Gem City, knowing Courtney was about to join him, made him feel the best parts of the last year. While he desperately missed playing with a band, there was something to be said about it just being him and his guitar, with no one else to rely on, singing his own music. After making it through the bridge with the harmonica, he loosened up and the short set went off without a hitch.

Courtney walked out confidently for their duet, and sang it perfectly- also a trademark of hers. He never understood how someone who worked as hard as she did worried about failing all of the time. *Or maybe that's why she works so hard?* He didn't know that he'd ever really get it. He did know that listening to the words they'd written together made him feel connected to her.

> *Bridges burned, rebuilt from ash*
> *A lover's hand brought back from the past*
> *Hearts can survive the regret and pain*
> *If there exists the promise to be together again*

The crowd loved her, and he kissed her much less playfully once they were finished. "I have never been so scared in my whole life." She breathed, his hands finding where they fit around her waist. They sat on a couple of folding chairs back behind the performance area.

"What? Why? You were incredible."

"I always knew that what you did, singing your own songs, was admirable, but I never really *got it* until right then when I walked out there. It's so much different than singing a cover. It felt like I was giving everyone something of mine to judge, and it was terrifying." She articulated the emotions perfectly- that was exactly what it felt like. She shakily placed her hands on his, her adrenaline fading into recovery.

"I know the feeling," he agreed. "But it's worth it, right? When you know people are listening to it or analyzing it? That's how it feels for me. Like whenever someone comes to talk to me after an open mic, it seems like we already have something in common."

"I kind of have a rock star crush on you right now, I want you to know that. I mean, I know you're my boyfriend, but you're different when you sing."

"I think I'm all right with that."

"Okay." She breathed again. "I'm pretty sure my legs are done shaking. Let's go have fabulous Fall Follies fun, shall we?" He gave her the best "you're-a-dork" stare, but she didn't appear to care.

♪ *"Bitch" – Meredith Brooks*

19

The trees that sprinkled the park were changing colors, and the streets were lined with pumpkins and paper luminaries to be lit later. As a kid, this festival was better than Christmas to her. She and Vanessa had gotten up much too early that morning to score prime seats for the parade, but it had absolutely lived up to her expectations: the cheerleaders, the band, the old cars, the candy- all of it. These were the types of things she'd gained when she'd chosen to move back. Strolling down the booth-lined path with Ethan squeezing her hand felt like living out one of her favorite movies.

"We have to buy, like, every available food item here," she insisted.

"Even those candy apples?" he replied, calling her out.

"Sure, as long as it's cool if I only eat the candy part off of it."

"You won't even eat a piece of fruit when it has been completely covered in sugar?"

"What part of 'I hate fruit' is not sinking in? I thought you accepted me for who I am." While Ethan was off getting her another treat he probably disapproved of, she glanced up from the kettle corn and saw Tyler- looking largely the same, though his hair was longer and he'd added a lip ring to his piercing collection. She hadn't seen him since homecoming the year before, and while she knew he and Ethan had had a falling out, the details weren't clear for her. He was walking her way with his arm around a girl she didn't know. She was prepared to ignore it, but he caught her eye a moment too soon.

"Hey, Courtney," Tyler offered coldly as they strolled by. The girl stopped short and turned back to face her. She was wearing an interesting ensemble. That was the nicest thing Courtney could think to say about it, anyway. She had on a black mini-skirt with fishnets and boots, which was a little 90s and could have been cool without the nearly see-through black top that showed off her purple bra.

"Courtney…" the girl said slowly.

"Ross, do I know you?" Just as she asked that question, Ethan reappeared with her cotton candy and did a double take of the present company. The girl met his eyes, and hers flashed with what could only be described as gleeful vengeance.

"You don't, but I know you. You're Fisher's pretty, pretty princess." Courtney's eyes narrowed. *Who the hell is this chick?*

"Sara, come on," Ethan let out, sounding more than irritated. *Okay, she has a name.*

"What? I was just going to say that if I'd known I'd be meeting *the* Courtney Ross today, I would have dusted off my tiara and picked out something more generic to wear." She gestured to Courtney's outfit dramatically. "It's the least I could do after stealing your boyfriend last year." The girl's dark eyes sparkled with what she certainly must have thought was a winning oration.

"What the hell, are you-" Ethan started in, but she interrupted him with her hand on his wrist.

"*Sara*, is it?" Courtney asked, her voice perfectly controlled despite the snap she'd experienced inside. "Don't be so hard on yourself, I'm sure your outfit will serve its purpose down on the corner later." Her mean-girl persona, rarely used but still in existence, was on full display at the moment, and she wanted to eviscerate this girl. "And just in case you're confused, thieves are supposed to hold on to the things they take." She looked the girl dead in the eye and saw her catching up. "Really good to see you, Tyler," she offered, and found him looking dumbfounded. "I hope you both enjoy the Follies." She gave the greatest smile she could muster and pulled Ethan by the hand towards the next booth. She heard the girl mutter, "Bitch," after her, but it didn't matter.

Her heart was pounding, but she walked calmly until she was certain they wouldn't run the risk of seeing them again. Ethan let out a sound that was a cross between a laugh and a sigh. "What…the hell…was that?" he asked very slowly. She sat down on a bench and felt tears prick at her eyes, though she wasn't sure why. The whole thing had been a fight or flight response.

"I'm from Scottsdale, you learn to fight with words. But let me ask you the same question. What the hell *was* that?" She willed her voice not to betray the range of emotion creeping up. Her anger towards the girl was lessening; she was just a stupid stoner chick, but there had to be something behind her words.

"She's no one, honestly. We went on a few dates last year after you and I…"

"Is she the reason we broke up? She said she stole my boyfriend, and I can assume she didn't mean Tyler."

"No! Court, no, I swear, I never cheated on you. I'm so sorry she just attacked you like that, she's sort of unbalanced, but I would have taken care of it, you just sort of… well, you kicked ass, I didn't really need to do anything." She couldn't tell if he was impressed or afraid. Maybe a little of both, which was wise considering her mood. She realized the less-than-amusing irony of the mid-October date. *We cannot be repeating the exact same timeline from last year.*

"You flat out said to me there was 'no one of importance' when we were apart. Clearly you were together long enough for her to know about me, and for her to develop some fairly strong feelings, I might add. It *was* you having the meltdown about Ben, yes? Like we were involved in the same conversation? Because you just let me walk into that having NO FREAKING IDEA who she was." She literally bit her tongue to keep anything else from coming out of her mouth. She didn't want to cry. Ethan looked repentant and kneeled in front of her, lessening the gap between them.

"I'm sorry. Maybe I should have told you about her, it just literally meant nothing. I was missing you, and she was there, that was it."

"Is that who you hooked up with the night you called me?" Her stomach was turning now, and she hated to admit it, but she had a slightly greater appreciation for his jealousy of Ben. Thinking of that girl's hands on Ethan made Courtney want to physically harm someone.

"No," he answered softly, placing his hand on hers. That had been a poor question. No answer would have made her feel better. She wiped the stubborn tears from the corners of her eyes and tried to shake off the whole encounter.

"I think I'm just gonna go find V," she told him, attempting to swallow the lump that had formed in her throat. It was becoming more difficult by the minute to keep her feelings in check, and she wanted to go home.

"Court," he said with no real follow-up. "If you want to go home, I'll take you, but I hate for this to ruin the whole festival. You love the Follies. Let me get you a snow cone and let's just chill for a minute, please? I'm sorry." He traced the lines in her palm with his thumb, and it made her nostalgic for when everything was new and they didn't have any baggage between them.

"Is there anything else I should know? To prevent future surprises?"

"No, I swear."

"That girl better hope I don't see her in a dark alley somewhere. I have way meaner things to say than that."

"Do you often frequent dark alleys?"

"I might start," she retorted, feeling some of the stress lifting.

"You were sort of scarier than Vanessa back there." This made Courtney give a genuine laugh.

"Yeah, well, you don't bring an emo chick to a cheerleader fight. She never really had a chance."

"Can I kiss you?"

"Have you ever asked before?"

"You've never been this intimidating before."

"You can kiss me. After you bring me a blue snow cone."

"Fair enough." He agreed and left to seek out the frozen treat. She took a mirror out of her bag and assessed her appearance. She at least reapplied a sparkly lip-gloss to look like she tried. Ethan returned with her requested item. She stood up to grab it, but he held it out of her reach. "Kiss first." She obliged and pulled him into her, trying desperately to get back to the picture-perfect place they were before.

♪ *"Don't Carry It All"* – *The Decemberists*

20

Is this a parallel universe? She looked like Courtney, and she kissed like Courtney, but this girl was not his sweet, anxious, mild-mannered you-have-to-get-to-know-her-to-know-what-she's-talking-about-half-the-time Courtney. It was sort of hot. And a little bit frightening. Running into Sara really hadn't ever crossed his mind; it seemed like so long ago that they had been together. *So much for her life-long friend Kacie,* he thought, imagining how she and Tyler must have gotten together.

He apologized at least six more times before they got to her house, and the shadow of the their earlier fight seemed to have faded some after snow cones and carnival games. "Do you want me to come in?" he asked, not quite sure where her head was.

"Again I say, have you ever asked before?" That response didn't help. He knew she was joking, but there was still a layer of ice to her words that he wasn't really used to.

"I suppose not."

"I'm sorry, I'm just in a mood. I'm not trying to be snarky." At least that statement was defrosted.

"It's okay, I know tonight was..." He searched for the right descriptor.

"Tonight was actually great. I mean, all things considered, right? Which is why I'm so annoyed that I let that girl get under my skin.

I had a freaking amazing time performing with you, and I got to eat massive amounts of sugar without you even trying to buy me a salad, and it's FALL outside. Do you know how long Phoenicians wait for fall? Forever. Because we don't have one, it's like an urban legend. Just ugh, her stupid fake red hair and stupid nose ring and stupid fishnets." She sighed, her hands making fists in her hair. "I know I should have taken the high road or something, I just... the whole 'stealing your boyfriend' comment made me want to..."

He had never seen her get mad at anyone, well, except himself, and he considered the idea that maybe all of this pent-up aggression could account for some of her anxiety. "I know, she's a bitch. I wish I could erase that part of our night."

"But you didn't think that always, right? I mean... you were *with* her. In all her 'I'm too emotionally damaged and angst-filled for traditional clothing' glory. I just don't get it. If that's what you like, then what were you ever doing with me? I'm not..."

"You're not what? Crazy? Court, I missed you, I was heartbroken. She was there, and then she was insane, and then she was gone. I promise you there is nothing more to analyze."

"Okay," she said after a long pause. "I promise I'll let this go. I just kept sitting here and thinking about the two of you. It's hard. I'm sorry I didn't really get that before." He knew she was referring to Ben, but he was glad she didn't say it. He pressed his lips to hers softly.

"I love you."

"I love you, too."

He let her go inside alone, hoping that tomorrow would bring a fresh start.

* * *

Ethan threw in a load of laundry when he walked into his house, realizing it was difficult to have actual clothing to wear if he was never home to wash any of it.

"How was the rest of the festival?" his mom asked when he walked through the living room, partially closing the open book on her lap. "You sounded great, I really like your new songs. Not so melancholy."

"Thanks, I think. It was... interesting I guess. Courtney and I ran into Sara and Tyler."

"I *see*. And how'd that go?"

"About how you'd expect it to, except for the part where Courtney totally ripped Sara a new one and walked away smiling."

"Seriously? Courtney, the girl who thanks me profusely for refilling her water when she comes over for dinner?"

"One and the same. Totally crazy. I don't know, I think we're good now."

"You think?"

"Yeah, it was awkward, explaining Sara, but it all ended well enough, I suppose."

"I wish I had been there to see it. I'd have liked to say some things to that girl myself," his mom muttered as he traipsed up the stairs. He forced himself to read the chapters for his Econ class and collapsed into bed.

♪ *"Love of Mine" – Nickel Creek*
"That's What You Get" - Paramore

21

The cups of coffee felt good in her hands; the morning was freezing. Perhaps not literally yet, but compared to an almost-November morning in the desert, it was like living in Antarctica. Her wardrobe had grown exponentially in scarves and coats. She had elected not to text Ethan and just to surprise him instead. It felt like as soon as everything started going smoothly for them, there was another speed bump in the road. *I guess that's just what a relationship is,* she thought, trying to remember the silly arguments she would have with Ben. But with Ethan everything was more intense- the good and the bad.

She watched him stroll out of the building with a couple of other people in conversation. He shot her the look that made her melt when she caught his eye.

"Hey, beautiful," he called as he sauntered up. He looked good no matter what he wore, but the leather jacket made her want to touch him.

"I could say the same to you," she flirted, tugging on the end of his jacket. She put the coffee in his hand and he sat next to her, putting his arm around her shoulder. "How was class?"

"Good, just notes and notes and more notes. I'll be glad when my science credits are taken care of."

"You can say that again. My geology class is the same."

"We should take a class together next semester."

"That is a truly terrible idea," she declared.

"What? Seriously? Why?"

"I have a hard enough time concentrating in class some days just because you're in my head. I can't even imagine trying to focus with you sitting next to me."

"Come on, it wouldn't be that bad."

"You are unaware of what goes on up here, then," she claimed, pointing to her temple. "It is much more interesting than sedimentary rock, I can promise you that."

"Care to elaborate?" he teased. She felt better bantering with him; even the cold wasn't as bothersome. They finished their coffee and he walked her to her first class of the morning. "Can I see you tonight?"

"Later, yeah. I have plans with this girl Bri from my Poli Sci class to go over a project, but can I call you when I'm done? You could always go to the house if you don't wanna drive all the way home."

"Sure, sounds good. I'll see you later, then." He kissed her more seriously than was necessary, sending shivers down her spine, but she gathered that he was letting everyone who walked by know that she was taken. Still, it didn't stop her admiring him from the back when he walked away.

* * *

November passed quickly, and though the weather cooled down, things between her and Ethan did not. She tried to set boundaries, feeling like it couldn't be healthy for them to be together as much as they were, but the newly-independent part of her didn't care, and she wanted what she wanted.

Clothes were haphazardly finding their way into her suitcase the day before she left for Thanksgiving at home, and he was successfully making packing a very difficult task.

"Do you want help?" he asked, kissing her neck while she stood, staring into her closet.

"Is this your definition of helping?"

"Maybe." She sighed, fearing if she turned around that his dark eyes would pull her in, and she'd end up going home without any shoes.

"Give me ten minutes. Put on some happy music to motivate me to make decisions." He sighed but did as she asked.

"It's five days, how many things do you need?"

"I don't know, that's the problem. I could be lounging at home the whole time, or perhaps my friends missed me so much I will have a jam-packed social calendar. One must be prepared."

"Jam-packed, huh?"

"Just with my friends, babe," she tried to reassure him. He hadn't asked about Ben, but she knew the thought was in there.

"I know," he responded, the room soon filling with Nickel Creek.

"I like this song," she told him, throwing two more sweaters and a skirt into the open luggage.

"Me too." He lay on her bed, idly thumbing through his phone while she went down her mental checklist.

"Done and done," she announced a half hour later.

"I think we should work on your time estimation skills."

"I think we should work on your patience."

"Yeah, that's not gonna happen. You know me. Come here." He scooted over on the bed and she hopped up. "What do you think of this?" he asked, handing her his phone. There were photos of an apartment up on the screen, and she flipped through them slowly.

"This looks nice! Are you thinking of moving out already?"

"Well not until summer probably, but this guy in my English class lives there and has some good things to say. There's just usually a waiting list, so I thought I might put in a deposit and get on it."

"What is this planning-ahead business? It's like you're a responsible adult."

"I know, it's a little concerning, right? But I'd like to have my own space, and then I could actually ask you to come home with me sometimes, not just invite myself over here."

"Well I love it when you're here, but I get wanting to have your own space. I say, go for it. I'll come along with you to look at them in person if you want."

"Yeah? Cool." He took back the phone and tossed it on the floor. "Am I allowed to distract you now?"

"Not needed. You have my full and undivided attention." He pulled her in close and brushed her lips, the beginnings of a scruffy shadow tickling her face.

* * *

The automatic doors slid open, and she stepped out into the 75 degree air, her suitcase rolling behind her. She had to admit it felt weird. Like it wasn't quite her home anymore, but part of her still belonged there. The red beetle pulled up to the curb as promised and tears sprang up unexpectedly when her mom got out and hugged her.

"I missed you," she told her mother sincerely.

"I missed you too, sis." Her mom only called her that when she was feeling particularly sentimental, and it made her heart swell. They loaded her bags and got on the road.

"So, am I going to find that workout equipment has taken over my room?"

Because all of the working out your father and I do? No. It's a wine cellar now."

"You're so creative," she teased.

"So tell me things! How is the house and school and Ethan and Vanessa?"

"Mom. You talk to me every other day. You already know all of those things."

"Well, maybe there are new goings-on. I don't like being out of the loop."

"Nothing new. Everything's really good, actually. I like it there, and I'm starting to make some friends that I think I can hang out with, like out of school, so that's positive."

"Good. Have you thought about rushing a sorority?"

"Not this again. Mom, I had enough female bonding for the rest of my life cheering in high school. I think I'm ready to be done with it."

"Just saying, I think you'd have fun, and it would give you a lot larger social circle."

"Thank you for the suggestion, but I'm good for now."

"All right, all right."

Her mom caught her up on all of the neighborhood gossip and agreed to take Courtney to Ajo Al's for Mexican food that weekend, even though she refused to pick up Thanksgiving dinner from there. They hadn't even pulled in the driveway when she got a message from Ashley.

> A: So I'm totally stalking you and I know your plane landed already, so can we go out now?

Courtney laughed. She had made it a point to keep up with her friends online as much as she could, and she also enjoyed the tipsy-sounding voicemails from them around 3am on the occasional weekend. Ethan got a kick out of them too, and she wished he were there to bring her worlds together.

> C: I'm just walking in the door- give me an hour? Then yes :).
>
> A: See you then!

Ashley picked her up, being that Courtney's car was across the country, and gave her a squeal and a hug upon the answering of the door. Her friend was still her fairy-like adorable self, though she had traded in her long hair for a much sleeker shoulder-length style. "I missed you! You look so pretty!" Courtney got into Ashley's car with a million questions about her roommate and the dorms and classes; she didn't really ask where they were going. The Volvo pulled up in front of one of Courtney's favorite pizza places, and they got out.

They were chatting away happily all the way up to the hostess stand.

"Just the two of you?"

"No, we're meeting like eight or ten people, I'm not completely sure," Ashley responded, looking around.

"Whom are we meeting?" Courtney asked, confused.

"I see them- thanks," Ashley told the hostess and started to make her way towards the back of the restaurant.

"Everyone's in town, I sent out a text, and here we are. Mini-reunion." She wasn't kidding, and there were more than eight or ten people. A mish-mosh of tables had been moved together to accommodate them, and the girls grabbed two chairs on the end. There were hugs and hellos to go around from friends past, and Courtney felt an overwhelming sense of nostalgia. The nostalgia turned into something a bit stronger when Ben walked through the door and met her eyes. If he was surprised, he didn't show it, but he shot her a smile. *Oh, this is not smart.*

He looked good. His clean-cut hair had grown out some, and it made him even cuter. He made his own round of greetings to everyone there, and held out his tanned arms towards her when he arrived at the end of the table. She looked at him hesitantly, but stood up to hug him.

"I missed you," he murmured in her ear.

"It's good to see you," she responded, trying to keep her emotional distance.

"Well, that's gotta be awkward," Ashley noted a little too loudly. Courtney shot her a look, and she just shrugged an apology.

"Do you mind?" Ben asked her, motioning to the empty chair to her left. At least he pretended Ashley hadn't spoken.

"No, of course not," she told him, though her anxiety level was unbearably high, and her palms were starting to sweat. Thankfully the conversation around them picked up, and there were plenty of distractions. She did not fail to notice, however, that his arm rested casually on the back of her chair while he caught up with friends.

A lot of pizza and half-baked cookie later, her mom texted her to come home and help with food prep for the following morning.

"Hey, Ash, I gotta get home, is it cool if we leave here in a minute?"

"Sure, that's fine," though she seemed bummed to have to head out.

"It's cool, I can take you," Ben offered.

"I- um... that's really nice..." she stalled, hoping Ashley would rescue her from the obviously uncomfortable situation, but she was already back in her own conversation.

"It's just a ride, Court," he said more softly.

"I know. Yeah, that's fine, thank you." She could have killed her friend, but she'd have to take care of the murder plot later. They said their goodbyes to the crowd and made their way to his dad's BMW. He opened the passenger door for her as he always did before, and she just prayed that they could make it to her house without diving into the awkwardness of the atmosphere.

"You look good. Pretty," he told her once they were out of the parking lot.

"Thanks, so do you. I like your hair longer."

"Yeah?"

"Yeah." Things remained quiet for a few minutes while he navigated the surface streets.

"I wanted to tell you that I started seeing someone... I hope that doesn't sound crass, like I'm just telling you to get even or something, I think you know that's not me. I thought... well I thought it might make things less... this. If you knew, I mean."

Her heart dropped surprisingly. *Of course he's seeing someone, that's good for him. He's adorable and sweet.* "That's great, Ben, I'm really happy for you. It doesn't sound... I mean, it's good that you told me. I want you to be happy."

"Good, I was nervous to say anything," he admitted. "Are you happy? With him?" he questioned protectively.

"I am. Ohio is... what I wanted it to be."

"I'm glad. I want that for you too." They drove a bit further in another stretch of silence. "I, um. I know I shouldn't say this, but I'm going to anyway. I-" he hesitated, glancing at her in his peripheral vision. She started to ask him not to say it then, but he began before she had come to a conclusion about what exactly to spit out. "If I still had the choice? I'd choose you. I just need you to know how I feel. I don't know if it'll always be that way, but for now? It is."

"Ben..." she let out.

"I know that you're happy, and I'm not going to say or do anything to jeopardize that, okay? I'd rather be your friend than nothing at all, I just... while we were here and alone, I needed to tell you that."

"Okay. We can be friends."

"I guess we'll find out, at least, right?"

"I guess we will."

He dropped her off, but came in to say hello and Happy Thanksgiving to her parents first. He hugged her before he left, his familiar embrace leaving her guilt-ridden and confused, and then he was gone.

* * *

As was her routine, she called Ethan that night to talk and see how his break was going. She left out seeing Ben from the narrative. The information started to come out a couple of times, but she couldn't think of any good it would bring; it would just ruin his mood for the holiday. *You will tell him later. When you get home.*

Thanksgiving dinner with her family was pretty typical. Football was on TV, the windows and doors were open to let in the incredible weather, and her younger cousins were begging her to play Nintendo with them. It was nice to be around the familiar. Her mom dragged her out for a full day of Black Friday shopping, and she did find a couple of good deals- landing some really nice composition software that Ethan had mentioned, and a couple of pieces of jewelry and some great old movies for Vanessa. She tried to find something for Luke, but honestly thought he'd be good if she gave him a gift card to the hot dog stand in Gem.

> C: Happy Black Friday
>
> E: Yeah, that's not an actual holiday.
>
> C: At my house it is :) I got you a present

E: What kind of present?? One from the store with the pink striped bags?

C: No, an actual present.

E: That would be an actual present. All I want for Christmas is you :).

C: Okay Mariah. You'll like it, I promise.

E: If you picked it out, I'm sure I will. I miss you.

C: I miss you too. You should come here with me on one of our breaks.

E: Yeah? That would be awesome, I'm down.

C: Good :). I'll call you tonight ok?

E: K. Love you.

C: Love you.

Having him be willing to make plans so far in advance made her heart skip. While they had never really talked specifically about their lives down the road, she thought it was possible that they would travel them together. That both thrilled and overwhelmed her, and she had to stop the images of a long white dress from floating into her consciousness. She replaced them with images of a cap and gown, graduating from law school.

Ashley and Molly convinced her to go out with them that Saturday night, despite a wide variety of complaints that she had an early flight. She was wise enough to take her own vehicle this time, well, her mom's, anyway, and met them at the restaurant.

"Don't be lame, you can sleep on the plane," Molly chided, her blue eyes narrowing, as another protestation left her mouth.

"Whatever, she just doesn't wanna see Ben. The excuses you come up with are not very convincing, honestly," Ashley called her out as they headed across the parking lot.

"Oh, yeah, I bet that's uncomfortable," Molly reasoned, her hands raking through her short blond hair.

"Stop, it was fine. We are friends."

"Great, no issues then." They were meeting up with a lot of the same crowd at a popular sushi place. Courtney was not a fan; at least she was able to order chicken. Ben was there, but he respectfully kept his distance, offering a wave when she arrived. A lot of repeated chatter was passed around the table during dinner, and she was ready to go home when the check came. The goodbyes came with a little more heaviness this time, and she struggled with the familiar feeling of being pulled between two different worlds.

She strode out to her mom's car, straightening the cream colored sweater over her jeans, when she heard footsteps behind her. She turned around, her heart ready to pound, but she saw Ben and relaxed.

"Hey," he said calmly, walking up to her. She wished she didn't notice his broad chest in the blue sweater he was wearing. It was hard to keep the memory of his arms around her away.

"Hey."

"I didn't want you to leave without getting to say goodbye."

"I'm sorry, it's hard to know what's, like, appropriate."

"Courtney, it's me. It doesn't have to be this weird."

But it kind of does, she thought sadly. She might have believed him before the Sara incident, but the thought of Ethan hanging out and having dinner with that girl was enough to send her over the edge.

"I don't know. I don't want it to be weird..."

"Just, please don't be a stranger, okay?" His warm eyes searched hers, and it hurt not to be able to promise that much.

"Okay," she replied, without anything better to say as a replacement.

"Have a good flight tomorrow. I'm glad I got to see you again before you left." He gave her a sincere hug, lifting her off the ground.

"You too," she murmured.

She sat in her car for several minutes before turning the key in the ignition.

♪ *"Hands All Over" – Maroon 5*
"Fight Song" – The Appleseed Cast

22

His fingers were drumming out a beat on his knee while he waited at baggage claim. They hadn't really been apart since she moved back, and he was near desperate for her return. There appeared to be something to the whole absence and fondness of the heart or whatever. He missed her.

He had spent his Thanksgiving with his mom, sister, and grandpa, and was kind of disappointed Courtney didn't get to meet the old man. *Plenty of other holidays,* he told himself. He pulled out his ear buds when he saw her walk in, eyeing the active carousels. His shoulders automatically relaxed now that she had come back to him. He had to remind himself that as much as he wanted her, she had just left her family, again. He walked up behind her and put a hand on her shoulder, ready to offer his own if she was upset. "I know you said you'd meet me outside, but I kind of missed you." She jumped slightly at his touch, but the look in her eyes when she turned around was not one of homesickness. She put down her carry-on and grabbed his wrists, bringing him towards her and letting his hands rest low on her hips. He bent down wordlessly to kiss her, and she pulled his bottom lip between her teeth before finishing with him.

"I missed you too," she said quietly. *Apparently.* He picked up her larger bag from the rotating luggage line and held her hand tightly on the way to the car. Placing her suitcases in the trunk, he felt her arms snake around his waist and into his front pockets. *Her leaving occasionally might not be such a bad thing,* he thought as her thumbs traced his hipbones.

"You're eventually going to have to quit doing that, babe," he told her, all of the blood vacating his head.

"Why is that?" she flirted, pressing herself against him and kissing his back.

"Because I don't think I'll stop you, and I cannot be held responsible for my actions. We're sort of in an airport parking lot." She giggled softly and stepped back, allowing him room to turn around. His lips crashed into hers, but she met him with the same fervor.

"Take me home, Fisher," she murmured when things got more heated. She so rarely called him Fisher, and it kind of sent him into overdrive. It was probably unwise for him to operate a vehicle in his current state, but he managed to get them back to her house with her making promises in his ear all the way there.

They didn't leave her room all afternoon. "Babe, we need water. And food."

"I disagree," she insisted, her expression playful. He had no idea what happened in the desert, but the post-Phoenix version of Courtney was insatiable.

"Ok, *I* need water and food. You're obviously some type of super human today. But then, I promise I will keep you happy the rest of the night," he flirted, tickling the bottoms of her feet. She pouted and attempted to change his mind, kissing her way down his torso. "Courtney," he groaned, exhausted.

"Ok, ok, sustenance." She grinned, grabbing her jeans and a black pullover. "What time is it? Do you just wanna go out and get food? I haven't been here to shop or anything," she explained, making a face at her hair in the mirror.

"I'm not sure, that sound good though," he answered, looking around for his phone. She grabbed hers, but the look on her face suggested she found information other than the hour.

"What's wrong?"

"Nothing. It's almost five, so that's an appropriate dinner time if we're senior citizens, right?"

"Sure."

"Let's go then- we have to help you regain your energy." She smiled, but there was worry in her eyes.

"Hang on, what's wrong, seriously?" She sighed and chewed on her lip.

"Nothing's *wrong,* really. I just need to tell you something, and I don't want to. Like, I don't want to fight with you, I just want to stay in this room and have you look at me like you've been looking at me all afternoon. I missed you so much."

"Court, just tell me then." He sat on the edge of her bed and waited.

"Do you promise not to get mad?"

"I don't know?" He ran his fingers through his hair, frustrated. He hated it when she did this. "I can't promise how I'm going to feel about something when I have no idea what you're talking about," he said, his tone growing annoyed. She looked down.

"I saw Ben while I was in town. On accident," she added quickly. "There was nothing, like, inappropriate about it, we were just at the same place with a bunch of people from high school. I swear I didn't know he was going. I didn't even know I was going, to be honest."

" 'To be honest?' That's kind of an interesting statement, since if you were really being honest you would have told me this days ago, instead of coming home and, I don't know, whatever this whole day was, you working out your guilt or something."

"That's not what I was doing! I missed you! Please don't make this into a bigger thing than it was. Please."

"Sure, I'll just tell you I had Sara over for Thanksgiving dinner, we'll call it even." He began putting his socks and shoes on, fully intending on leaving. She closed her eyes and looked toward the ceiling.

"Do I not get any points for telling you? Even though there was nothing more to it than seeing an old friend? Ethan, I *love* you."

"If you really want me to let this go, to believe that it was nothing, then hand me your phone."

"What? Why?"

"Because I don't think you really had any intention of bringing this up, until you looked at your screen. So let me see why." He stood up, and she looked at him with a pleading expression.

"You can see my phone. I don't know that it will help, but I'm not going to keep things from you." She held it out tentatively.

> B: Hey pretty girl, I just wanted to tell you it was good to see you. I know you're with someone, and you seem happy so I'm not going to try to mess that up. I just need you to know that I'm always here for you. I hope I can see you at Christmas, even if for a minute. Have a good rest of your semester.

Ethan's jaw clenched and he took purposeful breaths. "I need you to take care of this. Or I will."

"What does that even mean?" she asked, and he could tell she was trying not to cry.

"It means that this is the last time I wanna talk about this guy. I get that you were friends, or whatever, but this is not a 'friendly' text. So I need you to make it very clear to him that this is the end of it. Or I will make it clear for you."

"I am not really okay with you like giving me an ultimatum right now. I gave you the phone. Obviously I'm not hiding anything. I will talk to him, okay? But it feels like you're telling me I can never speak to him again, and I don't know if that's something I can promise. We have the same friends; I'm not going to run out of a restaurant because he shows up. I didn't do anything wrong." There were tears collecting in her eyes, but it didn't make him back down as it had before.

"It's *killing* me that you seriously think this guy just wants to be your friend. He is in love with you, and I'm starting to feel like you want to keep it that way."

"Ethan, that's so unfair! I didn't do anything. I told him I was taken when you and I got back together. I haven't talked to him. This was not intentional."

"I get that you're this sweet and unassuming person, it's something that I love about you, but I can't handle him trying to lay the groundwork to get you back. I don't know if you understand this, but I don't really plan on giving you up."

"What are you talking about?"

"This text, it's letting you know the door is always open with him. So one day, when you're pissed at me, he's hoping you call. And he'll play the friend card, and he'll tell you that you're too good for me, or that he's worried I'm not treating you well, and depending on what kind of jackass I was being that day, it might work. It's the same game I've played with girls a hundred times. I know that's a terrible thing to say, but at least I'm honest about who I was. This guy… he's good." He could see the wheels turning, and her trying to decide if she believed him or not.

"I don't think that's what he's trying to do." She defended him stubbornly, but some of the certainty had left her voice. He kept telling himself to let it go, but it wasn't like it would be a one-time thing. She would be home for every holiday, and knowing that this douchebag was just lying in wait was setting his teeth on edge.

"Look, I'm gonna go home."

"You're leaving?" She sounded flustered.

"Yeah, I just gotta blow off some steam or something, I can't talk about this anymore right now." He got up to look for his keys.

"You know I never even would have been with him if you hadn't…" She seemed to think better of where she was going with her thought, but it was already out. His anger had been subsiding, but now returned with a vengeance.

"Is that really where we're going right now?" he challenged her. "Because I'm sort of done shouldering one hundred percent of the burden for what happened between us anyway."

"Ummm, what?" she replied, her eyebrows shooting up higher than they should have.

"The night we ended things? I wasn't trying to break up with you. I was trying to tell you that I was *struggling*, and you abandoned ship at the first sign of a leak in the boat. It all happened so fast, and I thought it was my fault for not being able to handle the distance, but what I really needed was for you to tell me it was okay for me to falter one. Freaking. Time. But you didn't. You let me go without so much as a decent conversation. So I'm not saying I had no part in it- but I'm not going to carry that around anymore. You hurt me too, when you didn't fight for us." He was breathing hard when he finished his diatribe. He didn't really know he had been holding that in, and he sure as hell hadn't meant to let it out right then, but there it was regardless.

"Are you done?"

"Yeah."

"I think maybe going home is a good idea." He laughed without humor. *Typical,* he thought.

"Go ahead and shut me out, Court. I'm sure Ben would love to hear about this, why don't you give him a call?" He turned, storming through the door. He could hear her crying before he got to the front porch, but he was done for the night. He slammed his fist into his steering wheel and let out a guttural yell once he was in the car. The angriest music he owned was set to blare through his speakers.

♪ *"In Repair"* – *John Mayer*

23

The soundless words she'd been holding in came out and rolled down her cheeks. She didn't know with whom she was more angry- Ethan or herself. Or maybe even Ben. Everything he'd said was spinning around in her mind, and it resonated somewhere inside. *He's not completely wrong,* she admitted to herself what she couldn't to him. *Dammit.* She had been quite content to let him apologize for everything when they got back together, and he'd never asked her for anything. Her heart hated that he walked out, but her brain didn't blame him. She hiccupped back the rest of her tears and resolved to take care of some things.

When a knock came softly at her bedroom door, her pulse skipped, thinking he had come back.

"Can I come in?" Vanessa asked.

"Yeah," Courtney said, forgetting that her friend would have overheard the majority of their argument.

"How's it goin' in here?" She approached cautiously in purple pajamas, her long hair braided down her back.

"Ugh, I don't know. Fine. Just coming to terms with the fact that I may not be right about everything. It blows." Vanessa laughed and lowered to the floor across from her.

"Wanna go TP his house tonight?"

"Yes. But no. I'm just so pissed that he's not wrong."

"Yeah, that happens sometimes. Care to elaborate, though?" Courtney went through the whole argument, and Vanessa listened patiently.

"I was trying to find a way you could still be right, but he's sort of on the money, girl. Especially about Ben. I mean, I've met the guy, and I like him, but he's doing exactly what Ethan said. You're going to have to shut it down."

"Uggggghhhhhh," she groaned, head in her hands. "I know. Okay. I'll call Ben, I'll take care of it. And then I will drive to Ethan's and throw rocks at his window or something."

"Yeah.... Maybe you let Ethan cool off tonight."

"Really? You don't think I should go?"

"Obviously you know him best, but he doesn't get mad very often... I mean, maybe call him first? You just don't wanna drive over there and have it turn into another fight, that's all I'm saying. He'll come around. Do you wanna watch *Can't Hardly Wait* and eat food that's really bad for us?"

"You're the bestest friend a girl could ever wish for," Courtney stated, the cheese factor intended.

"I'll get started on snacks, you have fun with that conversation." Her stomach twisted, but it had to be done. Vanessa shut the door behind her, and she pressed call.

"Hey you. I didn't expect to hear from you."

"Hey. How are you?" She had no idea how to dive into what she needed to say.

"Good, what's going on? You're back at school, I take it?"

"Yeah. I got your text."

"I figured, that's sort of how text messages work," he joked.

"Ben..."

"Court..."

"You can't send me messages like that. You know it's not fair."

"What's not fair? Did I say something over the line?"

"No, it's nothing specific, but at the same time yes. Like, you know I loved seeing you too. I do want to be able to catch up and I want to be friends, but right now..."

"Boyfriend not super pleased, huh?"

"Not in the strictest sense, no."

"I'm sorry. I'm not trying to screw up your life, you know I want you to be happy, right?"

"I know. I do, and I want the same for you."

"You know I'd be happier if we were together."

"Please don't."

"Okay, okay. I'll quit. I'm sorry. I know you're loyal to a fault, it's something I love about you. So I get it, okay? I promise no more questionable texts."

"I sort of have to ask for no more texts, period." She swallowed hard, knowing this wasn't going to go as well.

"For real? Like, this is the last time we're ever going to speak? You can't be serious."

"I'm not saying ever, no, I just have to put some distance between us for the time being. I'm sorry, I just can't-"

"There are more than two thousand miles between us, how much more distance does this guy need? If he's that jealous, then maybe there's a reason for it."

"Ben, stop. Please." He blew out a long breath, and she could picture him ruffling his hair.

"Okay. I'll do whatever you want, but I'm not taking back what I said earlier. You can call if you need me."

"Thank you for understanding."

"Oh, I don't understand, but I know you, and you wouldn't ask unless you felt like you had to. So I'll do it for you, not for him."

"Fair enough. I do miss you. I can give you that."

"I hope he's worth this."

"Have a good night," she concluded, not wanting to get further into her relationship than they already had.

"That's sort of impossible now, but thanks for the sentiment. Bye, Court." She had to let the residual hurt of that reply sit for a moment before putting the phone down.

Trying to shake off the feeling that she'd just lost one of her best friends, she rebranded it as fixing the rift between her and Ethan. She sent her boyfriend a quick message before heading downstairs, needing him to know she wasn't shutting him out.

> C: So… I almost drove to your house, but V convinced me to let you cool down first. I'm sorry I let you leave without saying anything. A lot of what you said was right, and I didn't want to hear it. We can talk more whenever you want. I took care of the text message situation, and we will not need to have any more conversations about Ben. I love you more than anything.

Her phone rang thirty seconds later on her way down the hall.

"Hi," she answered softly.

"Hi. I'm sorry I walked out."

"I don't really blame you."

"Well, I don't want to be that guy. I want to stay and work things out."

"And I don't want to shut you out. We'll get better at this."

"You mean we can't just decide never to fight again?"

"Well, that sounds easier, let's do that."

"Will I see you tomorrow?"

"I hope so."

"Then you will." They hung up and she knew they would talk more, but at least the bulk of the weight sitting on her chest was dissipating.

♪ *"All My Life"* – The Foo Fighters

24

That wasn't the last time he and Courtney had a conversation about Ben, but it *was* the last time he left in the middle of an argument. He learned a lot of things about her their freshman year. In addition to her obsession with color-coded flash cards, and that she was really terrible at yoga- probably because she wasn't allowed to talk through it- he also found that she was constantly his biggest fan, and could always be more easily won over when she was mad if he was shirtless. The latter realization came in handy often.

"The last day of school is supposed to be relaxing, you know," she complained, sweating in her white tank top and gym shorts.

"I promise I will help you relax when we get all of this into the apartment," he swore, removing his t-shirt when they set down the sofa at the top of the stairs.

"Ridiculous," she muttered, her eyes roaming over him.

"What's that, babe?" he challenged.

"Nothing," she sighed, picking up her end of the couch. Jared showed up a bit later with his own truck, but at least he'd brought a couple of his friends, bribed with the promise of free pizza when they finished. Courtney was much happier directing from atop the kitchen counter.

"You're so helpful," he told her lightly, exhausted but glad they were done. He gave her a sloppy kiss and wrapped her in a sweaty hug.

"Blech, you need a shower," she voiced, but didn't push him away. Again, being shirtless usually did the trick.

"That can be arranged," he flirted.

"Get a room, guys," Jared said, downing his own slice of pie. He'd seen a lot more of his old friend after he showed up to one of Ethan's open mic performances a few months prior. Tin Roof was no longer in existence, and that made their friendship much easier. As it happened, they were both looking to move out of their parents' houses, making a rent payment much more manageable.

"Sort of the point of the apartment, dude." Courtney rolled her eyes and went to start unpacking the boxes in his room. He had sort of been banking on her OCD tendencies to get everything put away.

"So, does Courtney have any cute friends?"

"I'm sure she does, but why would she set them up with you? You are like the poster boy for a one-night-stand."

"That's the nicest thing you've ever said to me, Fisher."

"Why don't you do something useful? Like hook up our TV?"

"And what exactly are you going to be doing?"

"Just going to see if my girlfriend needs any help."

"Right."

"Whatever. I'll get started on the kitchen in a minute." Neither he nor Jared had much stuff, so Courtney and Vanessa had made it a mission to find them furnishings they could afford, and he had to admit that V's skills at assessing Craigslist finds were unmatched. They had a decent flat screen, even if it was older, a gray sectional sofa, a simple wooden coffee table, and a plain but usable dining set for less than he made a week teaching guitar. Courtney took it upon herself to go to Ikea and buy every manner of kitchen utensil possibly available, though he had the notion that she just bought some of the stuff because it looked cool and she didn't know what it was used for. He walked into his new room and found the bed already made and clothes put away, guitars waiting to be hung on the wall and his desk organized with things he didn't even know he owned. Ikea was probably to blame.

"It amazes me how few things you have. Like, I'm almost done in here. I bought you new towels, they're in the bathroom. I got pink ones for me- tell Jared he can't use them."

"I will tell him. Thank you baby. I am pretty sure I'd be sitting in bean bag chairs and eating with plastic silverware without you."

"And it probably wouldn't bother you at all." She laughed. "But at least now I can come over too."

"I was gonna go start putting stuff away out there, unless you are going to force me to take a shower with you right now, in which case the kitchen can wait." He flirted, his hands circling her rib cage and making their way down her back.

"I didn't realize I was such a tyrant. I'll have to scale back my demands," she shot back. "But I'm sort of in the zone right now, so I'll come out and help you in a second. I really am almost done in here, ya crazy minimalist."

"One kiss," he suggested, and he ran his fingers through her hair. She'd been wearing it straight more often now that it had grown out to her shoulders, and he liked that he could do that. One kiss turned into many, and he couldn't have cared less about unpacking. However, she eventually kicked him out to get to work.

"I got a message from Luke this morning that he'd be around this weekend. Are he and Vanessa..." he pried once she joined him in the common area.

"On again. I think. Or at least she was going to have dinner with him, so possibly?"

"Okay. Just wanted to avoid awkward an conversation with both of them."

"I hope so, though. Luke drives me crazy, but I kind of miss having him around."

"Do I need to worry about you and Luke now?"

"Ugh, shut up. Maybe I need to worry about your and Jared's little bromance, huh?"

"Oh, you definitely do. Fisher's my soul mate," Jared interjected, listening to their banter from the living room.

"How sad my friend Bri will be to hear that."

"Sorry, Fisher, you're out. Tell me about my new soul mate."

"I already informed her of your reputation, so don't try to pretend you're boyfriend material. But she said as long as you can dance without hurting anyone, she'd meet us out one night. You're welcome."

"Such a low opinion of me! I just crush a lot." He grinned. "But she's cute?"

"Of course she's cute."

"How cute?" Jared asked Courtney, but looked at Ethan over her shoulder. Quickly, he held up both his thumbs as an endorsement. She was, indeed, cute; a curvy brunette with a penchant for tight clothing, but his girlfriend didn't need to know that he noticed.

"Cuter than you," Courtney snapped back, but Jared didn't even care after looking at Ethan.

"I'll pretend like I didn't hear that. You're my new best friend Courtney Ross."

"Yeah, yeah. Save your charm for someone it'll work on."

"You're just jaded because you've been with this guy for too long, you can't even recognize my skills. Fisher, you've blinded her to other men."

"You've uncovered my master plan." He had to admit that having his own place was starting off exactly as he pictured it. The three of them got around to putting everything where it belonged, and Courtney even mopped and vacuumed while he and Jared hooked up the PlayStation. "You're kind of a sexy little housewife," he told her once they were back in his room.

"Yeah, I'm not really sure that's a compliment. Maybe try, 'super hot girlfriend who helped me all day but will someday be a badass attorney.'" *Ah, you have offended the feminist.* He took a breath, prepared just to apologize and move on. He wanted her far too much to get into an argument about appropriate PC terms.

"That just rolls right off the tongue. I wasn't suggesting you would be a housewife, I'm sorry, can I just say thank you for helping me and that you look incredibly hot all sweaty and make-up-less?"

How One Attempts To Chase Gravity

"You can say that," she said, sliding over to him.
"I thought I was too grubby for you to possibly touch," he teased her.
"Maybe we fix that." *This is the best apartment ever.*

♪ *"Deep Inside of You" – Third Eye Blind*

25

That summer passed too quickly. She only went home for a couple of weeks, wanting to pick up as many hours as possible at the firm. They had her writing more complex motions and helping with the calendar at that point, and she wanted to learn as much as she could. That, and the thought of leaving Ethan all summer didn't sit well with her.

"So, are you aware that it's our technical one-year anniversary next week?" she expressed to him one night after he made her dinner at the apartment.

"Technical?"

"Well, from when we got back together."

"Ah, I see. And what date are you considering the actual anniversary?"

"The date of the Train concert."

"That was a good night," he responded wistfully. He had been doing well as far as how people were receiving his solo stuff; he'd gotten a few gigs playing at some low-key events and parties, but she knew he missed it.

"Well? Is anyone good coming to town this summer? I will get us tickets… it's been a while since we've been to any big-name headliners." They went to local shows all the time, which was fine, but she missed being able to sing along to every song.

"Let's just see." After searching around for a bit, they found that Third-Eye Blind would be playing in Columbus towards the end of the month.

"Do you even want to see them live?" she asked, knowing he'd much prefer see The Appleseed Cast, who was also playing in a few weeks in Cleveland.

"Sure, I'm down. I know you love them." She kissed him and let herself get excited. The decision was also made in the back of her mind that she'd buy the other set of tickets too and surprise him later.

"You're the best boyfriend." She smiled, falling slightly into his lap.

"Who would've thought, right?"

"Me," she assured him. "I've gotta head out to meet Bri and Vanessa for dinner. What are you doing tonight?"

"I'm gonna catch up with Luke later, I think, but just messing around with some old songs now. You sure you have to leave right this minute?" he asked, kissing her intently.

"I'm sorry, I do. We can hook up later if you want?"

"Sounds good. Don't get into too much trouble."

"Oh you know me," she teased as she walked out. And she loved that despite the light-hearted nature of her statement, he really did know her.

♪ *"Accidentally In Love"* – *Counting Crows*

26

Vanessa's face was the picture of annoyance. Not that it was all that different from her normal face, which Ethan liked to think of as *mildly irritated*. Normally, he was fine hanging out with V while Courtney did whatever it was she did to get ready. But normally it wasn't this awkward.

"So. How are classes so far?" Ethan tapped his fingers on their coffee table as he spoke. Vanessa started back to school the previous week, and Luke had gone back to Bowling Green, no doubt adding to her stressed-out demeanor.

"Just dandy." The tension was just getting ridiculous. Ethan pulled out his phone, fully intending to put in his ear-buds while he waited, but decided to shoot off a text to Luke to make him aware of his girlfriend's unpleasantness.

> L: Yeah man, I know. She's been on full radio silence with me since I left yesterday. Don't tell her, but I'm headed there now. Like a half hour out. Where will you guys be?

Thank god. At least the whole night wouldn't be spent with Courtney catering to Vanessa's mood.

> E: Sweet. Not sure, probably just at Upper Crust for pizza or something.

L: I'll text when I'm closer.

E: See ya.

Ethan looked back up at Vanessa, who was still staring awfully intently at the wall, and he had half a mind to tell her anyway, Luke's directions be damned. Courtney chose that moment to bound down the stairs in a pink dress he'd never seen before, however, and he didn't care nearly as much about V's mood.

"Took you long enough. Can we just get this third-wheel dinner over with?" Vanessa complained, crossing her arms dramatically.

"Well, yes and no." Both Ethan and Vanessa shot her quizzical looks. "I just invited Jared. He was going on about having nothing to do tonight, so I told him to meet us."

"When did you talk to Jared?" The idea of Courtney and Jared being overly chummy called up some less than friendly feelings toward his roommate.

"I didn't. He posted his complaints online, so I texted him to come. Stand down mad dog."

"Point taken," Ethan admitted, feeling a little bit embarrassed that he was so transparent.

"I am *not* going on some sort of double date with you guys and *Jared*. I'm lonely, not desperate."

"It's not a date. It's pizza. And you can both roll your eyes at Ethan and me and tell us how lame we are. Get in the car." Courtney didn't wait for an answer, she just pulled Ethan out by his pinky finger, and he pretended not to notice Vanessa shooting daggers at his girlfriend's back. *Should be a good time.*

* * *

Vanessa twirled the straw in her Diet Coke and glared at everyone else. Mostly Jared, though he didn't appear to care. Courtney squeezed Ethan's hand under the table, and he just hoped Luke showed his face soon.

"So what classes are you taking now, V? Is there like a History of Polka Dots 101 or something?" Jared seemed to really want to know.

"No. There isn't."

"Vanessa Roberts, don't pull snarky bitch on me. I will happily tell the story of you hitting on me on a bench outside of school sophomore year of high school-"

"Oh my god, shut up. I didn't hit on you."

"I beg to differ. Fisher, if a girl practically sits on your lap and tells you you're too cute to be single while doing *something* with her nails, do you call that being hit on?"

Ethan had to laugh out loud at Vanessa's absolute fury directed at his friend, and even more at watching Courtney try *not* to laugh next to him. "Yeah, I'd have to say that's definitely flirting. Sorry V."

"Why have I never heard this story?" Courtney demanded.

"Hey, I've never heard it either," I insisted.

"There were extenuating circumstances, *Jared*." Even Vanessa was smiling at that point though. "Interesting that you remember it in such detail. Maybe I wasn't the one with the crush?"

"Well, that may be the case, but I crushed on everyone." Jared grinned his signature shit-eating grin, and the energy at the table shifted.

"That's true, actually. I had to turn this guy down several times in high school- he's not easily dissuaded," a voice said from behind Ethan.

Jared looked up and grinned again. "Well, who could've possibly taken no for an answer from you?"

Luke slid into the booth next to a shocked Vanessa. "Are you just going to let him talk to me like that? I guess chivalry really is dead," Luke deadpanned to her as if there was nothing out of the ordinary. Instead of responding, Vanessa just kissed her boyfriend and led him out of the restaurant and back out to his truck. Luke gave a small wave on their way out.

"Did you know he was coming?" Courtney asked Ethan.

"I might have."

"And you let her sulk around all night and make our lives miserable?"

"What can I say? I'm a romantic." Courtney just shook her head and attempted to convince Jared for the eightieth time to actually pick a major at community college.

When the pizza arrived at the table, Ethan predicted that Courtney would pick off all of her peperoni despite the fact that she was the one who ordered it, and she would insist that she just liked the flavor left over on the cheese. He also knew that Jared would eat more than half the food and claim to have forgotten his wallet.

"What are you thinking about?" Courtney asked him when Jared went to try to grab some beers at the bar.

"Ah, nothing. Just that life is pretty good. That's all." That brought a smile to her face, and she scooted fractionally closer to him as they ate.

♪ *"I Really Want It" – Great Big World*

27

Courtney missed her mom. Fiercely. It would be the first Thanksgiving she'd ever spent away from her family, but it just didn't make sense to spend the money for her to fly home for four days. Not when she had Ethan and Vanessa to keep her company.

> C: Are you making the stuffing waffles?
>
> Mom: No. We just decided to cancel Thanksgiving since you won't be here. We will eat cereal.
>
> C: And the cranberry syrup? And the pumpkin cake?
>
> Mom: Well, no pumpkin cake. You're the only one who doesn't like pie, so we're having pie.
>
> C: :(
>
> Mom: You're going to have fun at Ethan's. Don't be sad.
>
> C: Fine. They better not make me eat fruit. Or pie.
>
> Mom: Maybe you should take your own desserts.
>
> C: There's already a pumpkin cake in the oven. It just won't be as good as yours.
>
> Mom: Probably not. But good for you for making it ;)
>
> C: I love you too, Mom.

Courtney sighed and went to her closet to find a holiday appropriate outfit. She'd be meeting Ethan's grandpa for the first time, so there were some nerves going on, but really she just felt lonely.

> C: Can I come over early?
>
> E: Of course. Everything okay?
>
> C: Yeah. I'm just blah.
>
> E: I'm sorry. I should have stayed with you last night.
>
> C: It's fine. Just… don't make me eat pie, okay? Or cranberries.
>
> E: How would I make you eat these things?
>
> C: By creating a situation of social awkwardness if I don't eat them.
>
> E: Ah, of course, the old socially-awkward-environment trick. You got it. You do NOT have to eat pie or any type of fruit.
>
> C: Love you. I'll be there soon.

* * *

Ethan was out and at her car door before she even turned off the engine. It was *cold* in Ohio at Thanksgiving. She'd forgotten, and now she missed her t-shirts and patio table of days of yore. He pulled her in for a hug, and she sort of melted at that.

"I have to get the cake," she explained as he began to pull her towards his mom's house.

"You're the only person I know who eats cake at Thanksgiving."

"To be fair, I eat cake for any and all occasions."

"True. I can't wait to have some. It can be a new tradition." Her heart warmed at his words, thinking that this really could be the first of many holidays together.

"I also brought you a present."

"A present that I should open right now because it would be inappropriate in front of my entire family?"

"No. It's perfectly appropriate. You'll love it." Courtney grinned mischievously and grabbed a gift back from the back seat.

"You're crushing my spirit." He took the bag anyway and even looked mildly excited.

"That's fine, but I'd rather crush it inside. It's really freaking cold out here. She nudged him with her hip, which came to about his mid-thigh, and they made their way into the house. He leaned down before they walked through the door.

"I really like this dress. Just thought I'd mention it." He smirked, and she appreciated her new favorite black dress. His house smelled of the holiday, and she felt more at ease once she was inside. It felt like family.

"Happy Thanksgiving!" his mom called from the kitchen.

"To you too! Thank you for inviting me."

"So this is Courtney, I take it?" An older gentleman stepped into the dining room where Courtney was stashing her cake.

"Yes, sir. Nice to meet you." She held out her hand and he shook it firmly. He was tall, like Ethan, with gray eyes and olive-toned skin. He still had a full head of gray hair, which she was sure Ethan was happy about.

"Grandson- she calls me sir."

"I know. I told her just to call you 'old guy,' but she has something about respecting her elders, I don't really get it." Ethan smiled, and she felt like she could see him as a kid in that moment. He was cute with his grandpa.

"Yeah, yeah. You'll be old one day too, and you'll have wrinkly tattoos. Good luck to you." He was certainly a spy old man. "Anyhow, Courtney, you can call me Robert."

"Robert it is then."

He looked at her cake pan suspiciously. "It's a pumpkin cake. I have a thing about pie." *You sound completely stupid.*

"My wife never liked pie either," he declared. "Cake is good by me." Courtney wore a happily bewildered look as she followed him into the kitchen to see if she could help with anything. By *help*, she meant sorting napkins or organizing silverware, not actual cooking.

"Did you bring *Harry Potter* Clue again?" Taylor piped up when she entered.

"I may have thrown it in my trunk."

"Sweet. Can I take a picture of it for my insta?"

"What is an 'insta'?" Robert asked.

"Don't worry about it, Grandpa, way over your head." Taylor waved him off as she checked her phone. It was weird that she was getting older, and Courtney felt exactly the same age as she did the first time they met.

"Now, young lady, I served in Korea. I assure you there is very little that's over my head."

"I'll teach you how to use the app, Robert. It's actually pretty user friendly." She just liked this guy. She kind of wanted him to adopt her as his granddaughter.

"Ethan... if you don't marry this girl, I might." His grandpa winked at her as only grandpas could.

"Dad! They're young, leave them alone!" Mary chimed in from the potato-mashing event in the kitchen.

"I was married at nineteen, and no one was happier than Emily and me. I'm just saying."

"I got it under control, Grandpa, don't you worry about it." Courtney shot Ethan an incredulous look, but he just went about his business setting the table. As she looked around, she realized the feeling of homesickness from earlier had nearly faded away, and was instead replaced with a feeling of *home*.

"You might want to open that gift I brought you before you get all sweet and lovey."

"You think that something in this bag is going to make me love you less?"

"Only time will tell." Courtney suppressed a grin at his expense. It was tradition in her family to give this gift on Turkey Day, and since she wasn't at home to partake in the festivities, Ethan was the recipient. He narrowed his eyebrows and took the tissue paper out of the bag with a turkey on the front. His expression only became more confused as he pulled out a knitted masterpiece.

"You got me an ugly sweater." His tone was neutral.

"Not just any ugly sweater. This one is special." He spread it out onto the table and saw that there was an electric guitar knitted onto the front and it said *Rock Star* across the top.

"I think that's a very nice looking article of clothing there, Grandson."

"You would. And Court? Just so you know, I'm wearing this everywhere we go until Christmas. To my open mics, to class, everywhere. And I'm going to make sure everyone knows you're with me."

"That's fine. I have my own. It has a doughnut on the front."

"God you're going to be a good lawyer. You counter all of my best moves." Ethan laughed genuinely this time. "You win." He slipped the sweater over his head, and unsurprisingly, he still looked hot.

"Yeah, I know." Courtney didn't bother to hide her grin this time, and it earned her an ugly-sweater-hug from her boyfriend.

♪ *"Here We Go"* – Drew Holcomb and the Neighbors

28

The rest of sophomore year passed in a blur. He wasn't completely sure how they were at finals already. In his mind, they were still eighteen.

"Can we somehow infuse strip poker with studying for finals?" He was completely serious in asking this question; his motivation to study was nowhere to be found.

"Yeah… that didn't work last semester or last year, but kudos to you for not giving up." Courtney had her particular system of papers and textbooks set up around her on the floor and her coffee table.

"Couldn't you like, fail finals and still end up with Bs?"

"Nope."

"Liar." He knew her annoyance level was rising; he could see it in the purposeful deep breaths and the number of times she'd blinked in the last five minutes.

"Are you actually going to study, or are you just going to keep asking questions while I try to study?"

"I just need a break, babe. Come grab food with me."

"Go ahead and go; I'm in the middle of something." She chewed on her lip and it was not helping his current situation.

"Let me distract you for twenty minutes." He climbed carefully onto the couch next to her, mindful of her piles of notes. He slid in behind her and wrapped his arms around her middle, tickling her lightly.

"Ethan." Her saying his name usually had a different effect. This wasn't so playful.

"Babe, come on, please just take a quick break. You look so hot sitting here in your messy bun with your books. Talk nerdy to me."

"Flattery will get you nowhere right now. I'm seriously in the middle of something. This final is going to kick my ass, and it's in twenty-four hours. Please."

"You always do well though." He was resigned to the fact that she was in study mode, but it didn't mean he liked it.

"Ya. I *always* do well because I *always* study. Don't make it out like everything is so easy for me." She chewed on the end of her pen with an anger he didn't know had been there.

"I didn't mean it was easy," he sighed, scooting back out from behind her. "Just that you're too hard on yourself. That's it. I will leave you to it. Do you want any food?" He reached for his keys on the coffee table and immediately knew it was a mistake. A precariously placed cup of coffee fell in slow motion across one of her notebooks before he could get to it. "I'm sorry!" he shouted before she could get a word out. He picked up the cup as quickly as possible, afraid to look at her.

"Please just go get your food." Her fingers were pressed against her temples, and there was some definite deep-breathing going on.

"I'm so sorry, tell me what I can-"

"Please just *go* and let me deal."

Ethan just shook his head and headed for the door. He had yet to discover a way to bring her back from wherever she went when she got overwhelmed. He glanced back before opening the front door to assess her level of freak-out, and she was assessing the level of damage to her notes.

"And you better bring me back a freaking piece of chocolate cake." *All right.* He breathed a little easier. If she was demanding baked goods, they were okay.

♪ *"Ships in the Night"* – Mat Kearney

29

Being away at college was a strange experience. She'd been at UD for two years, so when she returned to Ohio after a quick trip to Phoenix that summer, she wasn't sure whether to say she was leaving home or headed home.

It had turned into a bigger argument than was normal when Ethan told her he couldn't go to Arizona with her. Even now, as she walked through the airport and searched for his face, it stung that he wasn't arriving *with* her. It wasn't that he'd had to work; she'd known that would be an issue. It was just that it didn't feel like it was because of work. It felt like he didn't *want* to go because he might miss a show at one of the local dives where he played. They'd moved past it- she went to Phoenix alone, but she still had to work to shake off the feeling that he could have gone if it had been a priority.

She stood at the baggage claim carousel, waiting for her hot pink suitcase to appear, when she felt a pair of arms slide around her.

"Did you miss me?"

"I did." *I wouldn't have had to if you'd come with me,* she added silently. He bent down to kiss her cheek, and she tried to let everything else go.

"Are you still mad at me?" He turned her around so they were facing each other, and the softness in his eyes chipped away at her irritation.

"Not mad, no. I just wish you'd been with me, that's all. I did miss you." She breathed him in and let his arms settle around her.

"I promise we'll make it work at some point, babe. Okay? I swear."

"Okay, yeah. We will make it work."

He kissed her head and darted to grab her bag when it finally came around. He carried her back and put on the pilot sunglasses she loved as they made their way to his car.

"I thought you hated those glasses."

"Hate is a strong word."

"*You* said you hated them."

"But you like them." He flashed her his most charming grin.

"Well played, Fisher."

"That's my girl. Can I take you to get something to eat?"

"Well played again." He closed the hatch to his car, suitcase safely stored, and spread his legs wide to match her height. He gave her a real kiss- the kind she still hadn't gotten used to as evidenced by the fluttering in her stomach. She wrapped her arms around his neck and kissed him back, letting him know he was forgiven.

"And then can I take you home and show you how much I missed you the past two weeks?" he murmured close to her ear.

"And that's the game." She grinned and ran her fingers through his hair.

* * *

That night, after making good on his promise, Ethan pressed his forehead against Courtney's and kissed her lightly.

"So..."

"So," she responded.

"I've been thinking about something."

"Oh yeah? Were you going to share these vague thoughts?"

"Stop," he chuckled. "I'm serious."

"Okay, go for it." She leaned back so she could look into his eyes. He did appear serious- almost nervous. "What's up?"

"Well, just that I'm here all the time, or you're at my apartment."

"This is true."

"And Jared isn't sure what he's planning on doing this fall, so we're month-to-month on our lease right now."

"Okay..."

"I just... are you really going to make me come right out with it?"

"I think I am. I'm not totally sure where you're going."

"Would you want to get a place together? Or... I sound like an ass asking if I can move in here with you, I don't know. I've never had this conversation before."

"Oh! You want to live together."

"Well, yeah. I do. Do you?" His face changed from nervous to confused in that moment.

"I...don't know? I mean, I've always thought of us living together. I just didn't think about it *right now*."

"Okay. Can you think about it?"

"I just... I don't know, maybe I'm being silly."

"You are a lot of things, but silly is not one of them. Tell me." His eyes searched hers for understanding.

"I always sort of pictured us being engaged or something before we lived together. I don't even know why...it's not like we've ever been super traditional."

"Oh. Okay. I guess that makes sense, I just didn't know you felt that way." He put a bit more space between them, making Courtney's heart race. *He practically lives here anyway... what would the difference really be?* But even as she asked it, she knew it would be different. There would be no space that was her own, and she just didn't know if she was ready to give that up.

"I'm sorry... I do want us to live together..." She thought about blaming her parents and saying they wouldn't allow him to live there. But she and Ethan had a fairly good track record of honesty, even when it was uncomfortable, so she decided against is.

"Don't apologize, I get it. We'll get there, for all of it. No rush."

"I love you." Her heart was still racing in her chest, wondering if he was holding something back.

"I love you too, babe." He kissed her and rolled over, apparently going to sleep. Courtney lay awake for hours, second-guessing her reaction and her decision. *He was putting himself out there and you just brushed it off like it was nothing. He wants to live with you. Every day. Like two adults who live together and share a closet. Oh god, my closet.* The closet was color coordinated and divided into work clothes and school clothes. And all of the hangers matched. Ethan's closet was basically just two hampers- one clean and one dirty. *But he loves you and deals with the post it notes and the meditation and the hormonal outbursts.* She tried to close her eyes and just sleep. *Would a normal person just say yes?* She had started to understand that she couldn't trust her "gut" as others would, because her gut always told her to prepare for the worst. She didn't really have a game plan for preparing for good things to happen.

She slid out of bed and into the hallway, slowly creeping to Vanessa's room. She knocked lightly.

"Murgh."

"Oh good, you're awake," Courtney said as she walked in.

"I am not awake. Go away."

"Ethan just asked me to move in with him and I said no but now I'm freaking out that he's going to break up with me and wondering if I'm an idiot for saying no please help."

"Ugh. I'll only help if you agree to breathe between sentences."

"Deal." Courtney breathed dramatically while Vanessa flipped on her bedside lamp.

"He asked *you* to move in with *him,* or for *him* to move in with *you?*"

"Ummmm he mentioned both as options, I guess. But I wouldn't really move out of this house, so I guess in with me."

"Yeah, no."

"No?"

"I am not going to be waking up and seeing Fisher all over the house for the next two years with his stupid abs that he thinks everyone wants to see. I mean, he's here enough as it is. There will be *no* guitars and amps and whatever the hell else comes with him sitting around this house and messing up my décor. Thank god you said no."

"Tell me how you *really* feel though," Courtney said, laughing.

"Yeah, well, I'm not one to mince words. And Court? I guaran-freaking-tee you he's not tossing and turning in there over this. He probably turned over and forgot about it as soon as his head hit the pillow. He's not going to break up with you."

"You think?"

"Yes. Now go to sleep and leave me alone."

"Goodnight, V."

"Goodnight, Court."

It would have been really nice if Courtney had been able to just let it go at that, but, well, she couldn't.

She re-entered her room and tried, unsuccessfully, to wake up Ethan as she got into bed.

"Ethan!" she whisper-yelled. "Are you awake?" She poked him in the shoulder.

"I wasn't, but now yes. I really hope you woke me up because you're feeling-"

"Shhh, no. Don't distract me. Are you upset about our conversation?"

"I'm a little upset about *this* conversation." He grinned and rubbed his eyes.

"Stop, you know what I mean. I haven't been able to sleep at all."

"You haven't slept? Babe, what time is it?"

"I don't know, like three. Just, I need to know how you feel."

"Court, you gotta sleep. And I feel fine. I asked because it would have been easy with my lease being up and I'm here all the time. It's not a crisis for us to wait. I've told you a thousand times that I'm not going anywhere, okay? We're good. Please sleep."

Instead, Courtney leaned in to kiss him, thinking sleep could wait just a bit longer.

♪ *"Such Great Heights" – The Postal Service*

30

Their junior year was almost at a mid-point, and he was about at his wit's end with Courtney's semi-annual "I'm going to fail all of my finals" breakdown. She was passive-aggressively sighing and picking up a pair of his socks from the floor and dramatically putting them in the hamper.

"Babe, I can pick up my stuff, just study for your test." He attempted to calm her, setting his water glass down on her desk. Her eyes flew to the glass and then shot daggers at him. *Ok, glass bad,* he tried to reason.

"Can you just… like, don't put a full glass of water next to my laptop. Please."

"I didn't set it *next to your laptop*. I set it on your desk so I could help you clean."

"And then when it tips over and my computer is fried?" she asked. *Annnnd we're at the tipping point of a full-blown meltdown.* He sat quietly, not wanting to poke the bear, so to speak. "Are you even going to respond? Like, have some respect for my things, Jesus." The frantic rate at which she was blinking and pressing her nails into her palm let him know it was going to be a long day of this shit.

"Yeah, okay. You know you're being completely insane." He knew using the word "insane" was not going to go over well, but that was precisely why he used it. She was testing his patience.

"Yes, Ethan. I'm insane for asking you not to put water glasses on my desk. How *crazy*. You should probably have me committed." He was putting his shoes on as she spoke. There was no recovering when she got like this. He stood up and downed the entire glass of water and slammed the empty glass back onto the desk childishly.

"I'm gonna go. Call me when you've transitioned back to your human form." He grabbed his phone and his keys and high-tailed it out of her room. There was a "thud" that followed him, and it took everything he had not to laugh, knowing she'd thrown a shoe at the door behind him.

He attempted to study after arriving back at the apartment, but ended up face down on his comforter when he trudged into his bedroom. The schedule he was keeping left him exhausted. He'd landed a job working at the campus radio station, and after a while they'd given him the option to sub in as a DJ for one of the later shows. Between that, his upper division classes, and still trying to make time for his own music and semi-crazy girlfriend, it had been a bit of a rough semester. Surprisingly, he actually stood a chance at a 3.0 GPA if he displayed a decent showing on his exams. *Only because Courtney proofed all of your papers,* he thought. She would pull a 4.0 as she always did, regardless of how many times she woke up panicked in the middle of the night, checking her Constitutional Law paper for errors.

The past year and a half had been near perfect. He never envisioned himself as the guy to have a college sweetheart, or to turn down the invitations to spring break in Daytona Beach in favor of a trip to D.C. to visit national monuments. But that's where things were, and there was nothing he'd trade for them. She'd thrown him a kegger for his 21st birthday that past June, and though he knew it stressed her out, she played it cool the entire night- stepping over the drunken guys on her back porch, ignoring the scantily clad girls, and never saying a word. She didn't even give him a hard time when he started to grow his hair back out and looked like a mildly insane person when it was going through the "in-between phase."

They still fought. Her anxious nature got to him, frequently. But he had stopped waiting for the day that the world didn't fall away when she touched him. He liked that she still got flustered when he worked to charm her, and that he could feel some of the stress leave her body when he put his hands on her, no matter how worked up she got. They just balanced. Most of the time.

Ethan put his fingers through his now-longer hair and resolved to organize his notes to study for his Econ exam.

>C: You busy?
>
>E: Not really. Are you less mad at me and my offensive glass of water?

His phone buzzed in his hand ten seconds later.

"What's going on?" he answered.

"Tell me that you don't have to work over break."

"I don't have to work over break."

"Really? Or are you just saying that because I told you to? Don't mess with my emotions," she scolded, making him laugh. Apparently she'd finished her paper satisfactorily. *Maybe you'll actually get lucky tonight.*

"No, the station is closed when there's no school. Spit it out already."

"You're coming to Phoenix with me. Well, I mean, if you want to. In less than two weeks."

"Seriously? When did that happen?"

"Just now. I was talking to my mom and she asked when I was going to finally bring you home. I know we've talked about it, and it just never seems to work out, but if you want the ticket, it's yours. Please say you'll come." The words were flying out of her mouth and her excitement rubbed off on him.

"Of course I'll come, don't be silly."

"Really? Like you don't even know how excited that makes me. I've wanted you to be in Phoenix with me every time I've been home. Okay. I'm going to start making plans so you can meet my friends and we'll do fun stuff, okay? I promise you're going to love it. Well, maybe not love it because it's sort of just a big desert, but it will be fun anyway."

"Court, don't worry. I'll be with you and I'll be on vacation. Where it's 70 degrees. There is no bad," he assured her, knowing she was fabricating some sort of metaphorical bar in her mind that the week would need to live up to. He gave her the courtesy of pretending her audition to play a mental patient earlier that day hadn't happened.

"You're right. I'm just... happy."

"I can deal with just happy."

They both lived through finals. He got the 3.0 by the skin of his teeth and managed not to shake his girlfriend when she went off another cliff after misplacing her flash cards for Latin American Politics. For ten minutes. And then they were in her bag the whole time. He was overjoyed to have her back when she showed up at his apartment the evening after her last test, a playful look in her eyes. "Kiss me," she demanded, guiding him backwards towards his room. He was turned on before they made it to the doorway. Relieved at her return to normal, he let her do whatever she wanted. She pressed his hips until he was sitting on the edge of his bed looking up at her.

"I'm sorry," she whispered, standing between his legs.

"I know," he murmured back, gripping the backs of her thighs. The look on her face was a mix of guilt and relief, but she spent the next several hours apologizing in other ways. Much more fun ways.

They didn't come out until the next morning.

Once the sun was up, she basically packed his suitcase, but he let her go, knowing it was just her way of dealing with the self-imposed stress of the trip.

"... and we can go to a Suns' game, and my friend Ashley is dying to meet you and said there will be plenty of parties, and we could even do a daytrip to Sedona and it would be so pretty, you don't even know, and then I'm sure there will be other stuff going on with-"

"Baby. Can you breathe, please?" He physically stopped her from folding clothes and put her hair behind her ears.

"Yes."

"I'm excited to be with you, and I don't know, see a cactus. It's fine."

"I can show you a cactus. We can go to the Botanical Gardens and see hundreds of them," she suggested, and he couldn't help but laugh. Sometimes he had to know when he was dealing with a lost cause.

* * *

Vanessa dropped them at the airport a day later, jealous that she didn't get to go.

"You know you'd have more fun if I was coming instead of Fisher," she complained one last time.

"Keep dreaming, V," he stated plainly. They thanked her and went to check in. It was really only his third time on a plane, so he just followed Courtney since she seemed like the expert. They made it to the gate, coffees in hand, and she proceeded to sit across his lap in the very uncomfortable terminal chair. She made him feel like a teenager when she giggled and kissed his jawline, but he was so much more content to be with her this way- in their twenties and able to travel together. It felt like the world was theirs.

"I just love you," she said softly, her nails scratching the back of his neck lightly.

"I just love you too. And I just like this shirt," he offered, pulling at the fuzzy gray sweater. She had changed clothes ten times that morning, but anything that showed off her figure and wasn't a winter coat was a winner at this point. He tickled her slightly while he sipped his surprisingly decent airport beverage.

"Are you two going on your honeymoon?" asked a sweet older lady sitting a couple of seats down.

"Oh, no, we're not married," Courtney replied back, looking embarrassed for being called out on their PDA.

"Oh, I'm sorry, you just had that look. You're very cute together, anyway," the woman complimented.

"Thank you," Courtney managed with a polite laugh.

"My late husband used to look at me the way he looks at you, when we were young. You wouldn't believe how fast time goes," the woman finished, getting up when they made the first boarding call announcement. His girlfriend just laid her head on his shoulder.

"She was a nice lady," Courtney murmured.

"She was. Do you, um. Do you think about that?" he asked, being purposefully vague.

"That?"

"Us, together. In a more permanent sense."

"Getting married? Of course. You know me, I think about everything. Not, like, in the context of right now, but it's in the someday column. I think... right? Am I freaking you out or something?"

"No, not at all. It's definitely a someday. We just never really talked about it seriously, that's all. But I want you forever, okay?" He was long past caring that she owned him. His heart had belonged to her at eighteen.

"Okay." She smiled, kissing him deeply. The announcement came for their group to board and he followed her onto the plane.

* * *

The crisp dry air in Phoenix was refreshing. He had never experienced that much sun in the middle of winter.

"How do you complain about living here? This is amazing. I don't even need layers." He demonstrated by peeling off his leather jacket and slinging it across his suitcase, his skin relishing the exposure in a soft blue t-shirt.

"Well, I'm not going to complain about you wearing less clothing," she flirted, tugging on the belt loops of his dark-washed jeans, "and this weather is the only reason people put up with living her from June to October, FYI." Her mom pulled up curbside in a black Infiniti, and he immediately thanked her for letting him come.

"We're happy to have you, it's probably long overdue." They loaded the car and he tried to get a feel for the city. It was expansive. He marveled at the sheer size of their house when they arrived. The whole town, or metropolis, rather, was nothing like anywhere he'd ever been.

"My dad will be back tomorrow. He's excited to meet you," she explained.

"That's cool. What's on the agenda for tonight?"

"Well, I was thinking I could sort of show you around, maybe grab some food, but then my friend Ashley wants to take us to a party one of her friends is throwing."

"Sounds good to me, but I really need you to show me around this house or I might get lost." She raised her eyebrow at him flirtatiously and he followed her up the curved staircase. In opening the door to her bedroom, he was flooded with memories of video chats and late night phone calls from their senior year. The room looked largely the same, though with fewer personal effects, since those had been moved to her house in Dayton. "Being here is weird," he uttered, looking around.

"Yeah kind of."

"It feels smaller than I imagined. Like I dreamt of being here with you for so long, it just seemed this far off place that I'd never see."

"And yet, here we are," she said, smiling.

"Here we are."

♪ *"Teenage Dream"* – Katie Perry

31

Having him standing in her teenage bedroom, his muscles flexing under her fingers as she danced them around his hips, made her feel eighteen again. She couldn't count the number of nights she'd wished he were with her.

"Do you still have that cheerleading uniform in there?" He nodded towards her closet, smirking.

"That I had to give back when I graduated. Sorry to shatter the little fantasy you had going on."

"Oh, come on, I had to at least ask, right? I assure you there are plenty of other fantasies stored in there." The butterflies fluttered from her stomach into her chest. It was so surreal that what was once only in her imagination was playing out in front of her. She let him kiss her hungrily, pressed up against her cheery yellow wall, until the sound of her mom coming up the stairs shook them out of their bubble.

"Okay, then." She sighed, pushing him back a step. "On to the rest of the house." She finished the tour, including the room where he'd be sleeping. On the main floor. Very far away from her room.

"Did your parents design this house specifically to keep me away from you?"

"Yes, I believe that this day was at the forefront of their minds when we built it," she teased. "You can deal for four days, we practically live together the rest of the year."

"I know, I just like having you next to me at night. I'm going to have to steal one of the hundred stuffed animals from your room."

"Hey! I am a girl, I'm allowed to keep them."

"Don't worry, I won't tell anyone when you're a big shot lawyer that you have every Beanie Baby ever made." She smacked him playfully.

"I'm gonna go get ready. If you want to shower, everything's in the bathroom across the hall. Or you can hang out with my mom and let her know what your intentions are with me and where our relationship is going. I'm sure she's been dying to get you alone for a long while," she told him, eyeing him mischievously.

"I love that you think you're scaring me. Honestly, it's cute." He kissed her again and her stomach flipped. "Now go get ready so I can impress all of your friends."

"There's the arrogance I know and love." She grinned, and left him to his own devices.

* * *

Ashley honked her horn repeatedly from the driveway. "Do me a favor and don't make my friends fall in love with you, okay? It's bad enough watching the crowd at your open mic nights increase exponentially with girls I *don't* know lusting after you."

"I make no promises. Sometimes I don't know my own power."

"Ethan!"

"You're being ridiculous, but okay. I promise not to make your friends fall in love with me. I'll be a total ass and they'll have to ask me to leave."

"Better." They made their way out to the car and Courtney was happily surprised to see Molly in the passenger seat of the Volvo. Her blond hair was cut short and sassy; it almost made Courtney want her shorter hair back as she ran her fingers through her own.

"Hey! I didn't know if you were home yet!" Her friend got out and hugged her briefly before turning her attention to Ethan.

"Just drove up like an hour ago, it's so good to see you! And you must be Ethan?"

"That I am, and I'm gonna go with Molly?" he guessed, holding out his hand.

"Good guess," she responded, sizing him up.

"Okay, okay, get in the car, I wanna meet him too," Ashley said, her voice carrying out through the open sunroof. She and Ethan packed themselves into the backseat and he introduced himself to Ashley.

"So you're kind of like really pretty, then," her friend mused in true Ashley fashion, just moments after shaking his hand. *Will she never develop a filter for what comes out of her mouth?*

"That's what the pageant trophies all say, yeah," Ethan deadpanned.

"Wait, what?" Ashley asked. "You do like beauty pageants? Those exist for guys?" Courtney rolled her eyes. *Some things never change.*

"No, but I'm kind of flattered that you bought that. Or offended. I'm not sure yet, but I think I like you," he threw out, making Ashley giggle with a flirtatious edge. Some of Courtney's high school jealousy about her friends' abilities to be carefree and fun made an appearance, which she hated. She ignored it and focused on enjoying the fact that her boyfriend was there. And that her friends loved him. Ashley drove them to a house party in Tempe, and Ethan volunteered to be their designated driver.

"Are you freaking kidding me? I'd have gone to Ohio too if *that* was waiting for me," Ashley gushed when he went to get them drinks.

"Seriously, pictures you've shown us don't even compare. Please tell me he's terrible in bed or has an IQ of 25 or something. *Something.* Like no way it's fair for a decent guy to look like that and be a musician."

"Ummm… he does leave socks everywhere. And his comma usage is terrible. He also plays a lot of PlayStation, usually to avoid me when I'm in my neurotic mode. I don't know, he's kind of amazing," she said sincerely, though she left out the part about his ridiculous jealous streak, knowing she had a minor one of her own. Or how he refused to give her a straight answer when she asked him questions he thought were silly, and would merely tell her little known facts that he learned on "Behind the Music" instead. The last one really annoyed her.

"I sort of hate you," Ashley mentioned casually.

"Just don't tell Mike that I covet your boyfriend, deal?" Molly asserted, Mike being her off-again, on-again boyfriend of several years.

"Deal." Ethan returned, and the four of them hung around for a while but eventually decided to get late-night tacos at Jack-In-The-Box and take them up to Ashley's parent's house for a hot-tub soak. They lived in an expansive home overlooking the desert; Courtney had forgotten how magical the view was at night. It made her think of prom when they snuck out and went skinny-dipping with their boyfriends. It was a happy memory, but she thought it unwise to bring up anything in relation to Ben.

"I think I like Phoenix," Ethan commented, holding her hand and pulling her onto his lap amidst the bubbles. Ashley had scrounged up a pair of her brother's old swim trunks, and Courtney was wearing one of her friend's bikinis that was probably a size and a half too small, but it didn't seem to bother the man with his arms around her. Ashley had brought a boy back from the party, and Molly was waiting in front of the house for Mike to show up half the time they were there, but it was a genuinely good night. It felt like a piece of her life with Ethan had been put into place, even though she hadn't realized it was missing. She'd needed for him to see her here and to know that he fit in this part of her world too.

♪ *"Stubborn Love"* – The Lumineers
"Play With Fire" – Vance Joy

32

Molly's boyfriend dropped them at Courtney's late that night on his way back home, and Ethan was wavering between being exhausted and getting a second wind. Seeing her with her friends, hearing their stories from high school; it was like falling in love with a whole other version of her.

She grabbed them each a bottle of water from the fridge and was startled when he came up behind her.

"So, I'm thinking that it's really late, and it's probably safest if I walk you to your room."

"You make a good point," she murmured turning to face him. "It's a pretty dark hallway."

"How quiet can you be?" he asked. She held a finger up to his lips in a shushed motion and pulled him up to her room.

"Do you remember when we used to fantasize about having a teleportation app on our phones?" she asked quietly once they were safely behind a closed door.

"I remember fantasizing about a lot of things. Some of which I plan on demonstrating for you momentarily." He grinned as he grabbed her hips until they fit with his. He let all of the creativity of his teenaged imagination guide their encounter, and the feeling of nostalgia was overpowering once they were tangled up in her bed. They proceeded to say goodnight for the next hour until she relegated him to the guest room.

* * *

Disoriented, he woke up early the next morning, but was content when he realized his location. He got ready before making his way out into the Ross' kitchen. Admittedly, he'd thought Courtney was insane when she packed him a host of short-sleeved shirts and only one jacket, not believing it could possibly be as warm as she said, but he was so glad it was. Being cold all of the time was tiring. *You could totally live here,* he thought. It did not appear that Courtney was up yet, but there was a middle-aged man with graying brown hair standing in the kitchen. Ethan cleared his throat to announce himself.

"Good morning. Mr. Ross, I would imagine? I'm Ethan," he said, holding out his hand toward the man with the coffee. Her dad's face was tired, but his smile was welcoming.

"Ethan, good to finally meet you. I've only been hearing about you for three years. Please, call me Greg. Coffee?"

"Yes, please." Courtney never talked too much about her dad, as he was usually traveling, but he seemed like a nice enough guy. "So, um, I saw a car in the garage under a cover... I asked Courtney what it was, and she just said 'old,' so I take it it's yours?"

"Ah, yes. That's my sixty-nine Roadrunner. Do you know cars?"

"I have a 1980 Nissan Z that my grandpa and I fixed up. That car is my life. Well, other than Courtney and school obviously." He backtracked quickly, realizing saying his car was his first priority didn't exactly scream "son-in-law material."

"Ha, don't worry, I won't tell her you said that. So do you wanna see it?" he asked, seeming excited to have someone to show it to.

"Yeah, definitely. Does it run?"

"Hell yeah, it runs. You wanna take it out?" He figured joyriding with his girlfriend's dad before breakfast would probably be enough to earn him some brownie points, so he followed Greg into the garage and helped him take off the cover. The car was clearly a custom paint job, a serious royal blue. It was a really solid machine, and even had the original steering wheel with the cartoon Roadrunner on it. Courtney's dad started it up and the engine was thunderous. He backed it out of the garage so Ethan could get in.

"Let's see what she can do then," Ethan suggested, looking forward to the adrenaline. The man looked like he was sixteen and showing off his first car, which Ethan realized it may have actually been. They took it north of the city, and he let the engine rip. It was even a rush in the passenger seat. After zipping around for a bit, he pulled the car over.

"So are you interested in driving it back?"

"Seriously?"

"Sure. I haven't had that much fun in a long time."

"Absolutely." Ethan hopped out of the car and traded him places. He adjusted the seat and mirrors, really not wanting to crash this vehicle. He shifted into gear and pulled it back onto the road.

"Well, punch it," her dad encouraged him. He pushed the car as far as he was willing to go, being that it wasn't his own and he didn't know the roads well. It was something he supposed he would have enjoyed doing with his own dad at some point growing up. If his dad wasn't a complete sack of shit. He let that thought go into the wind rushing past his ears as they sped down the road.

They pulled into the garage, and a surprised Courtney peeked her head out of the door. After he killed the engine, she gave them an interesting look. "So I see you two have met, then?"

"We did."

"And you let him drive?" she addressed her dad.

"It would appear that way."

"He has never let me drive this car ever," Courtney complained, directing her attention to Ethan. *Well, shit,* he thought, not knowing it had been a big deal.

"Courtney, you refuse to learn how to drive a stick. I'm not going to teach you on a vintage car. Learn, and I'll let you drive it," her dad let out what sounded like a well worn-in speech.

"Yeah yeah, I've heard it all before. Now come in and have breakfast."

"Thanks for taking me out," he managed before Courtney grabbed his hand and marched them into the kitchen.

"There you two are," Mrs. Ross stated, setting the table for breakfast. She really was a pretty lady, he gathered, and he saw a lot of Courtney in her face. "Courtney insisted we have breakfast here, and requested something other than cinnamon rolls. I'm not really sure what you've done to my daughter, but you are going to help do all of these dishes." She gestured towards the sink.

"No he doesn't, stop it," Courtney retorted

"Nah, I'm down to do dishes."

"I was just kidding, but I like that you agreed anyway," her mom teased.

After breakfast, she took him out to see "the sights," as she called it, but he was under the impression she was using the tour as an excuse to take him shopping.

"I'm sorry you got stuck alone with my dad this morning. I hope it wasn't awkward."

"You apologize for weird things, babe. I got to drive a vintage car at very high speeds. It was a fantastic morning."

"Okay, then, I take it back." She smiled, relieved. "I got us tickets to the Suns game tonight, and tomorrow night there are a bunch of people meeting up at Dave and Busters if we wanna do that."

"Is that like one of those arcade-restaurant places?"

"Yeah, we don't have to stay long, but I told Ash we'd come by."

"Sounds good to me," he reassured her, kissing her cheek.

* * *

He felt like he had finally met the cheerleader in her at the Suns game the previous night. She'd always said she was a fan, but he didn't really believe it until seeing her energy at a live event. The whole trip was proving to be very eye-opening into the world of Courtney Ross. While he was waiting in his assigned room for her to get ready for Dave and Busters, his phone rang, displaying Crawford's name and number.

"Hey, man. How's it goin'?" he answered, surprised.

"Fisher, glad you picked up. It's going well, actually. Really well. How are you?"

"Good. I'm in Phoenix at the moment. You guys are on the road, yeah?"

"Yeah, we've been playing with Eight Degrees Down for a couple of months. It's kind of a kick-ass show. That's sort of why I called."

"Okay?"

"The other opening act, a three man group called Ire, I don't know if you've heard of them, but anyway, they had to drop the last two months of the tour because their front man got arrested and can't cross state lines or something equally as stupid. I didn't really get the full story. Anyhow, I wasn't kidding when I told you I pitch your solo stuff to everyone, and the tour manager got the okay for you to fill in for those eight weeks, doing your own set, whatever you want."

"Are you being completely serious right now?"

"As a heart attack, man. I would not call you if it wasn't the real deal." Ethan took in a slow breath.

"When are we talking?"

"You'd come meet us in Indianapolis the third week of January, and ride out the Midwestern leg of the tour. You'd be back by mid-March. I know you've got school, but this isn't the kind of thing that falls out of the sky more than once." Ethan ran his free hand through his hair while he paced the very beige guest room.

"I don't know. Jesus. I'd have to figure out school, my mom would kill me if I just left without a plan. Ummmmm. Maybe I could take some classes online for this semester and a summer session to catch back up. And then my job..." he was rambling more for his own benefit than for Crawford's.

"I totally get that I'm just throwing this at you right now, and I hate to make it more pressure-filled, but our tour manager sort of needs an answer ASAP. Do you think you could let me know by Monday?"

"Yeah, of course. Lemme make some calls and see what I can work out. This is kind of surreal." He breathed. He had given up on the dream of touring and was happy with where his life was headed, but how could he turn this down when it was right there for him to grab?

"For the record? I think you should do it. School will be there when you get back. But totally your call, no hard feelings if the answer's no. I'll catch up with you this weekend."

"Yeah, I hear you. Thanks man, for talking me up or whatever. I really appreciate this."

"No thanks necessary. Talk to you soon." Ethan stared at his phone for a few solid minutes, not entirely certain that call had been real. He shot off an email to his advisor, hoping she was still checking her inbox during break. He wanted to say yes to the tour, but not at the expense of the time and effort and money that had gone into UD so far. And then there was Courtney. He wanted to go upstairs and tell her right then, but he thought it might go over better if he had an actual plan before springing it on her. It took several minutes for him to decide if he could keep quiet about it, but he landed on waiting to tell her until he had more information.

* * *

He thought the arcade-restaurant concept was one he could get on board with. The beer was overpriced, but the atmosphere was fun. He'd also missed seeing his girlfriend in clothing that didn't involved scarves and sweatshirts. He met a host of people whose names he didn't remember when they first got there, and he elected to play a few video games and grab a drink while she chatted with some girls he believed she said were on her high school cheer squad.

When he sauntered back towards the group, he noticed a guy looking at her with an expression he wasn't totally fond of. And then the guy started to look familiar. Ethan couldn't be certain since he'd never met him, but the look on the guy's face pretty much solidified that he was Ben. Courtney was oblivious, now messing with her phone in the absence of her girlfriends. He'd be protective if anyone was sizing her up that way, but the couple of beers he'd had, plus the history of hating this dude, made his chest tighten.

He slid into the chair next to Courtney, her back still towards him. Pushing her hair to one side, he kissed her neck playfully, his hands on her stomach.

"Well, hello to you too," she answered flirtatiously.

"How is it possible I still want you this much after all this time?" he asked as she turned around to face him.

"Hmmmm, because I'm-" He didn't even let her finish. Knowing Ben's eyes were still on her, he wanted to make a point. He kissed her like they were very alone; his hands wandering up the back of her shirt and his tongue dancing with hers. She reciprocated to a point, but pulled back.

"Babe, if you wanna get out of here, I'm down, but we are in public."

"Sure, I'm sorry. You have the tendency to do this to me."

"Well, I kind of like that power." She smiled, ruffling his hair. "Just let me say bye to a few people first, okay?"

"Of course."

"Are you heading out?" a voice came from behind him. Courtney looked up, and her voice died in her throat. Finding it, she replied, "Yeah, I think so. Um. Ben, this is Ethan. Ethan, Ben." Ethan stood up before turning around.

"Hey man, nice to meet you," he managed, shaking Ben's hand. He wished they weren't the same height; he'd have liked that advantage. *She's here with you, that's advantage enough.*

"Yeah, likewise. So Court, you never mentioned that your boyfriend's name was Ethan. Is that like a super common name in Ohio or..." Ben asked, switching his focus to Courtney.

"What do you mean?" she asked, her face going pale.

"Just so odd how the other guy you dated there had the same name, right?"

"Not odd. Just one and the same," she got out.

"Good to know. Hey, listen, it was great to finally meet you. You must be a hell of a guy to get her back after the crap you put her through before. Congrats," Ben spat out, his fists clenched. *Let it go, let it go,* he kept telling himself. But he couldn't.

"Don't be a sore loser, dude, it's not a quality she finds attractive," he said plainly, goading him.

"Ethan, don't, just let him go," Courtney said, grabbing his wrist tightly.

"Well if she's into assholes who make her cry now, then I probably wouldn't stand much of a chance anyway. Listen to your girlfriend and let me walk away." Ethan took a step forward, but Courtney was in front of him before he got any momentum behind it.

"We're leaving," she said firmly, though there were tears on her face. *Ironic*, he thought, that Ben was the one making her cry now. She hurried them to the borrowed Infiniti and burst into tears. His first instinct was to comfort her, but something Ben had said was bothering him.

"Why didn't he know you were with me, specifically?" He waited for her to calm down enough to answer.

"I don't know, I didn't think I needed to rub it in his face that I was back together with you *one week* after moving. I thought it was enough that he knew I had a boyfriend." He got her logic, but it still stung.

"Yeah, I guess I get that at first, I just thought you would have told him after the other text messages. I don't know."

"Did you know? That he was there?"

Shit. "What do you mean?"

"When you kissed me like that. Was that for show because you knew he was there? Don't lie."

"I've never even met him, how would I have known he was there?" *Answering a question with a question is not the way to go*, he scolded himself. He'd always had a hard time not being straight with her.

"You're really not good at this. You know what he looks like. Did you see him or not before your very public display of affection?" Her tears had moved from upset to angry more quickly than he would have liked.

"I didn't know for sure it was him. I thought it might be. But I still don't get why that pisses you off."

"You know exactly why it pisses me off. You did that on purpose to hurt him."

"You're seriously defending that guy right now? After what he just said? Like it is taking everything I have not to go back in there and finish our conversation. The only reason I'm out here is because of you. Please don't speak up for him." Disbelief was flooding his system. "And to be honest, you seemed pretty content with my affections until you saw him. So feel free to explain that to me."

"You are so thick-headed! You knew he was there and you set out to embarrass me."

"*Embarrass* you? We've been together for three years, Court, and I still want you as much today as I did the night we met. The fact that I can't keep my hands off you is not really something I thought you were embarrassed by. Or is it just because it's him?"

"Ughhhhh!" she yelled. "You know exactly what you did, and I hate it when you act like I'm crazy and you have no idea what I'm talking about! It's infuriating!"

"Then paint a picture for me as exactly what I did wrong. I thought that might be him, yes. And I wanted to make sure he knew what was mine. It's not like I stood on the table and made an announcement. I kissed you, I'm not seeing the crisis you're making it out to be." Frustration was oozing out of him.

"What was *yours*? I'm not something to... ugh *dammit* Ethan. If you thought you saw him, you could have just told me you wanted to leave to avoid a confrontation, but instead you fueled the fire. For no REASON! I am *with* you. I have never given you a reason to feel like you have to provide evidence of that fact to anyone."

"Please don't recite your Gender Equality textbook to me. You know exactly why I wanted him to see us together. The only reason I even noticed the guy was because of how he was looking at you. I can tell you with one hundred percent certainty that he would have done the same thing if the roles were reversed. I know that I don't *possess* you, okay? Don't make it sound like I'm that guy, because I'm not."

"No, you're not. But you're also not the guy who has to prove himself to anyone. The Ethan I know would have played that off like it was nothing, because he'd know at the end of the night, no matter how any other guy looked at me, I'd be going home with him. But instead you ruined our last night here together." She started the car, and he assumed that meant the conversation was over. *That's probably for the best,* he thought. He was having a really difficult time swallowing that somehow he'd become the asshole in this situation. They were quiet on the way home except for her occasional sniffle. It started to sink in that maybe his decision-making skills hadn't been on point that night, but he was nowhere near apologizing yet.

♪ *"Breathe" – Michelle Branch*

33

Courtney pulled into the garage and stepped out wordlessly, slamming the door to the car. It felt childishly good. She expected Ethan to stop her, or to apologize, but he followed her inside and went straight to the guest room, the door clicking behind him. She couldn't recall a time they'd gone to bed not speaking. Hot tears sprang back to her eyes and she trudged up the stairs in defeat. *Maybe you should cut him some slack? Did he really do anything that bad?* She hated questioning her instincts when she'd made such a point of being angry. It was taking a lot of will power to ignore the flashes of her confrontation with Sara the previous fall. *It's not the same. It's one hundred percent not the same.* Her arguments weren't even working on her. Her hand rested on the door handle, but she turned away in favor of going back downstairs to speak to him. When her foot hit the third step, her phone buzzed. She wondered if he was having the same crisis of conscience and was too afraid to come upstairs. But the text wasn't from Ethan.

> B: Court, I'm so sorry. I lost it seeing him all over you. Can I call you? Please, just let me apologize over the phone.

She sighed, wishing it had been Ethan trying to make amends. Against her better judgment, she agreed to Ben's request and closed the door behind her when she went into the bedroom.

"Hey," he offered pitifully.

"Look, you asked to talk to me, so talk. I really have no idea what the hell happened tonight, so do you care to explain what you were thinking?"

"I wasn't. I saw you guys together and I thought I could deal, but then you told me his name, and I just didn't get it. How after he broke your heart you could be with him. It's not my business, I know, we haven't been together for a long time, I just still feel... I feel protective of you. It took me back to being in high school, and I was jealous. That's not an excuse... I shouldn't have said what I did."

"No, you shouldn't have. That is a true statement." She let out a breath, some of her anger going with it.

"I'll apologize to him if it will make things okay between us."

"That is a terrible idea."

"Yeah, I kind of figured, but I had to offer."

"Okay, well, you offered. You apologized. So I'm gonna go."

"Wait."

"What?"

"I have the feeling this may be one of that last times I get to talk to you like this. I want to tell you I'm applying for grad school at ASU next year."

"Okay? That's great."

"I'm afraid the next time I see you it will be too late, and maybe that's me being paranoid, I know we're only twenty-one, but I didn't know where you were applying for law school, and if it's back here... well, I wanted you to know I'd be here."

"Ben, please... I can't-"

"I'm not going to interfere with you and Ethan again, I swear," he interrupted. "You've told me you're in a good place, and that can be enough. I just wouldn't have forgiven myself if I didn't at least let you know my hat was in the ring, okay?"

"There is no ring, okay? Thank you for the apology, but I really have to go."

"Goodbye, Court." Her heart was heavy as she hung up the phone. It felt like she had traveled to Phoenix in a time machine rather than a 747. Having these arguments was getting old. She steeled herself for what would probably be another couple of rounds with Ethan if he were in the mood to dig in his heels, but she would never sleep otherwise. For good measure, she threw on an old muted blue t-shirt of his that she'd stolen over the years, and the shortest pajama shorts she could find. *No harm in helping along the reconciliation,* she assured herself. Tiptoeing down the stairs felt juvenile, but she did it anyway. *You're twenty-one years old.* But that didn't really change the fact that she didn't want to run into her father in the hallway going to her boyfriend's room at one am. *Too awkward to think about.* The tiptoeing recommenced.

She knocked lightly on the door, and wasn't surprised when he didn't answer, imagining that there was some very angry music in his ears at the moment. She opened the door a crack and saw exactly that, him stretched out on the bed. Even mad, he was beautiful. She eyed the scripted tattoo on his forearm he'd gotten on spring break, after insisting they do at least one stupid thing. It was a line of lyrics from the first song they'd written together. *"Is it the moon pulling the tides, or her smile reflecting in my eyes?"* She longed to trace the words with her fingers and forget the fight had ever happened. That day was clear in her mind. She'd tried to convince him not to do it... it was like tattooing her name on his skin, she'd told him, but he declared he'd happily do that too. He was always so certain about everything; it was the antithesis of her own worried manner. *All emotion,* she reminded herself, trying to understand his actions towards Ben.

He looked up warily and saw her in the doorway, pulling his ear buds out. "If you're hoping to fight, I'd rather you just go to bed. I can take a cab to the airport in the morning," he let out, looking exhausted. His tone was icy and not something she was used to.

"Ethan, stop. I'm taking you to the airport. I don't wanna fight. I just... we've never... I wanted to talk to you."

"Then talk. I really don't have anywhere to run, so get it all out." His brown eyes seemed more harsh than warm that night. She swallowed hard, not expecting the level of hostility she was encountering.

"Can I just lie down with you?"

He sighed, his shoulders heavy. "Can we just do this in the morning? Tonight you told me that I embarrassed you, you defended your ex boyfriend to me when he called me an asshole in a restaurant full of people, and then you made me leave like a dog with my tail between my legs. It really hasn't been a great evening. Please..."

"Okay," she whispered, unable to hide the hurt in her voice. She turned and left his room, watching his eyes drift up towards the ceiling and the headphones go back into his ears. As her feet stepped slowly, she waited for him to stop her, but then accepted that he wouldn't. Her alarm was set early enough that they could go to breakfast before she took him to Sky Harbor, but she had a pit in her stomach about him leaving. It was doubtful he would agree to stay for the holiday no matter what she said at that point, but the thought crossed her mind to try.

With sleep appearing like a lofty goal, she got up and wrapped his Christmas present instead. She'd had a graphic design student work on logos of his name along with some photos of Ethan playing various shows. The kid came up with four awesome images that he could use for an album cover or as part of a website design. She had them printed on cardstock, and wrapped them carefully in addition to a flash drive of the digital proofs. She paced for a while, debating on whether or not to try to talk to him again, her mind falling down the well-traveled rabbit hole of what-ifs. *What if he's done after this? What if he's put up with your anxiety and uncertainty for so long and he can't do it anymore? What if he finally realizes there are girls drooling over him everywhere he goes, and they would probably be happy to go to Myrtle Beach for spring break?* For the last one, she resolved to tell him they could do spring break his way this year. No Congressional hearings, just the beach and body shots. She even wrote it down in a card on top of the gift so she couldn't freak out about the crowds and the ocean later on and change her mind.

♪ *"Damage" – Jimmy Eat World*
"Diamonds" - Johnnyswim

34

The guilt about sending her away was weighing on him, but he just couldn't bring himself to lie down on this one. It felt like freshman year all over again, like nothing had changed. He was tired of having the same fights and dealing with the same crap. He wanted things to move forward. *Maybe this tour is coming at a good time*, he thought. But when he imagined leaving without knowing she'd be there for him when he got back, his heart sank.

His advisor had responded, and it looked like he'd be able to swing changing classes and still graduate on time if he took a summer session. Even the manager at the radio station had been cool, offering him the opportunity to do a podcast from the road for their website. His mom didn't sound thrilled in her text, but at least he had been able to lead with the fact that he'd still be enrolled at UD. That just left Courtney.

He quieted his mind with his headphones and tossed everything into the suitcase. He grinned slightly at the fact that she would be horrified by everything being stuffed into his luggage, without rhyme or reason, and finally surrendered to sleep.

* * *

Too few hours later, he felt her crawl into bed. It was easy to want to let go of the night before with the scent of her shampoo around him.

"Can we go to breakfast before I have to take you to the airport?" she asked tentatively, running her fingers along his tattoo.

"Yeah, that's fine. I'm sorry I didn't want to talk last night..." he spoke carefully, making sure he wasn't implicating an apology for anything else. *Not there yet.* She kissed his cheek and left him to get ready and grab the rest of his belongings. Courtney's father was at work already, but he thanked her mom sincerely for their hospitality. He really did enjoy being with her family.

"You're welcome here anytime," she said, hugging him. Courtney grabbed her mom's keys and they headed to what she said was her favorite breakfast spot.

"Listen... I know that last night was a disaster. While I don't think it had to come to that, I shouldn't have said that I was embarrassed. It wasn't what I meant. You know that I love you-"

"I have to tell you something," he interrupted, wanting to get it out before they made it into the restaurant. He saw fear cross her face as soon as the words left his mouth, and she pulled into the furthest corner of the parking lot. "Don't look like that. It's a good thing. Well, I think it is, but I can't talk about last night without talking about this first."

"Okay?"

"I got a call from Crawford yesterday. Their manager wants me to replace one of the openers for the last two months of the tour they're on. It's all approved, I just have to say yes."

"Are you serious?" she asked, excitement ringing in her voice after she processed the information. "But, wait, how? When would you leave?"

"In a few weeks," he responded, his eyes looking anywhere but at hers.

"A few weeks? What about school?"

"I got in touch with my advisor right after I talked to Crawford. I'd be able to pick up online classes for this semester, and I'd have to take a full summer session to stay on track, but it's possible."

"Wow… so you've already decided to go then."

"Of course not, that's why I'm talking to you. I just wanted to have my ducks in a row. Please don't act like me being responsible is somehow a slight against you, okay?" He really needed her support on this.

"Okay…"

"What are you thinking? I need you to talk to me."

"I'm thinking it's an incredible opportunity." Frustration rose in his chest. She was closing herself off, and he really didn't have the time to wait for her to decide to let him in.

"What are you really thinking? You know that I would just give you the time to think about it if I had it. But I don't. You're the most important person in my world, so I need to know now if you're on board with this. Be honest."

"Honestly? I don't know what I'm thinking. When I got up this morning I was thinking I needed to apologize and get you to forget about last night using breakfast burritos, and that I was excited to give you your Christmas present. Now I'm thinking I'm not going to see you for two months and knowing that we're both aware of how well that worked out for us last time."

"Courtney! You cannot seriously be bringing up senior year right now!" He tried so hard not to yell, but it couldn't be helped. He rested his head on the dashboard in utter defeat. "I cannot comprehend how you think that is a comparable situation. We were eighteen and had known each other for three months. THREE MONTHS! We've been together for almost three *years*, Court. It is nowhere near the same. I cannot apologize for the actions of my teenage self when they have no bearing on this situation. We've had that discussion too many times."

"And how on-board would you be if I were leaving for two months and you knew full well there would be very attractive men throwing themselves at me on a nightly basis. Would you be planning a going-away party?"

"No." He answered truthfully, hating that she had a point.

"Thank you for not pretending."

"So I turn this down because women are going to hit on me? Like, have I not proven to you that I'm in this for the long haul? I know I would hate it if the situation were reversed; I won't try to deny it. But I'm asking you to trust me. I need to do this."

"I know you do."

"You do?"

"Of course. I've watched you work your ass off for three years, Ethan. I'm not going to tell you not to go."

"Okay?" Confusion spread throughout his body. He wasn't sure what the last ten minutes had been about if she was going to tell him to go.

"You need to go, and maybe the time apart will be good for us."

"Hold up, what do you mean by time apart? We're not breaking up while I'm gone."

"I'm not saying we should break up. Maybe we just take a breather."

"I think that's the worst idea ever."

"Really? You don't think a little emotional separation might make things better?"

"I told you not five days ago in no uncertain terms that I want to marry you. And now you want to tell me we need a 'breather'? Like, explain to me how this isn't just a passive-aggressive way of telling me not to go."

"It's not!"

"Yes it is. You know I'm not going to leave if you're not going to be here when I get back."

"I will be here when you get back. I'm not trying to break up with you."

"Then what the hell are you trying to do? You're taking all of the joy out of this for me." A look of shock and guilt flashed in her eyes. She was quiet for an almost uncomfortable number of breaths.

"I'm sorry. That is so far from my intention. I, um... I'm trying to protect myself, but I don't want to ruin this for you." It was rare that he got a glimpse into her mind when things were this heated. He watched her blinking back whatever else she was keeping unspoken.

"Protect yourself from me?" It hurt to hear her say that.

"From I don't know... being broken. I can't deal with you cheating on me. I'm not trying to insinuate that you've ever done anything wrong, I just know the way women are towards you, even in my presence. I would rather let you go than have you ripped away by someone else. Or many someone elses. I really don't know what goes on during a tour." His heart finally softened at her honesty.

"Look at me." With effort, she brought her shining blue eyes to meet his. "I am completely in love with you. Regardless of my actions last night, and how insane I make you sometimes, you *know* that." He grasped her chin in his hand. "There is no someone else. Anywhere. It's eight weeks out of the rest of our lives. And I'm not a cheater. Ever. You have to know that after what my dad did to my mom."

"What?"

"What do you mean what?"

"You never told me that... about your dad. I didn't know that's why they got divorced."

He searched his memory, coming up empty. "I thought I told you at some point over the years, but it's not something I talk about. My dad left my mom for his pregnant secretary."

"Oh my god, Ethan, that's awful." He wanted to move past this conversation as quickly as possible, but it was necessary for him to finally get it through her head that he wasn't going to stray. He would never be that guy. He convinced her to let it drop.

"Well, can I come see a show?"

"You can come and see ten shows."

"I'm really proud of you. I should have said that first," she told him, pulling him closer.

He breathed her in, getting the same rush he always did. His lips captured hers tentatively; he needed to feel her melt into him. She smiled against his kiss. "The back seat of this car is pretty roomy, wouldn't you say?" Her eyes sparkled.

"It's a definite selling feature," he agreed.

"Wanna feel eighteen again for just a while longer?"

"That part of eighteen? Absolutely." He smirked at her. She let out a hint of the girly giggle she used to give away so often, and they shimmied into the backseat as gracefully as possible. Her dark hair tickled his neck as she leaned in to kiss him teasingly, and it sparked memories of another such occasion, making him want her even more. Some things about high school really did live up to being the best days of his life.

* * *

Vanessa was kind enough to pick him up at the airport when Jared bailed, not entirely surprisingly. He was tempted to get on another plane and fly right back when he stepped outside into the biting cold, the gift Courtney had given him tucked carefully into his backpack.

"So, how'd you fare with the Rosses?" Vanessa asked once he was in her car.

"Just fine, thanks. I'm kind of a catch if you didn't know."

"Yeah yeah, so I've heard. Mostly from you."

"Doesn't make it less true," he shot back.

"Anything exciting happen? Any drama… offers to be a rock star… near fist fights?" she asked with mock anticipation. He took it that she was already quite aware of what went on. He rolled his eyes. Sometimes it felt like he had two girlfriends for as much shit as Vanessa gave him most of the time. "Yeah, I'm gonna need your side of the story. Courtney glosses over too much." Ethan acquiesced, knowing the ride home would be unbearable if he didn't. But it was actually a good segue into something he wanted to ask her anyway.

"…so I leave January twelfth," he finished.

"Wow. You're really going to do it. Good for you." Her reaction surprised him.

"Yeah?"

"Yeah. I mean, if you never do it then you'll never know, but you'll always wonder. It doesn't matter how much you love Courtney or care about school or whatever. You have to know for sure. If I would have gone to BG instead of design school? Well, life probably would be easier as far as my relationship with Luke- don't roll your eyes, and my mom probably wouldn't mention the state of the economy every time I go over there and how 'people aren't hiring designers like they used to,' but I never would have known if I was any good. And, as it turns out, I am." She flashed him a winning smile. "That being said, you know she's gonna be a hot mess to deal with while you're gone, and I do not thank you for that."

"Well, I'm sort of thinking of doing something that might help with the hot mess part," he said hesitantly.

"Like? I'm really not interested in hearing about however you're planning on keeping the magic alive while you're gone. I know we're friends, but you have Jared and Luke for these conversations."

"Just stop talking for a minute. I wouldn't even be telling you this, but I think I'll need your help at some point."

"I feel so loved."

"V," he said, his irritation showing. He hadn't actually voiced these thoughts aloud to anyone yet, and he was having a hard enough time convincing himself to do it now without her snark. She shot him a look, finally understanding he wasn't joking. "I think I'm going to ask her to marry me." Dead silence, for the first time since he'd met Vanessa, filled the car.

"I'm sorry, I think I just had a stroke. You think you're going to what?"

"I'm going to propose. I don't know when exactly. I was thinking if she came to a show while I was on the road, I could end my set with-"

Vanessa stopped him with her laughter. Now he was just annoyed and wished he'd kept it to himself. "Have you lost your damn mind?"

"I don't think it's that insane of a concept, V. We've been together for three-"

"No, no, no. I can get on board with the proposal. Well, I think I can. It's still processing. It's also the last thing I thought you were going to say. Literally, there are a billion other things you could have told me that would have surprised me less. Like you're not really going on tour but instead are serving an undercover mission for Inspector Gadget. That would be less shocking."

"I get it, you're surprised. Enough with the hyperbole and explain the 'have you lost your damn mind' comment."

"Oh, yeah, sorry. Still suffering from that mini-stroke. You can't propose to her on stage."

"Why not?"

"Because it's Courtney. And she will hyperventilate. She'll probably do that anyway, considering that when she's choosing classes every semester, she treats it like a peace negotiation in the Middle East- and that's just for a decision that lasts four months. You're going to be asking her for a lifetime. I beg of you, let her breathe into a paper bag somewhere private."

"You make a fair point," he admitted, despite his annoyance with her immediate shut-down of his idea.

"So… is she going to say yes? I mean, there's graduation, and then law school…"

"Well I obviously hope so. I guess there's only one way to find out. I just feel like we've been stuck in this pattern for too long. I need her to know that this is it for me. I'm not saying we have to get married anytime soon… we could be engaged for ten years, I don't care. But I want to be where she is." He ruffled his hair, not used to being this honest with anyone but Courtney.

"You're kind of making me swoon over here, Fisher."

"You wanna help me pick out a ring?"

"Now you're speaking my language." Vanessa flipped her blond hair confidently over her shoulder. While hoping she'd keep her remarks to a minimum, he was glad he had enlisted help. It was difficult for him to believe this was the plan too. *She'll say yes,* he thought persistently.

♪ *"Don't Leave" – Seven Lions, Ellie Goulding*

35

Her heartbeat was audible in her ears when they pulled into the motel parking lot. She'd agreed to drive him to Indy to meet up with the bands. They had spoken at length about how they would deal with the next eight weeks, and she felt sure it would be okay in the end. Sitting there, however, knowing they hadn't been apart longer than a week since choosing to be together again, was proving to be a bit much.

"You can come in a hang out for a while, Court, it's not like I'm joining the service. It's just a bunch of guys in a hotel. Stay, eat something."

"No, I don't want to be that girl. I'll be okay. I'll grab some food before I head back to school." Her hands were shaking and she wasn't entirely sure why. She shook them out, annoyed at her body for betraying her hard work at a cool exterior.

"Sprinkles," he said lovingly, running his thumb along her jawline. He hadn't called her that often in recent years; they seemed to have outgrown the nickname, but it calmed her almost instantly.

"Yeah," she answered softly.

"You know we're going to be fine."

"I know. You're going to be better than fine, you're going to be amazing and everyone will love you. But not too much," she corrected.

"Not too much, you got it. I love you. I'll see you in a few weeks in Columbus." She tried to kiss him with the intensity of eight weeks worth of hellos and goodbyes; she didn't know if it worked.

"I love you, too. Have fun." He carried his bag and guitar towards the entrance and she stayed for a minute, doubting the decision not to go in with him. His absence grew into something tangible. She found a suitable playlist for the two-hour drive home, and decided on a DQ Blizzard as her lunch. If there was ever a day it was appropriate, this was it, and she didn't want to miss out.

* * *

Courtney was surprised at the things she found to fill up her schedule. She'd always made time for the important stuff- school and work and Ethan and occasionally going out with her friends. Once she took Ethan out of the equation, save for their obsessive text messaging and daily phone calls, she had hours to waste. She actually watched TV, and went to the gym more than once a week, and read a book for fun. She loved college, but when she finally graduated from all formal schooling, she was going to have a stack of books to read with absolutely no academic purpose. *Pure fluff,* she thought happily. She even attempted to cook actual meals. Vanessa was impressed after she got over her fear of the food being poisonous.

Her boss, Dave Greene, surprised her one morning when she came into work.

"Hey there, Ross, you feel like coming to court today?" He practically tap-danced out of his office and over to the reception desk.

"Um, yes."

"Do you even want to know what for?"

"It doesn't really matter, but sure."

"Closing arguments in the Price case today," he informed her, his green eyes sparkling. He was a trial lawyer in the truest sense of the word; it was what energized him, but this case was a big deal. The guy was on trial for manslaughter. Originally it was a murder count, but Dave had argued it down.

"Oh my god, I can't believe it's actually coming to an end," she confessed. The case had been dragging on for a year. It had been a high-profile one to land, being that their firm was small and he and Jim hadn't been practicing together for that long.

"My closing is worthy of *Law and Order*, I swear to god. You're gonna love it." He ran his hand over his thinning brown hair and a grin spread across her face. She hoped that when she became a lawyer, she would have the same enthusiasm for the job.

"If I go with you, who's going to answer the phone?"

"I believe the term you're looking for is voicemail," he replied dryly. Her smile got bigger, and she was practically giddy about sitting in the courtroom all morning. They walked across the street to the Superior Court, and she took a seat in the back. Her boss winked at her before the judge came in. *So weird for him to be this happy at a murder trial.* She supposed he couldn't really look at it that way to be a criminal defense lawyer. At that time, she wasn't sure which field she'd like to pursue within law, but had to admit the trial atmosphere was exhilarating. *If you could ever get your craziness under control enough to speak in front of other people for a living.* Her fingernails dug into her palms while the both attorneys gave their final arguments, but Dave hadn't lied- his created a chill down her spine. They adjourned for the jury to begin deliberations, and he insisted on taking her to lunch to celebrate.

"Okay, that was a pretty kick-ass closing."

"Right?!" he said emphatically, pounding his fist on the wooden table. He spoke to her more like a peer than a boss, despite his years of experience. She liked that about him.

"Are you nervous?"

"Always a little, but I did my job." *True,* she thought.

"Well, I hope they come back soon. The waiting is killing me."

"No pun intended, right?" He grinned at her, causing her to throw a napkin at his head.

"Shut up."

"So, when are you starting LSAT prep?" he asked.

"I had my first class last week, my second one is tonight. I did okay on the initial practice test, but, well…"

"Hold on, don't tell me. The thought of being average makes you want to break out in hives." He gave her shit constantly for her perfectionistic attitude.

"Well, not hives, but it doesn't make me happy. I just have to focus, I guess."

"I hate to tell you this, girly, but the LSAT is nothing compared to your first year at law school." She nodded, ready for him to impart some sort of wisdom. "I'm just saying, don't *do* anything else that first year. Like, don't buy a dog. Shit, don't even buy a fish, because you'll feel guilty when you forget to feed it and have to flush it down the toilet. Plan on your boyfriend either leaving you or wanting to kill you, and don't get pregnant. Like, really don't get pregnant," he told her. She rolled her eyes at him, but the statement about the boyfriend made a familiar tightness creep up in her chest. She knew he didn't mean it specifically about Ethan, but it was a worry. Her LSAT prep instructor, Mr. Holt, had given a similar speech the first night of class, and the girl next to her had turned her engagement ring around so the diamond was hidden. It had seemed ridiculous at the time, and extremely sexist if she really thought about it, but she also understood wanting to be taken seriously and didn't fault the girl.

They moved on to another topic and enjoyed lunch. Upon walking back to the office, he brought the conversation back around.

"So I didn't mean to freak you out earlier… about law school. You're gonna be fine, you know that. Or even if you don't, I know that. If I passed, you can certainly pass. I was high most of the time." He laughed, making her shake her head.

"It's fine. I know it'll be hard, I'll just have to make it work."

"You will. And after you do, you come back here and see me about an associate position." The laughter had left his voice, and he nodded at her seriously before disappearing into his office. *Holy crap*, she thought. *Maybe staying at UD for law school has its advantages.*

The weeks passed slowly, but later rather than sooner she was getting ready to drive to Columbus for the night to see him play.

C: Getting ready to head out. I can't believe I actually get to see you tonight.

E: Drive safe, I can't wait. Are you dying to stay for the entire show? Or would it be okay if I sort of stole you away after my set... I may have made reservations.

C: No, no, steal away.

E: That's what I was hoping you'd say :). I'll see you tonight. I love you.

C: I love you too.

She'd been worried they'd hardly have any time together. This was a good surprise. She grabbed a long dress from her closet and hung it in the back seat, just in case the reservations were for somewhere fancier than her jeans and lacy black top. With an appropriate soundtrack on her stereo, she pulled the Mustang onto the street and followed her heart to Columbus.

He looked sexy in his trademark laidback rocker style, and based on the comments from the women seated around her, she wasn't the only one who noticed. Although she was kicking herself for not arriving there in time to see him backstage, she was there for his introduction. Sitting with hundreds of other people, she watched him light up the stage. It was reminiscent of the first time she'd heard him sing to her at the bonfire. Her heart had fluttered then, but watching him in his element, finally back performing for crowds of this magnitude, the butterflies had multiplied, not caring that she'd heard him sing a thousand times. He played well, but worked the crowd even better. It didn't feel like a brand-new opening act, though she knew her opinion was biased. While it would have been impossible for him to see her for the lights on the stage, she could have sworn he was looking right at her when he plucked out the songs she knew were hers.

"Hey, rock star," she greeted him when she got backstage. He picked her up without a word and kissed her squarely on the mouth.

"I. Miss. You."

"I'm right here."

"Not close enough," he complained. She kissed him back, possessively.

"You were absolutely amazing. I know I've seen you play maybe more than anyone, and you still rocked my world out there."

"I'll take care of that rocking your world business later," he teased in her ear. It sent a shiver to her core, and she wondered if his flirting would ever cease to affect her. "Lemme wrap up a couple of things and then we are out of here."

"Do I need to change?"

"Nah, the place is kinda hipster-y from what I understand, so you look perfect." He returned quickly, and he intertwined his fingers with hers on the way out the door.

♪ *"Forever For Tonight"* – *Blessid Union of Souls*

36

His palms were sweating when he held the door open for her at Rigsby's. It was a perfect night, having her there. Being on tour was everything he'd imagined it to be- crappy food, crappy accommodations, but great exposure. It also solidified for him that his future was probably not on the road. He actually found himself talking to the marketing and promotions guys about their jobs when he was waiting around a venue, and it made him even surer that his life at UD was the right track.

The ring Vanessa helped him pick out was an anchor in his pocket. It felt like the hopeful part of him was being strangled by the nerve-wracking fear that she'd say no. *She can't say no,* he thought, breathing slowly.

"Are you okay?" she asked as they were seated. "You're quiet."

"Yeah, I'm great. You're here," he reassured her, grabbing her hand. They ordered drinks and some sort of frou-frou appetizer. There was an easy quiet between them that he'd missed. It was a hard thing to achieve over the phone, but in person, just her presence was enough. The expression that crossed her face when she tried the sheep's milk cheese and fig preserves made him actually laugh out loud, lightening his mood. He looked at her for a long moment before making a decision to change the course of the evening. Motioning to their waiter, he paid the check and they walked hand in hand back to her car with a new plan. He directed her to drive him to a nearby grocery store.

"I'm sorry if I ruined our fancy dinner," she apologized nervously.

"Don't be. This will be better." She looked at him curiously when he instructed for her to remain in the car while he ran inside. It was one of those 24-hour mega-marts, which in this case worked in his favor. He picked up a pizza from their "hot and ready" section, chilled beverages from the cooler, and doughnuts from the bakery. After grabbing paper plates and plastic silverware to complete the supply list, he decided it was going to be the cheapest proposal dinner in the history of the world. It still made him grin to know she'd be much happier with this spread than with oysters and fifty-dollar entrees. He spoke to the barista working the in-store coffee counter and let her in on his plan. She looked incredulous, no doubt wondering why he'd be proposing in a pseudo-coffee shop with plastic chairs. He just grinned. Now, at least, he could set up their feast at one of the small tables without worrying about being interrupted. Finally, he went out to get her, loving that she was singing and dancing to Destiny's Child in her car. She jumped when he knocked on the window.

"You scared me! I sort of thought you were never coming back, but I'm glad you did," she said, getting out. His nerves were back in full force now that he had nothing but her to occupy his mind.

"I'm glad I could come through for you," he expressed, offering her his arm. She clapped lightly when she saw what he'd set up inside.

"You are the best." She plopped down happily in front of her pizza. His heart beat harder, and try as he might to focus on the present, his mind was fully entrenched in what was to come. They chatted easily through dinner, and he was mentally scolding the barista for staring expectantly at them the whole time. She gave a genuine laugh when he pulled the sprinkled doughnuts out of the bag, and he knew that was his shot.

"Do you remember your first birthday that we spent together?"

"Um, of course. Kind of a big night for me," she indicated, biting her lip.

"Kind of a big night for me too."

"Why?"

"Well, a couple of reasons... but you were the first girl I'd ever been with that I loved. It was an eye opening experience."

She smiled at him lovingly. "And what other reasons?"

"Well, I never told you this, or anyone, actually, because you know, I had a reputation to protect back then." He smirked. "But when I went to the mall to look for a gift, before deciding to give you my ring, this sales girl cornered me into looking at engagement designs."

"Seriously? Knowing you at eighteen... how did you not freak out and cancel our entire date?" she asked, amused.

"Well, I did freak out. Like, having a meltdown on a bench in the mall type of freak out. But it wasn't because I wanted to get as far away from that store as possible. It was because my first instinct was to imagine giving you one someday. That scared me more than anything else could have."

"Aw, baby, how have you never told me this story?"

"I think I was sort of saving it," he said, still working on his nerves.

"For..."

"Tonight."

"Tonight..."

"Courtney. When I think of where I was, what my ambitions were and the bar I'd set for myself before I met you, it's like looking back at another life. I knew you for a month before you left, and those four weeks changed everything for me. I, um-" He hadn't anticipated getting choked up, and he tried to breathe through it, reaching out for her fingertips. "I need you. Whatever that means and wherever it takes us, I'm in. I love you, and I think I knew that when you said you liked my abs, and when you yelled at me for calling you a hobbit, and when you called Tom Sawyer a badass in our canoe, and when you danced with me on the riverbank, and when you kissed me back at the Train concert, and when you tried to pretend you liked sushi, and when you insisted on proofing all of my research papers so I could maintain a B average, and when you didn't want to come into the hotel last month for fear of making me look uncool in front of my new tour mates. I could go on…" He swallowed, his mouth suddenly not cooperating properly. "But the point is that I'm in love with you, and it's only ever been you." He stood up, and the realization that had been growing in her eyes since he started his speech finally resounded with an almost audible "click" as he pulled the ring box out of his pocket and dropped to one knee.

♪ *"I Will Wait" – Mumford and Sons*

37

The sight of this jaw-droppingly beautiful man on one knee was enough to make her heart thrum against her ribcage, all knowledge of its job to beat regularly forgotten. She had one brief moment of bliss, wanting to melt into his arms before the request even came out. And then she stopped breathing. Her brain… true to its nature, began to throw out questions, concerns, worries, anxieties- really any manner of doubt available- in the form of metaphorical thought bubbles in front of her eyes. Her head filled with the advice from her boss and her LSAT instructor, as well as the image of the girl hiding her promise from the world at her desk. Fear cut like a knife, and she felt desperate, knowing she was about to ruin this moment and hating herself for it. *Just breathe. Just breathe and don't do anything stupid.* She searched his face for all of the comfort it provided, determined not to let him read her expression

"Let me say this before you respond, okay? I know that right now, your mind is probably in a million different places. I know you want to graduate and go to law school and get through the Bar, and maybe you don't know where marriage fits in. What I am trying to say, is that for me? The timeline doesn't matter, as long as I get to be with you. I will give you whatever you need- you know that. So whether it's in a year or ten that I get to call you my wife, I just want you to know that I'm in this forever." He took a breath. "Courtney Ross, will you marry me?" He had never looked more perfect than he did at that moment, with hope and adoration written across his face. It took her back to another such time when he'd asked her to stay with him, to be with him for real. She thought she might pass out when he opened the ring box... not because of her erratic breathing, but because he had just popped every single bubble of doubt that surrounded her, and they floated away powerlessly into the sky. The newfound weightlessness was making her head spin. *How does he know me that well?* For once, her mind was clear, and there was only one thought left with which to do anything. *Just choose the one thing that's ever made you feel free.*

"Yes," she breathed. "Whatever it takes to get there, yes." Tears filled her eyes, and she wasn't sure if it was just the realization that he wanted her to be his forever, or if it was colored with some embarrassment that he'd known she would hesitate. Either way, they spilled over when she saw him blink back his own.

"Yes?" he pressed cautiously, his voice heavy. "As in you will use the word fiancé and refrain from making out with other guys?" he asked, the smile on his face reaching his eyes. *So he was thinking of that night too,* she realized. She nodded for emphasis under the fluorescent glow of the store lights, and he slipped the ring on her finger.

"So sparkly..." she got out, her voice catching. He smirked and gave her a kiss that felt like the first one they'd ever shared- full of desire and perhaps a little left-over nervousness, but it was as strong and as certain as he'd always been.

♪ *"Love"* – American Authors

Epilogue: Five Years Later

He watched his fiancé flit around their room, trying to gather everything she'd need for the following day.

"You know this is ridiculous, right?"

"Shhh," she shot back.

"Do you just want *me* to go and sleep at Vanessa's parents'? And she can come here? The sheer amount of stuff you're packing is kind of concerning." Vanessa had flown in a week early from San Francisco to help with the wedding pre-game show, as he liked to refer to it.

"Not all of us are as naturally pretty as you- it takes supplies. And a highly trained team of hair and make-up specialists. Plus, it'll be like our last nostalgic hurrah. I'm actually looking forward to it."

"Insanity," he muttered. "I would marry you just like this. Jeans and no make-up and a ponytail." He grabbed her hips gently from behind and pressed his lips to her neck. She leaned into him momentarily. As much as he wanted her to be his wife, he was ready for the wedding part to be over and the honeymoon in Bali to be upon them. Having snuck a look at the mountain of lingerie she'd brought home from her bachelorette party, he was pretty certain it would be a trip worth remembering.

"I'd say you were the sweetest man in the whole world, if I didn't know that you were trying to get lucky." She raised an eyebrow sharply at him in the mirror above their newly painted white dresser. Her hair was long and dark, just as it was when he'd met her nine years earlier. He thought she looked even better now, if that was possible, and she had much more sass to go around since she'd won her first solo trial at Kramer and Green. Well, now Kramer, Green & Associates. His own hair was long again, but trimmed up closer to his ears than his jaw for the wedding. His mother insisted he not look like a hippie in his wedding photos. Courtney didn't seem to mind it when he looked scruffy.

"I have no idea what you're talking about." He flopped back onto their bed and let his legs hang over the side, stretching out on the all-white linens. She had imposed a two-week hiatus on any action whatsoever. Something about them waiting until their wedding night and it being special, blah blah blah. He suspected it was something she'd read on Pinterest.

"Sure you don't."

"Come lie down with me for a minute."

"Babe, there are, like, a million things to do."

"Then just add me to that list." He could tell she was biting her tongue trying not to smile.

"One minute," she acquiesced, grinning, and she lay down next to him. As was typical, her hand made its way across his stomach muscles and he stifled a smile, knowing he was about to blow the two-week rule right out of the water.

"You're going to be Courtney Fisher tomorrow," he whispered in her ear.

"Say it again."

"Courtney Fisher." His lips nipped at her jawline and he could feel her resolve crumbling.

"You don't play fair," she murmured, pulling his hips against her own. He peeled off his white t-shirt just for good measure, and resumed the trail he was making down her neck.

"Fairness is overrated. I like to win at all costs." He smiled against her shoulder. She sighed somewhere between contented and resigned. Her fingers found their way to her favorite spot at the base of his neck. Sliding her hands up above her head with his own, he dropped kisses anywhere he could reach, making her laugh. He didn't even miss the girly giggle anymore. "I am going to be the most kick-ass husband ever," he promised. He wished he could actually say that in his vows, but thought it might be frowned upon.

"Of that I have no doubt, baby." He kissed her intently, her lips parting, and he drank her in. The two-week rule was presently forgotten. Making love to her was as heart-stopping that day as it was the first time. She curled into him under their sheets when they came down from where they'd been. "You, Ethan Fisher, are a rule-breaker." She smiled, pulling one of his shirts over her head.

"I've been called worse."

"Well, I was going to wait until tomorrow, and send this over once you arrived at the venue, but I guess since we're being rebellious and all, I'll give it to you now." He had to admit his interest was piqued, being that he'd just gotten what he wanted. Kneeling in their closet, she pulled out a rectangular box wrapped in craft paper and decorated with Sharpie. This one had "Mr. and Mrs. Fisher" written all over it with hearts and wedding bells like a teenaged girl's notebook. He could not have loved it more.

"You want me to open it now?" he clarified.

"Yes now, hence the gift giving." He kissed her first, not really caring what was in the box, but then opened it carefully. His eyes widened when he finally saw the product name on the box.

"You bought me a PS4?" he asked incredulously.

"You did want one, right?" Nervousness crept into her voice.

"Um, yes I wanted one, I just... You're kind of the best wife ever." Her eyes shone at his remark.

"Well, now you can set it up tonight while I'm gone and mess with it."

He set the box down carefully next to their bed. "There is only one thing I want to mess with right now," he murmured, pulling her bare legs towards him. "How did I get this lucky?" She started to answer, but he cut her off with a kiss and tugged her down into the sheets.

She eventually did pack up their new-to-them SUV and get ready to leave for the Roberts' house. "You know I want you to sleep here, right? In case I didn't make that clear earlier. There could be a replay of-"

"Fisher..." she warned. "You can't see me before the wedding. Let's have one traditional thing about our relationship, okay?"

"Whatever you want, love." He kissed her and watched her drive away from the little Victorian house they now called their own.

♪ *"Marry Me" – Train*

Epilogue: Five Years Later

She took a long look in the mirror, butterflies dancing across her stomach. Or maybe they were elephants. Her dress was pristine, with gathered satin that resembled a cloud. Made of frosting. She wore a tiara around her hair piled artistically on top of her head, because other than when girls are five and playing princess, there aren't many times when a bona fide crown is accepted by the general public. Her engagement ring sparkled on her hand, a dainty white gold band covered in pave diamonds, and a small but brilliant center stone wrapped in sapphires. It was a vintage piece, and she knew she had V to thank for the exquisite find, though Vanessa never took the credit.

"You look like a cake topper," V told her, fluffing her dress for the fifteenth time.

"Yeah, I kind of like that vision," she agreed.

"You're good? Do you need anything? Water, champagne, getaway car?"

"Water, maybe. The others, no. I'm good." And she was. Ignoring the fact that her heart was trying to escape her corseted ribcage, that was the truth. Despite the long road traveled to get there, she'd finally arrived at happy. And ready. And sure. It took longer than she would have liked, but here they were. Vanessa kissed her cheek and left her alone in the small room adorned with framed canvasses of water lilies and wildflowers. Her dad knocked on the door, looking dapper in his tux.

"You ready?"

"I am," she said, hoping she didn't trip over the crinoline on the way down the spiral staircase. The whole thing moved in slow motion. The sound of an acoustic guitar played an original song Ethan had written for the occasion. Looking up, she saw him waiting for her, as he had been for the past five years since she'd said yes, a happy smirk on his face she was certain was for her benefit. The trellises of the outdoor venue were covered in vines, and twinkle lights sparkled like glitter. The ceremony was running just as it had at the rehearsal, but they hadn't shown each other what they planned to say once up at the altar.

When it came time to speak their promises, her heart stopped, looking into his deep brown eyes. "So, I really did write down my vows," he told her, a smile spreading across his lips, "because I know how you feel about the importance of notecards." A ripple of laughter popcorned through their gathered friends and family. "But I've always been better off the cuff, so here goes." He cleared his throat and looked down, gathering his emotions. "The night that I met you, you sort of rejected me, and well, that had never happened before, if I'm being honest." She grinned at the memory. "I didn't know what to make of this tiny cheerleader girl with a vocabulary that was a bit over my head, which is saying something," he gestured to reference his height, "but I knew that there was something I needed to be close to. You keep me grounded and focused on the important things; you are my gravity, and you changed my whole world. You inspired me, and you made me a better person. Today, I promise spend the rest of my life attempting to be worthy of everything you've given me."

Vanessa handed over tissues for the tears running down her cheek along with her vows before it was her turn to speak. His eyes never left hers, and she felt his fingers brush her palm in a calming motion before she began.

"Well, I do have notecards," she said, addressing the correct assertion from his speech. He smirked at her, and she just shook her head at the return of the fluttering feeling. "Interestingly enough, I also thought of the night we met. I believe the exact words played out in my mind were 'I am in so much trouble.'" She smiled as another laugh rose around them. "It's funny that you've always referred to me as your gravity. I'm glad to be that for you, but you are something else entirely for me. You are the feeling I get when swinging as high as I can, trying to *outrun* gravity and escape towards the sky. Exhilarating, and slightly terrifying, but you've always been what I needed. Today, I promise always to try to be what you need in return." His smirk was gone, replaced with a look of adoration, but it didn't make her heart skip any less. She couldn't imagine a better way to spend the rest of her life than flirting with him. He finally bent down to kiss her, and in true Ethan-style, dipped her back unexpectedly, but held her tightly as his lips found hers.

"I love you, sprinkles," he whispered in her ear when they stood back up.

"I love you too." She smiled against his cheek, not having heard that name in a while. She couldn't wait for the look on his face when he saw the white paper bags at every guest's chair, each filled with a sprinkled doughnut and tied with a piece of glittered ribbon.

* * *

The ting-ting-ting of champagne glasses pulled her out of her trance in looking into her *husband's* deep brown eyes. Vanessa was standing on a chair in her shimmering gold gown, calling everyone's attention for her toast.

"For those of you who don't know me, I am Vanessa, and I hold the esteemed position of Matron of Honor, as well as Courtney's very best friend since kindergarten. "I have also had the privilege of watching these two fall in love... twice," she added for effect, winking at them. "I will admit that sometimes it was infuriating to witness the spark that was so obviously between them while they tried to screw it up. There may have been yelling involved," she confessed, giving Ethan a look while he returned an innocent expression right back. "And yet here we all are, celebrating one of the best couples I have ever known. You really are supposed to be together. And yes, I still take credit for making all of this happen, so you're welcome." Their friends and family laughed and readied themselves to raise their glasses. Courtney's eyes filled with happy tears, thinking of how much she loved her friend for seeing her through to this moment... for always being there no matter their geographical location. "I offer a toast to you both- to the magic of Gem City summers, to taking chances, to breaking rules, to finding the right person, and to the happiness awaiting you in your long and exciting adventure together. I love you both dearly, congratulations."

A chorus of "hear, hear," rang through the air, and after clinking her glass to Ethan's, she stood and hugged Vanessa. Not just for the killer toast, but for the past twenty-plus years of having her friend as a guiding force in her life.

"I love you, you know?" Courtney asked genuinely.

"I know. I love you too, girl. Now go and dance with your super hot husband, will you? I'm about to do the same."

* * *

Before their first dance, Ethan grabbed the mic to address their guests. "I understand that the traditional first dance is supposed to be to the bride and groom's "song," he explained using air quotes. "The problem lies in that every song I know is somehow connected to my new wife." He winked at her. "I've played and written more songs for and about her than I might care to admit, but when she gave me free reign over the music for tonight, and I was wracking my brain for the perfect sentiment, there was only one that came to mind. While I took some liberties with the lyrics in the version you're about to hear, I played this for Courtney the night I first told her I loved her. Clearly it worked out for me then, and I want to start off our marriage with the same momentum." He grinned at her and nodded to the DJ. Heat pricked at the corners of her eyes again, knowing exactly what was about to play. His ability to just *get* what she needed never ceased to amaze her.

The DJ took back the mic and announced them. "Please welcome to the floor for their first dance as husband and wife, Mr. and Mrs. Fisher." She didn't know whether to laugh or cry when he pulled her close and placed a kiss just beneath her ear. Dan and Shay's "19 You + Me" rang through the speakers. He had recorded it with a full band, and re-written lyrics to be more about the two of them. It sounded better than the original.

"I love you, Courtney Ross," Ethan murmured against her cheek.

"Courtney Fisher," she corrected.

"Courtney Fisher," he repeated, and his lips found hers for the tenth time as her husband. She let the world fall away as it always had when they touched. Happily, she let the reality of the day, of the rest of their lives, wash over them both under the twinkling lights spread throughout the sky.

"I still like your abs." She smiled, looking up at him.

"I still like your ass," he smiled back, smirking and making her laugh.

"I'll love you forever."

"I'll love you forever too, sprinkles."

Thank you so much for reading! I would love for you to leave a review and share your thoughts!

New From Nicole Campbell:

**When The Time
Comes to Light a Fire**

Curious about Vanessa's rocky relationship with Zack Roads, or how she and Luke came to be? *When the Time Comes to Light a Fire* will revisit Vanessa's sophomore year at Gem City High School. Read on for an excerpt!

Visit NicoleCampbellBooks.com for updates and a chance to beta read or win a copy of upcoming books!

Acknowledgements

Being new to this author gig has meant a steep learning curve, but I am continually amazed by people's willingness to help- to read, review, promote, and to share their thoughts on what I've written. The response to *What Comes of Eating Doughnuts With a Boy Who Plays Guitar* has been incredible, and I have to admit that I think I like *How One Attempts to Chase Gravity* even more (sorry, Courtney, it was fun developing Ethan's character). There are so many people who made writing and publishing this book possible:

My husband and son for ignoring the fact that my face is constantly in my laptop and for loving me anyway. My friends and family who shamelessly promote my books for me... even in the checkout lines while shopping... when I'm standing right next to them. I also appreciate the fact that none of my friends have told me to shut up about my book yet. They are awesome.

Lastly, this amazing community of book bloggers, beta readers, and Instagrammers that exists in the blogosphere. I am truly in awe of your willingness to read something I've written and give honest feedback with nothing in return. I appreciate you more than I can say; I get positively giddy when a new review comes out.

Thank you, thank you, thank you, and I hope you enjoyed the end of Courtney and Ethan's story.

  Facebook: https://www.facebook.com/NicoleCampbellBooks/
  Instagram: @NicoleCampbellBooks
  Website: NicoleCampbellBooks.com

A Note From the Author

Writing a book was sort of one of those things that I thought about and never actually intended on doing. I spoke to a seventh grader in my English class about the idea for the book one day while I was teaching a creative writing unit, and she *insisted* that I at least write it as a short story. I took that as a challenge more than anything, and I sat down that afternoon and outlined the plot in some random spiral notebook. Exactly four weeks later I had completed the draft. It became a complete obsession for me, I couldn't stop. At this point I have a hard time remembering what life was like before I started writing, and I am so thankful for that initial conversation with one of my (now favorite) students. *Gravity* is the end of Courtney and Ethan's story, but I will publish one more book in the Gem City collection from Vanessa's point of view (it will be a prequel released sometime next spring), and I'm maybe embarrassingly excited to be in her head for that long, AND to get to write more of Luke. He's the best. All in all, I can't imagine *not* writing, and I am eager to get into my next series as well to move a little bit away from just straight Contemporary/Romance. I love chatting with readers, so please comment on my blog or social media, I will totally respond!

♪ *"Girls Just Wanna Have Fun" - Cyndi Lauper*

Excerpt From: When the Time Comes to Light a Fire
Prologue: Summer Before 8th Grade

Minnie Mouse would get more attention in a bikini. Looking in her bedroom mirror, Vanessa tied the strings of her new bathing suit around her neck, wishing her mom had let her buy the one she'd really wanted. She sighed at the red polka-dotted boy-short bottoms reflected back at her, remembering their conversation.

"Vanessa Roberts, no thirteen year old girl has any business showing off her butt cheeks. I will not be spending money to have you looking like a street-walker."

"Oh my god, it's a swimming suit." Vanessa's eyes rolled back in her head, hard.

"Roll your eyes at me again, and you're liable to spend the summer in your room with no need for swimwear." The tone in her voice wasn't playful, and Vanessa readjusted her expression.

"Yes, Mom." She put the beautiful purple suit with the bows back on the rack and stomped slightly to the dressing room.

Her bedroom door opened, bringing her back to the present, and she glanced up in the mirror at her best friend. Courtney's dark curly hair looked wilder than normal, given the humidity, though she had tried to tame it with bobby pins into a high ponytail. Her friend assessed the bathing suit situation.

"I don't know what you're complaining about. I think it's cute."

"Ugh, don't patronize me. I look like Minnie Mouse, and Brad James is never going to look twice at me."

"I thought you were hoping to run into Luke something-or-other?"

"Yeah well, apparently he's with Elena now, so I set my sights elsewhere," Vanessa admitted begrudgingly. Courtney's ensemble was much like her own; though her short muscular build filled it out very differently than Vanessa's more slender frame. Courtney just raised her eyebrow. "Whatever, let's just go." They bounded down the stairs with their over-stuffed pool bags to let her mom know they were ready to leave.

*　*　*

The pool was crowded, but she supposed that was the point. The air smelled of chlorine and warm grass- it was effectively a run-of-the-mill Gem City summer. She and Courtney found a spot in the near-shade, and her eyes scoped out the boy situation.

"I hope your mom will let me come back next summer too. Then I can almost pretend we'll be going to high school together," Courtney mused with a frown.

"My mom will let you come back anytime. She loves you. You don't talk back, so she might like you better than me," she smiled. "And don't depress me. I wish we were going to high school together too. You don't think you guys will ever move back?"

"I don't think so. I miss it though." Vanessa sighed. Her other friends were *fine*, but she and Courtney had been through everything together since they were five. The Ross' moving had done a number on her. The thought of the two of them not cheering on the same team and obsessing over boys had a melancholy effect on her demeanor. She also wasn't sure who she was going to cheat off of in math.

"Well, summers it is then, friend."

"Summers it is. So, where is this Brad character?"

"Basketball court. Black shorts, blue t-shirt." She flipped her long blond ponytail over her shoulder as if he could see her.

"He's cute. But *who* is the other guy?" Vanessa had to smirk.

"That would be Luke Miller."

"Things are making much more sense now."

"Stupid Elena."

"I don't know her, but I'll second that."

"Whatever, two more years and we'll be in high school, probably cheering varsity," she added, giving Courtney a lazy fist bump at that prediction, "and most importantly, getting our licenses. I just wish we could skip freshman year. I want a *car*. I want boys to take me out on *dates*. I want to listen to my music as loud as I freaking want. And I want a super hot jealousy-causing boyfriend."

"I think I'd probably settle for a sort-of-cute mathlete at this point, but I like your ambition," Courtney confessed, looking as she always did when she went into low-self-esteem mode.

"Stop, you're adorable. Come on. Give me your perfect boyfriend checklist." Vanessa plopped her sunglasses onto her face and prepared to mentally correct her friend's choices.

"My what?"

"Shut up, your checklist. Don't lie and say you don't have one. For example: tall, cute with a good smile, football player, preferably, because you know how I feel about the uniforms, smart enough to hold a real conversation, great sense of humor- not like 'oh he laughs at amusing jokes,' but like 'oh my god he is hilarious and my sides hurt from laughing.'" Courtney was looking at her curiously, but she didn't care. "And I want a guy who can make me mad. Just a little bit."

"Um, ok? Everyone makes you mad. Except for me," Courtney retorted with a smirk.

"Ha, until now," Vanessa replied. "No, you know what I mean, like a guy who's not afraid to argue. Someone strong." She sipped her lemonade. "Your turn."

"I don't think I have quite the extensive list you are looking for, friend."

"I call bull. Tell me anyway." Courtney made a Kermit-the-Frog face at her, but she knew she'd give in.

"Fine. Also tall. Ummm nice?"

"Nice?"

"Well yeah, nice, like easy to be around. And likes to read."

"So you want to date a nice book-reader."

"Yep."

"You're hopeless."

"And I'm your best friend. What does that say about you?"

"That I need to save you from yourself and make sure you don't date a librarian." Courtney promptly threw a handful of ice from her cup of water at Vanessa and stuck out her tongue.

♪ *"What About Your Friends"* - TLC
"So What" - P!nk

Excerpt From: When the Time Comes to Light a Fire
Chapter One: Two Years Later

Vanessa breathed in the scent of what was left of the summer sun heating the asphalt outside of the gym. It was the last cheer practice before the start of school, and she was officially one week away from having her license. *No more parent drop offs,* she thought blissfully as she watched her mom's Durango pull back out onto the street. She trotted easily into the gym to warm up.

"Ohmygod, thank you for being here early," Jessi practically yelled, placing a death grip on her forearm as soon as she made it over the threshold of the gym doors.

"I'm here, I'm here, what's the deal?" Her friend's green eyes were shining, and her dark red hair was pulled into a messy bun atop her head. She was practically vibrating with anticipation over something.

"I need a favor. Like a big favor. Flavoricious. Flavorful. Favor. Please say you'll do it."

"English. And I'm gonna need more information. Like, any information really."

"You know that guy Josh I've been wanting to go out with forever and ever and ever?"

"From Ohio State?" Vanessa raised her eyebrows suspiciously. When Jess said "forever and ever," it could have meant since yesterday. She really didn't remember the first time her friend had mentioned him.

"Yes! Well, he's in town for the weekend and asked me to go out, but he can't like, pick me up at my house, you know my parents would flip their tea kettles. And my car is kind of out-of-commission at the moment. You see why this is an emergency right?"

"Not particularly, no. And last time I checked, tea kettles didn't flip. Just borrow your mom's car."

Jessi rolled her eyes. "The whole reason my Jeep is in the shop is because I curbed it so hard I popped the tired and jacked up my alignment. My parents told me I would never sit behind the wheel of either of their cars again."

"Still unsure how this equals a flavoricious favor from me," Vanessa let out, becoming annoyed. *Always with the drama.*

"Say you'll come with me."

"I could say it, but it wouldn't be true. I am sort of missing the key components to be able to do that. Namely, a license and a car. Plus, why would I come on your date?"

"Don't be dense, he's bringing a friend. Didn't I say that?"

"Nope."

"Oh, well he is. And aren't your parents out like playing Jenga on Friday nights or something? I'll have my mom drop me at your house this afternoon, and we can take the other car; we'll be back before they're home. I'll even drive so you're not like breaking the law." Jessi tapped her foot impatiently as if Vanessa were somehow annoying *her,* and she used the phrase "breaking the law," as if she meant "breaking a nail."

"It's Bunco. And you've lost your mind."

"Did I mention his friend is *cute?* Like Leo in *Romeo and Juliet* cute. You haven't been out with anyone since Michael, come on. It'll be fun. We'll just go play pool for a while and then go home, no big deal.

Your parents will never even know we were gone." It was a low blow mentioning Leo. *Not good enough*, she argued in her head.

"You literally just told me your own parents won't let you take their cars because you're an awful driver, but you want me to give you the okay to drive the car of one of my unsuspecting parents?" Vanessa side-stepped the red-headed devil to get to the mat and begin stretching. The conversation was getting more ludicrous by the moment, and the mention of Michael annoyed her.

"I would do it for you, but whatever. Be afraid to have any fun." Jessi stomped past her, pouting as she warmed up her scorpion. Vanessa sighed, wishing her friend hadn't helped her out of rather sticky situations that past year. She would probably still be grounded if it weren't for Jess's ability to spin a story at the drop of a hat. It wasn't a lie; she *would* do it for her.

"You swear to god we'll be home before eleven?" Jessi's expression turned from glowering to elated immediately, lighting up her full lips and wide emerald eyes.

"Cross my heart. Eeeeee!!!! I love you!" Vanessa almost lost her balance with the force of Jess's hug.

* * *

There was still sweat dripping down the curve of her spine from a particularly brutal conditioning session after practice. She had headed out the door of the locker room and was rummaging in her bag for her phone when she ran face first into a wall. A human wall.

"Jesus, look where you're going," she relayed, annoyed. She tried to fight the redness she knew was spreading over her cheeks when she realized it was a very cute, broad shouldered, grinning human wall.

"I am so very sorry for letting you run me over. How rude of me," he retorted with amusement. From the looks of him, he was headed to the weight room. She realized, horrified, that her hand was still resting on his arm where she'd placed it trying to catch her balance. Her horror deepened when she recognized who said arm belonged to, which was the new starting wide-receiver of their football team.

"I, um, well. It's possible I wasn't paying attention. I'm sorry for almost tackling you," she managed evenly, regaining some of her composure and trying to salvage the situation. She took in his dark wavy hair and bright blue eyes. He was still smiling at her, and it didn't help her focus.

"I think I might be all right being tackled by you." His grin widened, and she realized he was flirting with her. It also struck her that she was in gym clothes, and there was literally no part of her that wasn't sweaty. She bit her lip in uncertainty of how to react. "Just to make sure the rest of the students are safe, I think I'll walk you to the parking lot. I wouldn't want you to run over anyone else." He changed his initial trajectory and fell in step with her in the direction of the junior lot.

"How safety-conscious of you."

"Just looking out for my fellow man," he smirked, glancing sideways at her. She tried to flip her long blond ponytail over her shoulder and failed miserably. It just sort of flopped there, a sticky sweaty mess. *Seriously. Could this not have happened any other day?* "So, should I just call you blondie? Or do you have an actual name?"

"Vanessa. Roberts," she replied tentatively.

"Good to know, Vanessa Roberts. I'm Zack. Roads," he stated, mimicking her structure. "And tell me, why haven't I seen you around?"

"I don't know. Have you been looking?" she asked flirtatiously, not particularly wanting to say it was because she was a freshman last year. He was only a year older, but he seemed moreso. Everyone knew who he was... high school football was sort of a religion in Gem City.

"Well, I'm looking now," he replied without missing a beat. "Will you be at Vader's bonfire next weekend?"

"Is that an invitation?" It was taking everything she had not to clap her hands and jump up and down. Vader's parties were legendary, but she had never been invited.

"It is. I'll see you there, then."

"Sounds good. Thanks for keeping the sidewalks safe," she mentioned as they walked through the gate to the parking lot.

"All in a day's work. I'll see you next weekend, Vanessa Roberts," he flashed those white teeth again and headed back towards the gym. *Oh.My.God.* She could not *wait* to see her friends' faces when she told them where they were going next Saturday.

* * *

"Are we seriously doing this?" Vanessa asked incredulously while Jessi took her hair down for the tenth time. "And just make up your mind about your hair, will you? You're stressing me out." Vanessa's own long blond hair was done in a loose fishtail braid, and she elected for a simple white t-shirt and jeans, having no expectations of anything glamorous happening that evening.

"Of course we're 'seriously doing this,' it's just playing pool, not a bank heist, V."

"Yeah, yeah. I'll feel better once my mom's SUV is back in the garage."

"Chill, we'll be back in a couple of hours." She sighed, fluffed her shiny red hair one last time, and rubbed her glossed lips together. "Let's go." Vanessa took a breath and committed to the transgression. *You're all in now.* Despite her friend's driving record, she figured letting the licensed driver operate the car was better than them getting pulled over with her behind the wheel.

"I swear to god if anything happens to this car-"

"Stop, we're driving like two inches." Vanessa shook her head.

"Who is this friend I'm supposed to be entertaining anyway? Is he actually cute or was that just a carrot you wanted me to chase?"

"Ummmm."

"Um? Jesus, Jess."

"No, I mean, I assume he's cute because Josh is cute, I just haven't actually met him," she replied, clicking the garage door to close.

"Awesome."

"It'll be fun! Come on, stop acting like Kim. If I wanted someone to be a downer, I would have asked her to come." Vanessa pursed her lips at that.

"Whatever. Kim's not bad."

"No, no, I love her. You know what I mean, she's just all mom-ish."

"Ok. I'll attempt to be more cheerful." Jessi simply smiled victoriously.

They arrived at *The Eight Ball* without incident, and Vanessa plastered on her most charming smile as they strolled in to the pool hall, the smell of old smoke flooding her nose. Dodging a precariously placed cue on the way to a table towards the back, she watched as Jessi ran up behind a broad shouldered male and threw her arms around his neck playfully.

"Hey there," he smiled, turning around.

"Hey yourself," Jess replied, her eyes shining. Vanessa stood, feeling bored already, waiting to be introduced. Not at all surprisingly, she was now invisible.

"Hi. I assume you're Josh?" she interrupted the couple's hello. He was moderately attractive, but had a weak jawline. There was nothing she could see to warrant the lengths they'd gone to in order to get there.

"Oh, yes, silly me. Vanessa, Josh, Josh, this is Vanessa, or V. Whatever," Jess giggled, flipping her hair.

"Hey, good to meet you," Josh responded, holding out his hand. She shook it, but wasn't totally fond of the way his eyes rolled over her skin. "My buddy Matt's around here somewhere, I'm sure he'll be back in a sec. You guys wanna play?"

"Sure. I'm crap at pool though. You'll help me?" Jessi asked him. *Could she be more obvious?* Vanessa thought, knowing it was going to be a long couple of hours if she was already this annoyed.

"Of course babe." Vanessa didn't really play the helpless female role very often. Being that she had a pool table in her basement, she was actually pretty decent at the game and offered to break, sinking two balls.

"Nice shot," she heard from her right. She leaned back up, away from the green felt surface of the table, and locked eyes with a completely average looking guy. She mentally calculated his stats. *Five-ten, probably one-eighty, meh hair, meh face, meh.*

"Thanks," she offered lazily. "Matt?" she asked, hoping he would say no.

"The one and only." *Charming.*

"Vanessa, nice to meet you," she said, realizing that Jess and Josh were not even pretending to play the game. "Do you feel like playing?" *One hour and forty-five minutes to go.*

"Yeah, cool," he agreed, taking the stick from Josh's hand easily, as he was otherwise engaged. They played a boring round of pool, she won, and he pretended to have let her do so.

"Sure dude, whatever you say," she retorted, watching the clock on the other side of the hall. She jumped when her gaze came back down and he was next to her. Too next to her. She took a step back but he caught her fingers and interlaced them with his. *Ummmm, no.*

"Since I let you win, I think you owe me," he smiled, leaning in to her. He smelled like stale peanuts and faint body odor, and she resisted the urge to dry heave.

"Yeah, I don't really think-" she began, but was interrupted by his hands on her back and his mouth brushing her neck. This time she stepped back much more forcefully, her hands on his chest. "Ok, *Mitt*, I get that you don't know me, but I don't like hook up in dives like this. Or with complete strangers. Sorry." *So not sorry.*

"Don't be such a tease," he responded, completely ignoring her intentional name failure, pulling her wrist back closer to him. Her heart rate picked up, and she was done. Wrenching her wrist from his hand, she walked away and ignored his almost-grab of her elbow.

"Hi, we're leaving," she stated very loudly when she found Jessi making out in some shadowy corner. *God this was such a stupid idea. Gross.*

"Ummm, why would we be leaving?" her friend questioned with a tight smile.

"Ummm, because this guy's awesome friend just assaulted me. So we're out."

"Oh my god, could you be more dramatic?" Jess's eyes were shooting killer glances at her, and she could not have cared less. She pulled her friend out of Josh's earshot.

"We are *leaving*, Jess. I am not about to let this random nobody put his hands all over me so you can make out against some wood paneling from the 70s."

"Really... you're insulting the décor of the pool hall? Whatever. I'm having fun. Leave if you want." Fireworks of feminist rage were now shooting out of Vanessa's ears.

"You know I *can't* leave without you," she hissed.

"Sure you can. Here are the keys," she quipped, plopping them into her hand. "I'll have Josh drop me around the corner from my house or something and walk home."

"You have got to be kidding me. You are unbelievable."

"Just stick it out another half hour, I swear we can leave then," Jess negotiated.

"Not a mermaid's chance in hell. See ya later, *friend*." Vanessa turned on her black leather heel and clicked her way out of the building, a storm brewing in the back of her brain. The cooler night was a welcomed sensation. She got in the car and carefully considered the option of just waiting there until her maybe ex-friend came out and making her drive home then. *This is what you get for letting her talk you into shit*, she berated herself. Her mind also raised the worry that she could be in there a while, now that she assumed Vanessa had left. *Screw it.* She put the keys in the ignition and adjusted the mirrors, determined to make it home without getting arrested. Hands were white-knuckled at ten and two the whole way.

Her fingers visibly relaxed when her house came into view. And then the urge to vomit came- because her mother was sitting in the rocking chair on their front porch, and her expression was not jovial. A stream of expletives rolled through Vanessa's head while she tried to come up with a plausible reason that she took the car. *Someone needed help... I had to get a first aid kit... Jessi was sick and I had to take her home... dammit!* She pulled the car carefully into the garage and got out, determined to make her mother actually listen this time. *This is just so typical that I get caught when I actually did the right thing.* With fear in her eyes, she tip-toed up the stepping-stones to the front porch as if it would help.

"I cannot imagine a story good enough to get you out of this," her mom iterated, a humorless smile on her face. Her mom really was quite pretty. She had honey blond hair and warm brown eyes that just never seemed soft when looking at her daughter. Vanessa immediately launched into the half-baked story of Jessi not feeling well and needing to take her home, and her mother stopped her about thirty seconds in.

"Try the next story."

Vanessa knew she could just tell her the truth, but also knew she'd probably never be allowed to hang out with Jess again. Despite her rage, she shouldn't have expected more, and didn't feel like losing her friend over it.

"I went to go play pool."

"And in your mind, you thought breaking the law was the best way to get there?"

"No, I-"

"It really doesn't matter, Vanessa. I thought you were taking things more seriously. I thought this year would be different... you seemed to care. But now I can see that I was wrong. You're just as self-centered and impulsive as you've always been. There will be no car for your birthday. There will be no birthday, period. Or parties, or sleepovers, or television, or phone. You are grounded until I feel like ungrounding you." Her mom rarely yelled when she was this mad. It was more of a crazy-calm. Like her head might spin around at any given moment from holding it all in. Vanessa felt tears begin to overflow.

"Mom, please just *listen* to me. I'll tell you everything that happened, I'm sorry I made up a story, this really isn't my fault."

"Of course not. Nothing's ever your fault. Do me a favor and save it. Put your phone on the counter and go to your room." Choking back an angry sob, she felt her teeth grind together and marched her way into the house, practically chucking her phone into the kitchen. *That's what*

I get for doing the smart thing and leaving, she thought, furious at the fact that her sophomore year was shaping up to be a big fat disappointment. The tears came in a torrent once her door was slammed shut, the injustice of the whole night washing over her. *Whatever, she's just been waiting for a chance to bust me anyway. Nothing I could have done would have made any difference,* she argued with herself, her mom's words ringing in her ears. Makeup and pajamas forgotten, she stared at the wall with hostility until sleep finally came.

Made in the USA
Columbia, SC
25 February 2021